"Wicked sensuality and a hero to..."
Christina Dodd

DEBRA MULLINS

author of
A Necessary Bride

Three
Nights...

*More Passionate Adventure
and Glorious Romance
from*
DEBRA MULLINS

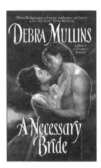 

Also:
THE LAWMAN'S SURRENDER
DONOVAN'S BED

"Debra Mullins mixes adventure, tenderness,
and humor with a deft hand."
Teresa Medeiros

She grabbed his arms with desperate fingers as the heat of his kiss bubbled through her.

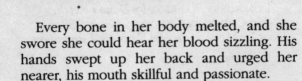

Every bone in her body melted, and she swore she could hear her blood sizzling. His hands swept up her back and urged her nearer, his mouth skillful and passionate.

She'd been kissed before. Once, four years ago. But that swift peck could not compare to the inferno that exploded within her as Lucien DuFeron devastated her senses with one touch of his mouth.

"Do you still intend to bite me?" he teased, his lips barely rubbing against hers as he spoke. "Or perhaps I should bite *you*?"

The former threat now struck her as amazingly erotic. Speech deserted her, and she could only make a small sound of supplication when he teasingly scraped his teeth against her sensitive mouth.

"Tell me," he demanded. "Say it."

"Yes." Barely had she breathed the word when he slowly took her lower lip between his teeth.

Rational thought spun away. She clung to him and surrendered to his skill, her body a vibrant, thrumming instrument, lost to the touch of a virtuoso . . .

Other **AVON ROMANCES**

ATTENTION: ORGANIZATIONS AND CORPORATIONS
Most Avon Books paperbacks are available at special quantity discounts for bulk purchases for sales promotions, premiums, or fund-raising. For information, please call or write:

Special Markets Department, HarperCollins Publishers, Inc., 10 East 53rd Street, New York, N.Y. 10022–5299.
Telephone: (212) 207–7528. Fax: (212) 207-7222.

DEBRA MULLINS

Three Nights...

AVON BOOKS
An Imprint of HarperCollinsPublishers

AVON BOOKS
An Imprint of HarperCollins*Publishers*
10 East 53rd Street
New York, New York 10022-5299

Copyright © 2004 by Debra Mullins Manning
ISBN: 0-06-056166-1
www.avonromance.com

First Avon Books paperback printing: March 2004

Avon Trademark Reg. U.S. Pat. Off. and in Other Countries, Marca Registrada, Hecho en U.S.A.
HarperCollins® is a registered trademark of HarperCollins Publishers Inc.

Printed in the U.S.A.

10 9 8 7 6 5 4 3 2 1

For my sister,
Kathleen Mullins Enberg,
the "idea man."
Thanks for being there.
And for
Eric Maldonado.
We'll make a romance writer
out of you yet!

Part One

Before

Chapter 1

Cornwall
November 1810

Aveline stared at the drab stone walls of Thornsgate, clutching her cloak around her with icy
fingers that had nothing to do with the chill in the
late November air.

Everyone said that Thornsgate's master had a
heart as black and empty as the pits of Hell. That he
was cold, ruthless. That growing up as the baseborn
son of a duke—spoiled though he had been by the
wealth of the father who'd acknowledged him—had
made him hard and bitter.

Aveline chose to believe there was some good in
him. Somewhere.

In the house, a clock struck eleven. Whispering a

prayer beneath her breath, she began the long, lonely trek up the winding drive to the forbidding manor.

Lucien DuFeron reclined in the overstuffed chair near the fire, a glass of fine French brandy in his hand. He stared into the flames, his mind on the coming sunrise. The large ruby ring on his finger glittered as he lifted the glass to his lips.

He was getting tired of appointments at dawn.

Contemplative, he swirled his brandy and leaned back against the soft burgundy cushions of the chair. The same thing happened at each early morning encounter. He showed up. He shot. He won the match. Nothing ever changed.

Perhaps he should hire someone to see to the duels for him. At least then the outcome wouldn't always be so certain. With a dark chuckle, he drained the glass.

A knock sounded at the door. He scowled. The servants knew he preferred to be left to his thoughts the night before a duel. "Come, blast you!"

The door creaked open to reveal the hesitant face of his butler, Stavens. "Your pardon, sir, but there is a lady here to see you."

"A lady?" He sneered. "I never knew you to refer to Charlotte as a lady before."

The butler colored at the reference to Lucien's mistress. "It is not Mrs. Everston, sir. It's a lady—a young one. She refuses to give her name."

"Indeed?" Arching one thick black brow, Lucien refilled his empty glass from the decanter on the table beside him. "Well, we don't see many ladies at Thornsgate, do we, Stavens?" He capped the decanter. "Show her in."

"As you wish, sir." The butler withdrew, and a moment later a woman entered the room, her features shadowed by the hood of her dark blue cloak. All he could see was her pale hands where she gripped the garment with tense fingers. She glanced around her, and one burnished curl spilled out from beneath the hood.

His curiosity caught, Lucien slowly rose to his feet.

She stepped back, and he had to smile. His size often intimidated people; it had helped much in his youth when the wellborn boys at school had thought to torment the Duke of Huntley's bastard son. He had earned their respect with his huge stature and ready fists.

And their fear.

But he didn't want this mysterious young woman afraid of him. Quite the opposite.

He bowed. "I am Lucien DuFeron. How may I be of service?"

He saw her hesitation in the stillness of her body. Then she slowly loosened her grasp on her cloak and reached up to pull back the hood.

Desire struck like an arrow.

Hair the shade of warm honey glimmered in the firelight, its beauty undiminished by the sedate knot in which she wore it. Delicate curls swept her small ears and teased her neck. Her smoothly curved cheeks held a delicate peach tone, like the inside of an orchid, and looked to be petal-soft.

Above the slight dent in her chin, her full, lush lips captured his attention, bringing to mind all manner of lusty images involving that siren's mouth on various parts of his body. His loins tightened in immediate response, and he raised his gaze to meet hers, expecting some acknowledgment of the attraction to show in her face. Exotic green eyes surrounded by gold-tipped lashes watched him with unflinching caution.

Arrested by this sudden—but not unwelcome— surge of lust, he gave her his most sincere smile. "Again, lovely lady, how may I be of service?"

Either she was too innocent to understand the innuendo or she simply ignored it. "I have come to speak to you on a matter of great urgency, Mr. DuFeron."

"Indeed?" He swept a hand toward the other chair. "Do sit down, that we may discuss this urgent matter in comfort."

She hesitated once more, watching him as if he might pounce on her at any moment.

Smart girl.

He smiled again. "Please, do sit down."

Watching him from the corner of her eye, she slipped past him toward the chair. As she went by, he laid his hands on her shoulders. She gasped with alarm and spun around to face him, leaving her cloak dangling from his fingers.

Which was what he had intended.

"May I take your cloak?" he asked, every inch the congenial host.

She swallowed hard and gave a small nod. "Yes, thank you."

He turned away to lay her cloak over a nearby settee, the smile fading from his face. Good God, she had a body made for a man's hands. For *his* hands.

Turning back to her, he gestured for her to sit down. As she moved to obey him, he closed his eyes in torment at the view of her from behind. The prim green dress with delicate embroidery around its modest neckline and hem could not disguise her generous bosom, her slender waist, her lushly curved bottom.

He clenched his hands to stop himself from reaching for her. She was *made* for sex.

She perched on the edge of the chair like a young novitiate, hands folded in her lap. "Thank you for seeing me, Mr. DuFeron."

"It is my very great pleasure, I assure you." He forced his fingers to relax and took his seat. Since he couldn't caress her skin, he instead ran his hands over the smooth brocade armchair covering. "I cannot help but wonder, however, what matter can be so urgent that a lovely lady like you would take her reputation in her hands and pay a call on a man in the middle of the night."

She flushed. "I realize my behavior is incredibly unseemly, sir, but only the gravest of circumstances would force me to such a turn."

He nodded in understanding. "Of course."

She took a deep breath, treating him to a thoroughly enjoyable view of her magnificent breasts as she did so. Then she said, "My name is Aveline Stoddard. I have come to beg for Lord Chestwick's life."

The change that swept over his features stunned her.

"Indeed," he said, his tone icy. "Are you his wife then?"

She lifted her chin with pride, though her fingers shook. "His daughter."

"His daughter." A slow, wicked smile parted his lips, and his dark eyes gleamed with interest.

Aveline trembled but held her ground. She had known this would be difficult. Lucien DuFeron did not look like the type of man who forgave easily. Everything about him intimidated her, from his great height to the blatantly sensual cast to his blunt features. His broad shoulders barely fit in the chair, and his big hands looked as though they could crush stone. His dark brown eyes, thick black brows, and proud Roman nose must have been inherited from his French mother, as he looked nothing like his father, the fair-haired Duke of Huntley.

He was rumored to be frighteningly intelligent, devastatingly charming when he chose to be, and a crack shot.

It was the last that worried Aveline.

Her father, Lord Chestwick, had gambled away every penny they had, and the bulk of his markers belonged to this man, Lucien DuFeron. Panicked by the sum he had lost in their last game, her father had foolishly accused DuFeron of being a cheat and so found himself with a dawn appointment to meet the deadly marksman over a set of dueling pistols.

She could not . . . *would not* . . . let that happen.

"Your father owes me a great sum of money." He picked up a glass of spirits from the table beside him and sipped, watching her over the rim.

She maintained the proud posture her mother had taught her. "I'm aware of that, Mr. DuFeron."

"He also insulted me." He replaced the glass with a small click. "Called me a cheat."

"He sent you an apology." She couldn't quite hide the rebuke in her voice. "A gentleman would accept it."

"Indeed." Amusement flickered across his features. "A *gentleman* would. But you and I both know that I'm no gentleman, Miss Stoddard."

She raised her chin another notch. "A gentleman is as a gentleman does."

"Quite." A knowing smile playing about his lips, he studied her for a long moment before he reached for his glass again.

Aveline's heart sank, but she refused to let her fear show. "Does this mean you still intend to meet him?"

"That depends."

"On what?"

"On you." His deep purr triggered unexpected ripples low in her belly.

"Indeed?" She threw his mockery back at him. "How so? Surely you don't expect *me* to meet you for a dawn appointment."

He chuckled. "You could, Miss Stoddard, if you were to stay the night."

Rake! Hot color washed over her cheeks. "I am a

lady, Mr. DuFeron, not an opera dancer. I'll thank you to mind your manners."

"I never mind my manners, I'm afraid." He gestured with his glass. "There's the door, if you like."

She was tempted. "We were discussing my father and how much money he owes."

"Were we?" With a laugh, he drained the glass and slapped it back on the table. "Your father owes me three thousand pounds, my dear girl. How do you propose to pay it?"

Three thousand pounds! She paled. How could it possibly be so much?

He waited. "Well?"

"I have money, but not enough," she admitted, forcing the words through a throat gone suddenly tight. "I had hoped it was not so great a sum."

"I do hate to disappoint a woman," he drawled, raising his eyebrows. "But I have his vowels should you like to see them for yourself."

She waved a hand in defeat. "No, thank you, Mr. DuFeron. I believe you."

"That you should not do so readily, Miss Stoddard, for I am rather well known for my ability to bluff."

She breathed a sigh of relief. "Then that is not the amount?"

"It is indeed the amount." He chuckled.

"You are amusing yourself at my expense," Aveline gritted, clenching her hands together.

"I am."

"Have you no conscience, sir? Must you mock me?"

"On the contrary." He looked her up and down

with an intensity that stilled the breath in her lungs. "I find nothing at all to mock, my dear. Your beauty is quite flawless. And your love for your father quite . . . touching."

"And my fortune quite nonexistent," she snapped. "I cannot pay you."

"Oh, you can pay me, but perhaps not in the coin you expected."

She stood. "I do not like your innuendoes, Mr. DuFeron. Will you accept my father's apology or not?"

He tapped one finger against his chin. "I might. But there is still the matter of three thousand pounds."

She glanced away from his smug countenance. "I know."

"Come now." He stood, his great height blocking the firelight. "Is my suggestion really so terrible? Think of your father. Think of the weight lifted from your family's coffers if you and I were to work out an agreement."

She looked him dead in the eye. "The weight would merely shift to *my* honor, Mr. DuFeron. Either way, the cost is dear."

"Three thousand pounds is a lot of money," he agreed. "But what price do you put on your father's life?"

Her mouth fell open. "You said you would accept his apology!"

He held up one finger. "I said I might. Nothing has been decided. At this point, your father still owes me three thousand pounds, and I am scheduled to meet him over pistols in"—he pulled out his pocket watch and checked the time—"approximately seven hours." He shut the watch with a firm click.

She could only stare at him in amazement. "You treat the situation lightly, Mr. DuFeron. Is taking a life so easy for you?"

He shrugged. "It's hardly my first duel."

"I can't say the same about what you would ask of *me*." She turned away from him. "My father's life or my innocence, is that the bargain you propose?"

"I hadn't quite thought of it that way, but yes, I suppose it is."

"Hadn't thought of it?" She whirled back to him, incensed that the man had the power to rearrange the elements of her life like a child would his toy soldiers. "You are asking me to ruin myself for you."

He frowned. "Don't think of it like that. I certainly don't want you to ruin yourself. And it's not for me, it's for your father."

She ticked off the facts on her fingers. "You are proposing I spend the night in your bed in exchange for canceling the duel with my father. In addition, you also agree to forgive his debt to you. Whatever pretty words you put to it, Mr. DuFeron, we both know that one night with you will be my ruination in the eyes of Society."

"That's not quite true."

"What's not quite true?"

"It wouldn't be for just one night."

"What do you mean by that?" She held up a hand to fob off yet another glib comment. "No flummery from you, sir. Tell me *exactly* what you're asking of me."

He gave her a smile that made her want to slap his face. "My dear Miss Stoddard, as beautiful as you are, you can hardly expect one night with an untried virgin to compensate me for both my lost honor and three thousand pounds."

"*Your* lost honor!"

"I think three nights should do it, one for each thousand pounds your father owes me." He reached out to trace a loose curl by her ear. "And your father's life will be included in the bargain."

"Three nights!"

"Three nights. Take it or leave it."

One glance at his hard expression told her that she had no choice. There wasn't enough money to pay the debt—Papa's gaming had seen to that. And she knew her sacrifice was the only way DuFeron would give up the duel. She squeezed her eyes shut against the tears that suddenly welled up. "Very well, Mr. DuFeron. You have a bargain."

"You needn't sound as if it's a death sentence." He caught a lone tear escaping down her cheek with his thumb. "I plan on making sure you enjoy your time with me, my dear. I do know how to be gentle."

She pulled away from his touch. "I, too, have terms for this bargain we make, Mr. DuFeron. If this is to happen between us, I want my visits here to remain secret. No one can know about this. *No one.*"

He pursed his lips in thought, then shrugged. "I have nothing to gain by destroying your reputation.

As long as you follow through with your part and share my bed for three nights, I have no interest in advertising our affair."

She winced at that word "affair." At least he didn't try to disguise what was happening with a lot of empty promises and skillful lies. He seemed honest to the point of bluntness. There would be no talk of love, no broken hearts. They both knew where they stood.

She held out her hand. "Do we agree on all the terms, Mr. DuFeron?"

He took her hand, and she watched with a strange shiver as his fingers swallowed up hers. "I would add one more term. You must call me Lucien if we are to be lovers."

A small thing. "Lucien," she said with a nod. "I am Aveline." His fingers warmed hers, made her feel shaky inside.

He stepped closer, and she willed herself not to back away from him. She had to get used to him if this was going to work. She didn't want him to change his mind and recall the debt. Or, Heaven help her, recall the duel.

But he was so big. So very, very masculine in a way that scrambled her senses. Her body seemed to hum with awareness the closer he came. She didn't like it. She couldn't control it.

He cupped her face with his hand. "Let us seal our bargain with a kiss, sweet Aveline."

She resisted. "Please don't think that I mean to renege," she whispered, noting the frown that flickered across his face, "but staying tonight is impossible. Your acceptance of my father's apology will surely cause a fuss at home, and I will be missed."

"A kiss only," he agreed, "as reward for your father's continued good health."

She narrowed her eyes. "Continue in that vein, Mr. DuFeron, and you risk a bitten lip."

His dark eyes gleamed with humor. "You think such a threat deters me? I can't wait to see where that hot passion of yours takes us."

"You are the most—" The words fell away as he lowered his mouth to hers.

Sweet Lord in Heaven.

She grabbed his arms with desperate fingers as the heat of his kiss bubbled through her. Every bone in her body melted, and she swore she could hear her blood sizzling. His big hands swept up her back and urged her nearer, his mouth skillful and passionate. Her body knew she was in the hands of a master.

She'd been kissed before. All right, once. But the swift peck on the mouth from her second cousin four years ago could not compare to the inferno that exploded within her as Lucien DuFeron devastated her senses with one touch of his mouth.

"Do you still intend to bite me?" he teased, his lips barely rubbing against hers as he spoke. "Or perhaps I should bite *you*?"

The former threat now struck her as amazingly erotic. Speech deserted her, and she could only make a small sound of supplication when he teasingly scraped his teeth against her sensitive mouth.

"Tell me," he demanded. "Say it."

"Yes." Barely had she breathed the word when he slowly took her lower lip between his teeth. Rational thought spun away. She clung to him and surrendered to his skill, her body a vibrant, thrumming instrument, lost to the touch of a virtuoso.

He broke the kiss slowly, smoothing his hands over her back to soothe her as she struggled for breath and balance. "It will be good between us, Aveline," he murmured, pressing a soft kiss to her temple. "You will see."

With trembling hands, she pushed out of his arms. Her mind spun with the lessons he had taught her in the space of moments. How would she ever get through three nights in his bed and still remain the same person?

But a bargain was a bargain. And her father's life depended on it.

"I need to go home," she said, looking around for her cloak.

He scooped it off the chair, then tenderly assisted her in getting it over her shoulders. He smiled down at her as he tugged the hood in place. "My carriage will see you home."

"No, they will know I have been gone—"

He silenced her with a finger on her lips. "Trust me," he said. "My staff is well versed in discretion."

She stiffened at the reminder. "Indeed. Well, then I accept the offer of your carriage, Mr. DuFeron. It is very dark out this time of night."

"I will send it to fetch you tomorrow night at eleven o'clock," he said. "The driver will pick you up in the same place he lets you out tonight."

She nodded and turned away, but he stopped her with a hand on her arm. She lifted her gaze to his. His eyes bored into hers, serious with a hint of menace.

"Don't go back on your word, Aveline, or I shall have to go back on mine. I have no compunction about going to your father's house and demanding what you've promised."

She jerked away from his touch and gave him a cold stare. "Never fear, Mr. DuFeron. I will uphold my end of the bargain." She pulled her cloak more tightly around her. "See to it you uphold yours."

She swept from the room, the only woman to ever leave Lucien DuFeron speechless.

Chapter 2

"**H**a!" Lord Chestwick slapped his hand on the table. The rattle of the dishes made Aveline jump. "I told you it would all work out, didn't I? Told you he'd accept my letter of apology."

"So you did." Aveline picked up a slice of bread and buttered it.

"It came last night, after you were abed." Her father began slicing up his sausage. "Didn't want to wake you, but I bet you were happy to see that your dear papa is alive and well this morning."

"And thank heavens for it." Her stomach clenched, and she laid the untouched piece of bread on her plate with the rest of her uneaten breakfast. "I shouldn't have known what to do without you, Papa."

"There, there, pet." He shoved a slice of sausage

into his mouth and chewed. "Nothing for you to worry your pretty self about. All's well that ends well."

"But I do worry." She set down her silverware with a clank and fixed her sire with a sober stare. "Papa, you came very close to getting killed. If Mr. DuFeron hadn't accepted your letter of apology, I would be planning your funeral even now."

The baron laughed. "My luck is back, girl, don't you see? DuFeron has never accepted an apology before. It's back, I tell you!"

She glanced down at her breakfast as she wrestled with a flash of impatience.

"Now, now, don't make that face." Her father reached out to pat her arm with one chubby hand. "I know you're disappointed never to have had a Season. Now that my luck is back, I'll have the money for that in a thrice!"

"Papa, I don't need a Season! We need food, and repairs made to the house. Firewood. Wages for the servants."

"Posh." The baron leaned back, his portly frame making the chair creak in protest. "We have money enough for that."

"No, we don't. Papa, if you don't stop your gaming, I fear that we will soon have no food to eat."

"Now, pet, I won't let that happen. You know that." He sent her a beaming smile. "We'll get you to London in the spring, and there you'll meet a fine husband. I promise."

"I have no wish to marry." Aveline picked up the

bread again and forced herself to take a bite for the simple reason that she didn't want to waste the precious food.

"Nonsense, young lady! Of course you'll marry. That's the way of things."

"Then who will care for you?" She tried to smile at him.

"Never you mind about me. A woman's duty is to marry, and that's that. Once you have that Season, there'll be plenty of young bucks sniffing about, of that I'm sure."

"Perhaps I'll meet someone from around here," she said, trying to get his mind off the ridiculous idea of a London Season. "Then I'll be able to be close to you."

"Perhaps." His expression darkened. "As long as it's not the likes of that Squire Lofton."

"Squire Lofton is married, Papa."

The baron snorted. "Yes, he is, but that doesn't stop him from hanging about making calf's eyes at you, does it? The man's intentions are far from honorable, and I want you to stay away from him."

"Yes, Papa."

"I mean it, Aveline. You're a beautiful girl, but without a fortune behind you, you'll not attract the upper crust of Society. No, aside from your looks and sweet manner, you have only your reputation to recommend you. Have a care with it."

"I am not interested in Squire Lofton," she said honestly.

"Good." Rising from the table, he bent to kiss her

cheek. "I'm off to Melton's for the day to play a hand or two of whist."

Her jaw dropped. "Papa!"

"For sport only, my dear." He gave her a smile that didn't quite reassure her. "I'll be back in time for dinner."

Aveline turned in her chair as he started to leave the room. "Papa, please don't wager any more money. We haven't the funds to spare."

"Never fear," he said, waving a hand without turning around. "Your papa has it all under control!"

With that, he left the breakfast room.

Aveline stared after him, a sinking feeling in her stomach. How could he go merrily off to game at Lord Melton's after all that had happened? He didn't know about the bargain she'd made, but one would think that narrowly escaping the duel with Lucien would have brought her sire to his senses.

And if he were to find out what she had agreed to sacrifice to save his life, he'd challenge Lucien to a duel for besmirching her honor, and they'd be right back where they started.

With a groan of dismay, she buried her face in her hands. Was there nothing that would convince him to stop? What would she do if he got deeper in debt? Gaming was like a sickness for her father; he couldn't resist the tables. Even rusticating here in the country hadn't helped.

His obsession would see them in the poorhouse, or worse.

Her appetite gone, she tossed her crumpled napkin down beside her plate. If Papa intended to spend the day playing cards at Lord Melton's, then she clearly needed to make sure there was enough money to run the household in the event he lost—which he often did. Rising, she left the breakfast room and headed upstairs to her sewing room.

The sewing room had once been a small bedroom that Aveline had set aside for her own use, and it was there that she plied her needle to keep them all fed. She shook her head as she pulled forth a single key and unlocked the door to her private domain. As dearly as she loved her father, she found his lack of sense frustrating when it came to taking care of the family. More often than not, she felt as if she were the parent and he the child.

If only her mother were still alive. As the daughter of a vicar, Mama's strong morals had kept Papa's sins in check. Papa certainly hadn't behaved like this while she lived; it was only after her death that he had become so enchanted with gambling. He had driven them to the brink of poverty because of it.

Which is why Aveline had made the bargain with Lucien DuFeron.

An image of his dark-eyed visage rose in her mind, that sinful-looking mouth curved in a sardonic smile. A shiver rippled through her as she thought of those eyes gazing at her naked body—for she was certain a renowned rake like DuFeron would never honor her maidenly request for darkness. No, she had no doubt that he would eagerly view her most private attributes, parts of her body no one but her mother and nursemaid had seen. She didn't question that he would touch her in the most scandalous places, whisper the most erotic propositions, make the most shocking promises as to what he would do to her.

And she would do whatever he asked if it kept her father alive.

One of the servants called to another on the floor below, jerking her from her imaginings. With a start, she realized that she leaned against the wall as if her legs would not support her, her breathing shaky, her heart racing. Blood rushed to her cheeks. Good Lord, what if someone saw her?

She fumbled for the entrance to the sewing room and pushed it open, scrambling inside and closing the door behind her. Leaning back against it, she laid a hand on her pounding heart. How could the mere thought of a cad like Lucien DuFeron bring her to such a state? It was disgraceful! She should be steeling herself for tonight's ordeal, not panting about it like an eager bride on her wedding night.

It was all Lady Sarah's fault, she decided, struggling for composure. Her newly married best friend, Lady Sarah Cole, had educated the unwed Aveline more than was proper on the secrets of the marriage bed. If Sarah hadn't passed on such intimate knowledge, Aveline would not now be trembling at the thought of sharing Lucien DuFeron's bed.

Then again, she might have been trembling in fear instead. At least she knew what to expect.

Taking deep breaths to calm herself, she glanced around the room, comforted by the sight of her chair by the window and the familiar view of the road through the curtains. She crossed over to a trunk in the corner.

Kneeling, she lifted the lid and pulled forth several pieces of complex embroidery. She held one up to the sunlight and admired the evenness of the stitches. This one had always been her favorite, and she hated to sell it. However, her talent for embroidery was the only thing standing between her family and starvation. With a sigh, she chose two more pieces and closed the lid to the trunk. She would have to begin work on more pieces to replenish her stock. In the meantime, she would have her maid take these to the local modiste and see how much they would bring. It was the only honorable way a wellborn lady could make money.

Though after tonight, she doubted she could ever think of herself as "honorable" again.

She would go to DuFeron for the three nights he had demanded and submit to his advances, no matter what he asked. It was little enough payment for her father's life or the survival of her family.

Still, there was always the chance he would find some shred of decency inside his black heart and spare her the ordeal . . .

He would have to be gentle at first, Lucien thought as he peeled back the skin of the orange. After all, the girl was clearly a virgin, and he wanted to thoroughly enjoy his three nights with her.

Leaning back in his chair at the breakfast table, he pulled apart the juicy inner sections of the fruit and popped one in his mouth, savoring the tangy sweetness that exploded on his tongue as he pondered his course of action. Perhaps he would start with a cold supper beside the fire and some wine. Soothe her nerves, calm her fears. Virgins tended to be a skittish lot—or so he'd heard, anyway. He had a tendency to avoid the breed, as they usually came with irate fathers and calculating mamas.

But there would be none of that with Aveline. She was his to do with as he wanted. Sensual images flooded his brain, hardened his body, and heated his blood in seconds. He could hardly wait for night to fall.

Stavens chose that moment to enter the breakfast room. "Mr. Dante Wexford," he announced.

Lucien dropped his orange on the plate as his best friend strode into the room. "Blast it all, Dante, what are you doing here?"

A sandy-haired, slender man impeccably dressed in a bottle green coat and buff-colored breeches, Dante seated himself at the table with the ease of long familiarity. "You do recall Melton's card party, don't you? We were to go this evening. You even invited me to stay here at Thornsgate."

Lucien muttered a curse. "That's tonight?"

Dante raised his brows, amusement glittering in his piercing hazel eyes. "I take it you made other plans?"

"I did." Lucien shrugged. "I forgot about Melton's. I've had other things on my mind."

"So I've heard." Dante reached across the table and helped himself to a handful of grapes. "I stopped at the Hound and Hare, and gossip ran through the taproom that Lucien DuFeron had actually called off a duel."

"What of it?" Lucien scowled and picked up another section of orange, biting into it with a snap of teeth.

Dante chuckled. "My dear friend, you never call off a duel. Everyone knows that. Why did you do it this time?"

Lucien shrugged. "I felt like it."

"Indeed." Amused, Dante slipped a grape into his mouth. "She must be very beautiful."

Lucien merely glared.

"Now, now, don't lose your temper." His friend held up a hand in surrender, a devilish grin stretching from ear to ear. "Melton's games usually run well into the night. I shall simply stay out until the morning hours, does that suit you?"

"It does."

"So secretive," Dante gibed. "Very well, if you write me a letter of introduction, I shall go to Melton's alone and relieve the gentlemen of Cornwall of their fortunes."

Lucien frowned. "A letter? What the devil for?"

Dante's smile grew brittle for an instant. "My dear Lucien, you know that without your august presence, Lord Melton will not allow me as far as the doorstep."

"Blasted stiff-rumped sticklers."

Dante shrugged, the hardness fading from his expression to be replaced by his usual cocky amusement. "You too would share the disdain of Society if your father had not acknowledged you as his son."

Lucien gave a harsh laugh. "And a lot of good it's done me to have a duke for a father," he said. "Growing up at Huntley House was like living inside a tomb. And I can never inherit."

"But still, his acceptance of you has led Polite Society to receive you. That, and your dashed talent for tripling your investments on the 'change." Dante popped another grape into his mouth. "After all, you took that pittance your father gave you on your twenty-first birthday and turned it into a fortune to rival Huntley's."

"My dear Dante, you don't suggest that I am only received because of my 'golden touch'?" Lucien raised mocking brows. "How uncharitable of you. As if the *ton* would associate with me merely to learn my secrets of making money."

Dante snickered. "Whatever was I thinking?"

"Indeed." Grinning, Lucien scooped up the last piece of orange. "I assure you that the ladies of Society do not pursue me merely for my gold."

"No, they want something else just as hard."

Lucien's grin became a smug smile. "Jealous?"

"Hardly." Dante rolled a grape between his fingers. "I'm one ahead of you on the number of duels. We would have been even had you not accepted Chestwick's apology."

Lucien shrugged. "I'll still win the wager. Ten duels in a month, was that it?"

"It was." Dante leaned forward. "I have eight. You have seven. I'll have your hundred pounds in my purse before the week is out."

"We'll see about that." Lucien glanced at his

pocket watch and rose. "Let's see about that letter of introduction, Dante. I've business to attend to."

"I'm sure you do," Dante shot back. Tossing the grape back in the bowl, he stood and followed Lucien from the room. "But is your business blond, brunette, or redhead?"

Eleven o'clock came far too soon for Aveline.

Her father had not yet returned home, and she knew that he must have stayed at Lord Melton's and was even now wagering away every cent they had. It seemed she no sooner rescued her father from one folly than he began another. The frustration of it made her long to back out of her agreement with DuFeron.

But she'd given her word, and she had no doubt that the rogue would follow through with his threat to come to the house and demand she keep her part of the bargain.

At least this way, Papa would be safe from DuFeron's marksmanship.

The carriage was exactly where the scoundrel had said it would be. Keeping close to the shadows, she scurried to the luxurious conveyance, glancing back over her shoulder at every sound. Her limbs trembled, and her knees felt as if they would collapse from beneath her at any moment. What if someone noticed she was gone? What if someone sounded the alarm?

She climbed into the carriage and sank back into the sumptuous leather seats, her heart racing. She could hardly believe that she, Aveline Stoddard, daughter of a baron, was actually sneaking out of the house in the middle of the night for a rendezvous with a man, however reluctantly she did so. Her mother would have swooned to see the day.

The coachman called to the horses, and the carriage lurched into motion, whooshing her breath from her lungs.

Every wild story Lady Sarah had told her flickered through her mind. What would he do? Would he ravish her immediately, or would he put a pretty face on it with wine and sweet words? Which would be worse?

Her pulse skipping madly through her veins, she closed her eyes and concentrated on breathing, listening to the rasp of the wheels on the muddy road as the carriage took her closer and closer to her fate.

Chapter 3

Lucien decided to receive her in the parlor, a room he rarely used as its feminine décor, left by the previous owners of the house, did not suit him. But Aveline might find the room soothing, and so he ordered dinner set there and a fire started in the fireplace.

He was pouring the second glass of wine when Stavens showed her in.

She had clearly not given the butler her name, and she wore the same cloak as the night before, which shadowed her face and preserved her identity. Placing the wine bottle beside the two filled glasses, Lucien gave Stavens a wave of dismissal. The butler left the room, closing the doors with an audible snick.

She jumped at the sound. Nervous, obviously.

"I've given the servants the evening off," he said. "No one will disturb us . . . or betray your presence here."

"I appreciate your keeping your end of the bargain." With hands that trembled, she pushed back the hood of her cloak.

The firelight played over her honey blond hair and cast a warm tone over her smooth skin. Her eyes looked dark and fathomless in this light, and her lush lips quivered above her determined chin. Once more her beauty spoke to him, rousing his body so quickly even he was startled.

He wanted her badly. And tonight he would have her.

But Lucien had learned patience at a young age and was too proud of his prowess as a lover to rush something as special as initiating a maiden into carnal pleasure. So while desire nipped at his good intentions and demanded that he take her immediately, he forced himself to move slowly.

He offered her one of the goblets. "Wine?"

She hesitated. "I do not need my senses addled in order to keep my word."

"And I have no desire to take a drunken innocent to my bed." He gave her his most charming smile. "I want you comfortable, Aveline, and in control of all your faculties. Anything less would be an insult to both of us."

She let out a long, slow breath. "Forgive me, Mr. DuFeron, but this is my first time doing this."

"I'm aware of that. And my name is Lucien."

"Lucien," she echoed with a nod. Stepping forward, she took the glass. "Thank you, Lucien."

He caressed her cheek with the backs of his fingers. "I am not a monster."

She didn't move away from his touch, but her fingers tightened around the stem of the goblet. Then she laughed and took a large swallow of wine. "A monster? No. A rogue, perhaps. A rake, definitely."

"I don't dispute that." He traced the shell of her ear with one finger. "But I won't hurt you, Aveline. I want only to give you pleasure."

She shivered, whether from arousal or fear, he couldn't tell. "I pray it turns out that way."

"It will. But I won't rush you." He placed his hands on her shoulders. "Allow me to take your cloak."

She nodded, and he swept the garment away.

She wore a modest blue dinner dress that looked more suitable for an evening at the vicar's house than a seduction at the home of London's most notorious rake. Yet the cut and color of the simple garment emphasized the creamy youth of her skin and the supple roundness of her very feminine curves.

She looked beautiful, without artifice, and as tempting as a sugared cake to a starving man.

He turned away to lay her cloak across a chair—and to gain control of his sexual hunger. "Do you like the wine?" he asked, turning back to her.

"It's very good." She took another sip, watching him over the rim of the glass.

"There's food if you're hungry." He swept a hand

toward the laden table. "A fire in the grate. Companionable conversation."

"To soothe my ragged nerves?" Her smile held a hint of mockery. "Lucien, nothing can do that but the morning."

His name on her lips nearly distracted him from the drollness of her comment. Then he gave a bark of laughter as her meaning became clear in his lust-ridden mind. "You surprise me, Aveline. You accept the situation so easily. I had almost expected you not to come."

The smile faded from her lips. "I gave my word."

"So you did. It's just rare in my experience to meet a woman who comprehends the meaning of honor."

"There are many of us, sir." She raised her brows and sipped at the wine again. "Perhaps you have socialized with the wrong women."

"Perhaps I have." Amazed that he found her conversation as stirring as her body, he took up his own wine. "And you haven't answered my question. Are you hungry?"

"No." She set down her glass. "If you don't mind, I would like to bypass the niceties, as lovely as they are, and get to the point of the evening. My imagination is proving more fearsome than I'm sure the situation warrants."

Even as lust tightened his loins, he hesitated. "Are you certain? Perhaps your fears will calm as we get to know each other over a leisurely meal."

She shook her head. "I would rather get on with it. Unless you've changed your mind."

"I haven't changed my mind." He set down his

wineglass, her candor more arousing than any practiced flirtation. "I have no desire to hurt you, Aveline, and I detest missish tears on my pillow."

She narrowed her eyes. "I am never missish."

"Indeed, you are one surprise after another." He came to her and took her chin in his hand, forcing her to meet his gaze. "Are you a virgin?"

She jerked away from his touch. "Of course I am. What sort of lady do you think me?"

"It was an honest question. I've known many unwed ladies who were not virgins."

"A woman's virtue is her one true mark of honor. Why else would I give it to you in exchange for my father's life?" Her lips twisted in a bitter smile he'd never expected to see on a face so young. "It's all I have of value to offer a man like you."

A twinge of guilt surprised a frown from him, but he brushed the disturbing feeling aside. She was right. Her virtue was all she had, and she had agreed to gift him with it in exchange for her father's life. "I apologize for doubting you," he said. "If you're not hungry and don't feel the need for conversation, may I offer you more wine?"

"No, thank you." She folded her hands in front of her. "But please, feel free to partake yourself, if you like."

"No, wine isn't what I want." He took her face between his hands and looked deeply into her green eyes. Behind the bravado, he saw a flicker of uncertainty, though she didn't back away. He smiled at her courage. "I promise to make this as enjoyable for you as I can, Aveline."

Her expression remained sober. "I trust that you will, Lucien, or else I will have to suspect that your reputation is made up largely of exaggerated rumor."

He laughed with delight at her sharp wit. "You will have the opportunity to decide for yourself. Come upstairs with me."

"Let me bring my cloak in case the servants are still about."

He turned away and fetched the garment himself, laying it over her shoulders and tugging the hood over her burnished curls. Then he held out his hand, and she placed hers in his, allowing him to lead her out of the parlor and upstairs to his bed.

Aveline's heart pounded as Lucien led her up the stairs to his bedchamber. What was the matter with her? She could have played for time, could have lingered over cheese and wine until the wee hours, putting off the moment of truth. But no, she had spoken her mind, had forsaken the social pleasantries in favor of urging the rogue to take her to his bed.

Fool. What had she been thinking?

She'd been thinking they'd better get on with it, for to dress up what was about to happen served neither of them. This was not a love match, not even a seduction. It was a bargain, and the sooner she paid her part of it, the more comfortable she would be with the situation. He had followed through with his part, and now she must live up to hers. She resolved to make the best of things, even to enjoy herself if she could.

There was no turning back now.

They saw no one on either the stairs or the landing, making her realize he had told her the truth when he said the servants were gone. Even the butler must have departed after showing her in. Still, she was glad she had worn the cloak. It didn't allow him to see the anxiety on her face when they reached his bedchamber.

He opened the door, and the click of the latch seemed to unlock her fate. She followed him inside the very masculine chamber, assailed by the unfamiliar scents of a man's living space, then froze just inside the doorway at the sight of the huge bed that dominated the room.

The site of her honor's demise.

"Aveline." He turned her to face him with hands on her shoulders. "I'm not going to pounce on you like a wild beast. We have all night."

"I know. It's just . . ."

"It's new to you." He stroked his fingers over her cheek in what now seemed like a familiar caress. "I can go as slow as you'd like. In fact, it often draws out the pleasure."

"And will I feel pleasure?" She searched his dark eyes, seeking reassurance. "Or is it my role to lie still and submit to your whims?"

His mouth thinned, his brows lowering in warning. "Are you going back on your word, Aveline?"

"No." She met his implacable look with one of her own. "I only ask if I will feel pleasure in your bed."

He tugged the hood from her hair, stroked it back

over her shoulders so the cloak pooled on the floor at her feet. "I have much experience in bringing a woman pleasure." He traced a finger down her throat, never looking away from her face. "And I will use every bit of my knowledge to make your body sing with ecstasy."

Words deserted her as heat flooded her cheeks. She swallowed hard as his finger trailed across the tops of her breasts. To her mortification, she felt her nipples contract into hard little pellets. He glanced down at this evidence of her arousal and flashed her a knowing grin. "That's it." He slipped his other hand behind her neck to stroke her nape. "That's it, my dove. Let me touch you. Let me admire your body."

Soothed by his fingers caressing the back of her neck, she nearly jumped when his other hand cupped her breast through her dress.

"Shhh." His touch remained gentle, softly tracing and squeezing the plump mound through her clothing. "I love your body, Aveline. Your breasts are perfect." He lowered his mouth to brush her ear. "I can't wait to see you . . . all of you."

A sudden shiver of desire wracked her body, shocking her. But he merely chuckled and continued to stroke first one breast, then the other, murmuring soft words of encouragement between kisses trailed along her throat. His other hand kneaded the tension from her neck, and before she knew it, she leaned into him, arching her back so his hand could have better access to her breasts.

His palm caressing her sensitive flesh incited

amazing, unfamiliar tremors throughout her body. Her skin rippled along her arms, her nipples hardening until it was almost painful. An ache started between her legs, and every time his hand brushed her nipple, rubbing the tight bud through the layers of clothing between his flesh and hers, she wanted to moan.

But ladies didn't do such things. Ladies—

"Dear God," she whispered, startled when he brushed a kiss just above the neckline of her dress. "Lucien . . ."

"Trust me." His tongue flicked out, touched her collarbone. "There is much more than this, Aveline."

She clenched her hands on his shoulders. "Show me."

Keeping one hand at the nape of her neck, he pushed the door closed with the other, the little slam echoing with finality. This was it, then. The end of her innocence.

The beginning of womanhood.

Her breasts ached without his touch, and she found herself arching toward him, offering herself again. Her breath caught at the obvious hunger in his dark brown eyes as he gazed down at her, and for a moment, she was tempted to flee. But then he gathered her into his embrace, pressing her curves against his masculine frame, smoothing his hand down her spine to bring her even closer. Her pulse skipped wildly through her veins at the unfamiliar ridges and planes of his solid, male body. She'd never been this close to a man. Never imagined the strength and heat of his flesh, so different from hers, yet so right.

"Kiss me, Aveline," he murmured, brushing his lips against her temple, her cheek. "Show me that you want me."

How could he doubt it? That a practiced seducer like Lucien should need such reassurance had never occurred to her. She glanced into his eyes and was startled by the vulnerability lurking behind the honest lust to be found there.

"I do want you," she replied, tracing her fingers down the broad planes of his face. "Despite what brought us together. God save me, I do want you. I can't help it."

He gave a low growl deep in his throat and pulled her more tightly against him. "I won't hurt you. I'll make it good for you."

She touched his mouth with one fingertip. "I'm counting on it, Lucien. 'Tis all that keeps me from fleeing. That, and my honor."

"You're the most honorable woman I've ever met. I admire your character almost as much as I admire your body."

She stilled. "Enough to let me go?"

He gave a harsh laugh that seemed to mock both of them. "I can't. No, I can't do that."

Disappointment wilted her limbs for only a moment. But then she straightened up and faced him again, unflinching. "I didn't think so."

"Kiss me, Aveline," he said again, and this time she stood up on her toes to comply, pressing her lips against his. He met her halfway, taking control of the kiss, teaching her without words all the wicked ways they could pleasure one another with just their mouths. She was shaking when he finally raised his head, her mind spinning and rational thought forgotten.

He took her hand and flattened it against his chest. "Touch me. Don't be afraid."

She left her hand where it rested over his beating heart. "I don't know how."

With his hand over hers, he guided her palm over the rippling muscles of his chest. "Like this."

Even through his clothing, the heat of his body warmed her flesh. "So different from me," she murmured.

"That's the joy of it." He lifted her other hand and nibbled at her fingers. "Man and woman, so different, yet fitting together as if they should never be apart."

She swallowed hard, her gaze on his mouth as he nipped her fingertips. Who could have known that her hand was so sensitive?

"You're delicious. I want to taste all of you." Before she could blink, he had pulled the pins from her hair so that the honeyed mass tumbled down her back. Then his hands were at the fastenings of her dress as his mouth came down on hers, capturing her in a kiss as hot and blazing as the fire in the grate.

She didn't utter a syllable of protest. Her mind grew cloudy, and her body thrummed with strange, compelling emotion. She gave herself up to his obvious experience, astounded at the ways he touched her, the places he kissed her. Her dress dropped to her feet, leaving her clad in only her thin chemise. He peeled that from her body as well, following his skilled hands with his hungry mouth, kissing her everywhere.

Before she knew it, she was naked. He had her so hungry for his caresses that she didn't care if the candles were still blazing so he could see every flaw and freckle. She *wanted* him to see, and when he cupped her bare bottom in his big hands and rocked against her, she nearly went mad with wanting him.

He lifted her up and carried her the few steps to the bed, tumbling her back against the pillows. She reached for him, but he shook his head and stepped back.

"Let me look at you." His gaze swept over her with possessive heat as he shrugged out of his coat and jerked loose his fashionably tied cravat.

A blush swept into her cheeks at his open regard. She made to cover her breasts with her hands, then hesitated, torn between modesty and arousal.

"Yes." Cravat dangling from around his neck, he tossed his waistcoat on the floor and came to her, positioning her hands so that she cupped her own breasts, lifting them for his perusal. "Just like that. Stay like that."

"Lucien . . ." Shocked, she did what he asked, though she had never in her life touched her own body as she did now.

"You look beautiful. So desirable." He came forward again and gently parted her knees so that her most private place was open to his gaze. "Yes," he murmured, gazing down at her. "Yes, let me see you."

She couldn't. Embarrassment flooded through her, and she closed her legs with a small whimper of protest.

"No?" With a knowing smile, he bent down and brushed a kiss over her thigh, making her jolt. "We'll see how you feel about that later." With a slow caress of her leg, he turned away to yank off his boots.

He faced her again as he stood to rapidly remove the rest of his clothing. When he discarded his shirt, she stared wide-eyed at his powerful, hair-sprinkled torso. The muscles of his arms and chest rippled beneath his skin as he efficiently stripped off the rest of his garments, baring his impressive erection to her untutored gaze.

She shut her eyes. Lady Sarah had to be wrong. How could *that* possibly fit . . . *there*?

The bed dipped as he knelt on it. "Aveline."

Coward. She made herself open her eyes and look at him.

He gave her a rueful smile, his eyes crinkling at the corners. "I'm sorry. I'm going too fast, but you're so responsive . . ." His voice trailed off as he swept his gaze over her body. "I keep forgetting you've never done this before."

She let out the breath she hadn't even known she'd been holding. "It is all a bit shocking."

He grinned like the rake she knew he was. "Indeed, you'll be thoroughly shocked by dawn."

Wicked. That was the only word for the expression on his face. A tremor rippled through her, but she refused to let him see how he had unnerved her. She decided to be glad that he had such experience in the arts of love. That she found him attractive. Far worse for her if she had been forced to sacrifice her honor in the bed of a man half as skilled or half as appealing.

"Yes, I expect that you *will* shock me," she murmured.

"And pleasure you," he replied, sliding onto the bed with her. His heated flesh pressed against hers, their legs tangling.

"Dear Lord," was all she could whisper before he took her mouth in a scorching, deep kiss that drained all thoughts from her mind. He urged her lips apart with his tongue, taught her the delights of tasting and teasing, swept his hand along her waist, the curve of her hip.

She reached up to cling to his neck, lost in the sensations of her tender breasts rubbing against his hair-roughened chest. His lean hip pressed against hers, his sex hard and hot against her thigh. He was such a big man, he had her surrounded. Trapped. At his mercy.

The thought both threatened and thrilled her.

He seemed to be everywhere at once. One hand supported her head while the other caressed her thigh, edging ever closer to her female mound. He licked her breasts, wringing a moan from her at the delicious, unfamiliar sensation. He suckled, he nibbled, he stroked and teased until she threw back her head in surrender, parting her legs at his gentle urging, willingly giving herself up to womanhood.

All the while he murmured encouragement, told her how beautiful she was, how passionate, how responsive.

His hand slipped between her legs and pressed gently against her moist folds. She didn't have time to be shy; the intensity of her body's response threw her headlong into a whirlwind of sensation. He caressed her delicately, watching her face in between pressing soft kisses to her lips. He looked like he could spend all night doing just this, but she knew from the hardness of him that he was just as eager as she to complete their joining.

One blunt finger entered her slowly, and at the same time he touched her just *there* with his thumb. She bit her bottom lip and arched her hips and let loose a long, low moan such as she had never imagined would ever escape her lips. She begged him over and over again never to stop—never, never stop. And he didn't stop, kept easing his finger inside her, rubbing that aching place gently, oh so gently, until suddenly something inside her exploded. Her head spun, the world went dark, and pleasure spiraled through her, stealing the very breath from her lungs.

When he removed his hand, she came back to herself and gave a whimper of protest. He replied with a soft chuckle; then he shifted and lay on top of her completely, spreading her knees wide as he edged between her thighs. The blunt tip of him pressed against the entrance to her body, and he stopped there, waited for her to look at him. "This part will hurt, just this once."

She nodded—Lady Sarah had mentioned that.

He cupped her face in his hands and kissed her hard as he took her innocence.

She stiffened at the burning sensation of his entry, the stretching of her body to accommodate the length of him. It seemed as if he would never fit. She clung to his shoulders, wanting to pull him closer and push him away at the same time. The pressure was incredible, as if something resisted his penetration. Then a sharp, tearing pain, and he surged all the way inside her.

She cried out, and he stilled, hard and full within her, whispering reassurances in her ear. Then slowly he began to move, just a gentle rocking of the hips at first. His hand slipped between her legs, his fingers teasing the bud of sensation above their joined bodies that had brought her such pleasure before. After a moment pain faded, hunger rising within her like a slumbering beast awakened, and she realized that she liked his thrusts, wanted them, wanted *him*.

The tingling started again, a wave of heat flooding upward from the place where they joined. He wrapped his arms tightly around her, his face buried in her neck, his strokes growing harder and more urgent. Instinct urged her to spread her knees wider, immediately bringing him deeper into her and increasing the delicious friction. He gave a muffled groan at the movement and seemed to swell inside her. More, yes, more. She wanted that amazing feeling of losing herself again. Soon ... any moment now.

He thrust hard once, and again. Then pressed deeply into her, holding himself there as his entire body shuddered, and a hoarse groan ripped from his lips.

A ripple shuddered through her, then faded just short of where she wanted to be.

She closed her eyes, heart thundering in her chest, body strung more tightly than a harp string.

She stroked his shoulders and back as he collapsed on top of her, enjoying the feel of his heavy body on hers.

It was done now, and nothing would ever be the same again.

Chapter 4

He hadn't finished what he'd started.

Replete, yet shaken by the fact that he had just had the climax of his life in the arms of an untried girl, Lucien realized with a bit of chagrin that she hadn't finished.

She said nothing about the matter, merely lay with him sprawled over her, contentedly stroking him with her small, soft hands. His mistress—or any other woman for that matter—would have been clawing at his back, ranting and demanding her satisfaction.

But Aveline was like no other woman he'd ever known.

He raised his head and looked at her. She smiled at him, a shy little parting of the lips, and her eyes glowed with wonder.

He'd put that look on her face, and the mere thought of it made him hungry for her all over again.

"I forgot something," he whispered.

"What?" Innocence still lingering in her eyes, she continued to softly caress his shoulders.

"This." Still semihard inside her, he flexed his buttocks, moving his hips in excruciatingly slow circles. She gasped, her eyes widening with stunned delight. "Say my name, Aveline."

And as he dipped his head to tease her nipple with his tongue, she arched against him, her body clenching around him as she climaxed.

"Lucien," she cried. "Dear God, Lucien."

"Yes," he whispered and buried his face in her neck, awash in the sensations of her pleasure.

The night passed quickly.

When dawn's rosy fingers crept through the curtains fluttering in the window, Aveline slipped from the warmth of the bed. She winced as she moved across the room and scooped her clothing off the floor.

Not even when she'd learned to ride had she felt so sore.

She glanced back at the man slumbering in the bed and paused for a moment, captured by the sight of him. He slept on his stomach, the sheets tangled ropes around his legs, his naked body aglow in the golden pink morning light. She allowed her gaze to slide appreciatively over him, the well-toned muscles of his back, his compact buttocks, the solid sinew of his thighs and calves. Never in her life had she imagined that she'd be able to look upon a naked man without blushing from head to toe. And while the warmth did indeed creep into her cheeks, heat also tingled through her loins.

The wicked man had turned her into a wanton.

Three times. He'd taken her three times during the night, each encounter more sensually breathtaking than the last. He'd turned her this way and that, taught her things she'd never even imagined about how their bodies worked, and made her head spin with pleasure every time he touched her.

Oh, yes, she could see why he had the reputation he did. Every word of it well earned.

A clock downstairs chimed the hour, and she forced herself to turn away from him. She had to get home before her absence was discovered.

She walked over to the bureau and put her clothes down atop it, then reached for the pitcher and poured water into the basin. She washed the sleep from her eyes and, blushing furiously, took the cloth and cleaned away the evidence of their night together.

"Do you need help with that?" Even with the rumble of sleep still in his voice, the words dripped with sexual invitation. She spun to face him, crushing the damp cloth in her hand.

He still sprawled in bed, his dark eyes heavy-lidded and lazy. The sensual smile that parted his lips sent passion surging through her.

"I—I didn't know you were awake."

"I felt you leave. And I missed you." He gave her a slow looking-over with hungry, heated eyes.

Good Lord, she'd forgotten she was naked! With a squeak of dismay, she grabbed her clothing from atop the bureau and clutched it in front of her to cover her nakedness.

He roared with laughter.

Her face burned. "Stop laughing, you wicked man."

He only howled louder, clutching the sheets between his fingers and burying his face in the pillows.

"Just what do you think is so funny?" she demanded, her patience dwindling as he tried to get himself under control.

"You are." Still chuckling, he raised his head and wiped tears of mirth from his eyes. "I've seen every inch of your flesh, taken you half the ways a man can take a woman, and yet in the light of day you act like an untried schoolgirl."

Her eyes bugged. "Only half?" she blurted. And set him off again. Mortified, she closed her eyes and wished for the floor to open up beneath her.

"I was just teasing you." Amusement still tinged his voice. The sheets rustled, and the bed creaked as he rose.

"I know," she said with a sigh, opening her eyes. "I just—" Her words spluttered to a stop as her gaze dropped to his jutting erection. "Again?" she squeaked.

"'Tis a natural state for a man in the morning." He approached with a wide grin.

She retreated until her back hit the bureau. "Stop right there, Lucien. I need to get dressed and get home before I'm missed. We can continue this tonight . . ."

"Now." He caged her against the bureau with an arm on either side of her. His thigh nudged hers apart.

"Lucien, I—" Her words drifted away on a sigh as he nuzzled her neck.

"What is it about you?" he murmured against her skin. "We've only just met, yet I've this powerful hunger for the taste of you . . ." He tugged the clothing from her hands and tossed it behind him in the general direction of the bed.

"I have to leave." She said the words without conviction as he cupped both her breasts in his palms and teased the nipples to hard points. A mew of surrender slipped past her lips, and she wrapped her arms around his neck. "You know I have to leave."

"Then let me kiss you good-bye." He bent his knees and lifted her suddenly, her legs hooked over his arms, her buttocks braced against the bureau.

"Lucien!" she squeaked. Then sighed, "Lucien," as he slipped inside her.

"Kiss me good-bye, Aveline," he whispered, beginning that slow thrusting she had come to know so well during the night. "Let me know that you'll miss me. That you'll miss this."

"Yes." She gazed up at him, thrilled to her feminine core by the possessive look in his eyes. Somehow he owned part of her now. Somehow, the bargain had become something more.

She brought her mouth to his, losing herself in his kiss, in the increasing tempo of his thrusts. The pitcher and basin rattled behind her as their movements shook the bureau. He lifted her legs higher, pressed deeper, taking her like a man who couldn't stop. The tension coiled within her, and she dug her nails into his shoulders as the force of it built.

The pitcher fell over.

The basin slid off the edge of the bureau and crashed to the floor in pieces.

Ecstasy shattered through her, and with a wild cry, she clenched her arms and legs around him as her body rippled with release.

He gave a hoarse shout, then thrust home, holding fast as he shuddered with his own completion.

They remained where they were for long moments, then he lowered her legs until her feet touched the ground again. The action caused his softened sex to slip from inside her, and she gave a little whimper of protest.

He continued to hold her tightly in his arms, their hearts pounding the same thundering rhythm, their skin slick with sweat. Finally, he gave a heavy sigh. "I'll send for the coach."

And with that, the first night of the bargain was over.

They shouldn't have lingered so long.

Aveline scurried down the stairs, well aware of Lucien's heavier tread behind her. The sun was nearly full up, and the alarm would be sounded within the hour if the servants at home found Aveline's bed empty.

Lucien had summoned the coach, and the well-sprung equipage awaited her outside the door, the horses whuffing and shifting in the cold morning air. She turned to face him, uncertain what to say.

He smiled, but the look in his eyes seemed detached. Aloof. Awkward silence rose between them. Then he took her hand and brushed a casual kiss across her knuckles. "Until tonight."

She gave a nod, then turned slowly toward the door, her emotions chaotic. How could he remain so cool after what had passed between them? Was she nothing more than a convenience to him after all? She had thought that since their night together had been so incredible for her, he couldn't fail to feel the same way. That he, too, must have been moved by the magic between them.

Silly of her. The man was a rake, an accomplished seducer of women. She had best remember that.

She stepped outside and hurried to the coach, conscious of the ever-rising sun. She could feel his gaze upon her, and she gave into the temptation to look back one more time as she reached the conveyance. He gave her a brief nod of acknowledgment, courteous yet still distant.

Annoyed at herself for seeking a knight in shining armor where clearly there was none, she held out her hand to the waiting footman and climbed into the coach. As she settled back into the luxurious seat and the footman shut the door, a thundering reached her ears. She glanced at Lucien, who frowned and stepped outside, his gaze fastened on something beyond her sight.

Aveline stuck her head out the window just as the

coachman urged the horses onward. The resulting jolt caused the hood of her cloak to slide backward off her head, and for an instant she held the startled gaze of the gentleman who had just raced his horse up to the doorway of Thornsgate. With a squeak of dismay, she popped back inside the coach, the image of Lucien's displeased countenance burned into her mind.

Who was that young gentleman? And now that he'd seen her, what would Lucien tell him? Would he break his promise of secrecy?

Heart pounding like a cornered rabbit's, she wondered if she stood on the brink of public ruin.

"And just who was that exquisite creature?" Handing off his horse to a sleepy stable lad, Dante took the steps at a leap, his gaze fastened on the departing coach.

Lucien scowled. "No one. Forget you saw her." Turning on his heel, he stalked back into the house.

"Forget her? Are you mad?" Dante trailed after him. "Who could forget that angelic beauty?"

"You can. I assume you want breakfast?"

"Of course."

"Come on, then." Lucien led the way to the breakfast room, uncertain why his mood had suddenly turned so black. How was it he didn't feel relaxed and amiable, as he often did after a most satisfying night of fornication? He'd had the girl several times during the night, not to mention this morning's romp. He should be feeling sated and lazy, not irritable.

It wasn't as if he were displeased with her. On the contrary. One never knew about virgins, but Aveline had proven a most apt and eager pupil once the nuisance of her maidenhead had been dealt with. He had no doubt she would show equal eagerness and enjoyment for the remaining two nights of their agreement.

And then she would be gone.

He frowned at that. He rather enjoyed her company—and he admired her practical approach to their agreement and her stalwart honor in following through to the letter. No missish whining or injured tears from Aveline at the loss of her maidenhood. She knew what she was about and resolved to accomplish her goal with a minimum of fuss.

He liked her, he realized suddenly. Not just lusted after her, but genuinely liked her as a person. *That's* why his emotions seemed at sixes and sevens. Such a thing had never happened before.

Bloody hell, he might even feel some regret at the end of their liaison.

"You're scowling again," Dante pointed out, as they reached the breakfast room. He went immediately to the sideboard and snatched a fat sausage from a platter. "Did your ladybird not please you last night?"

Lucien plucked the sausage from his friend's fingers and took a bite. "I told you to forget about her. If you want to continue to eat my food, Dante, then you must cease to be so tedious."

"Tedious? *Me?*" Dante stared, hazel eyes wide with astonishment. "Really, Lucien! Call me a rake, call me a Captain Sharp, even call me a sybaritic fool. But *never* call me tedious, I beg you." He gave a dramatic shudder.

Despite his own strange mood, Lucien cracked a smile and helped himself to a cup of strong, black coffee. "Forgive me, old friend. 'Tis the country that is tedious, not you."

"That I can understand." Taking up a plate, Dante began loading it with fluffy eggs and more sausages. "You really should have come to Melton's last night. 'Tis the only place in this rocky wasteland that boasts any civilized entertainment."

"You mean it's the only place with games rich enough for your liking."

"That, too." Flashing a grin, Dante sat down at the table with his overloaded plate and proceeded to devour his breakfast like a starving man. "I won last night, by the way."

"Did you indeed? A point to you then." Lucien took his seat at the head of the table.

"Which puts me ahead of you."

"For now." Lucien met Dante's gaze over the cup he lifted to his lips.

"First you called off the duel, and now I've won at cards. I shall win the grand game this year, Lucien. See if I don't."

"The end of the year is mere weeks away."

"And I suppose you think you'll win again?" Dante slanted him a glittering look of mischief. "You might yet be ahead if you decide to count last night's companion into the score."

Lucien put down his cup with an impatient click.

"Let it rest, Dante. She's just a lightskirt I paid for the night, nothing more. Certainly not worthy enough to be counted in the game."

"If you're certain." Dante snickered as he scraped the last of the eggs from his plate. "Though she must have given you a hell of a ride for you to send her off in your own coach."

Lucien schooled his features to reveal nothing. "I believe in discretion."

"You? Discreet?" Dante howled with laughter. "Wasn't it you who entered into a wager with me over that Italian countess? The one we both bet we could seduce?"

"The one we both *succeeded* in seducing." Lucien's mouth quirked with remembered humor. "And then the bet became which one of us could satisfy *la contessa* the most times in one night."

"The bet was a draw," Dante reminded him.

"It was." Lucien lifted his cup again and took a sip. "As I recall, she thanked us when she found out about that particular wager."

"Indeed." Dante sat back in his chair and regarded his empty plate. "We're a depraved pair of rogues, to be sure. Dante and Lucifer—Hell's Brethren, the scourge of society."

"Good Lord, Dante, you make us sound like a couple of pirates," Lucien said with a laugh.

"Society named us Hell's Brethren, not I. Though it does seem to fit. I do recall plundering the virtue of a lady or two."

"As do I." Lucien's thoughts drifted to Aveline again, and he impatiently pushed her to the back of his mind. Women were as common as rocks, and one was nearly the same as another. Why, then, did this brave little virgin linger in his mind?

Because she wasn't the same. She possessed the honor of a man, yet the passion of a woman.

And she wasn't a virgin anymore, either.

"Fond memories?" Dante asked slyly.

Lucien wiped away the smile that had crept across his face and gave an indifferent shrug. "Not unpleasant."

"Perhaps you will give me her direction when you tire of her." Dante's innocent expression didn't fool Lucien for an instant.

"And perhaps you'd better leave for London as soon as possible."

"Now is that the manner of a congenial host?" Dante rose from the table. "As it happens, I intend to leave for London later today, after I've collected my winnings from the gentleman who so kindly lost them to me. But for now, I am for bed."

"Peace at last," Lucien drawled.

"Your life would be terribly boring, had you and I not met so long ago at that house party," Dante said with his usual cocky grin. "You know it's true."

"Ah, but boring is very peaceful, isn't it?"

"Fine, then, if that's the way you want to be about it." Dante shook a playful finger at him. "But don't call upon me when you've wearied of watching the grass grow, you son of a duke. I shan't answer the door."

Lucien laughed and threw a piece of sausage at

his friend, who nimbly dodged it. "Only you could make the sobriquet 'son of a duke' into an insult."

"Part of my charm."

"Take your charm to your bedchamber with you." Lucien pulled out his pocket watch and noted the time. "I've an appointment with my man of business in less than an hour."

"Fenworthy is traveling all the way to Thornsgate to meet with you? From London?"

"Of course he is." Lucien rose and gave Dante his most superior look—spoiled, of course, by the chuckle he couldn't suppress. "I've got the golden touch, remember? My investments make Fenworthy a rich man. He'd travel to Hell to meet with me if I asked it of him."

"You do inspire people to do such things." The mischief dimmed from Dante's eyes. "Do you know, Lucien, I *am* tired. Perhaps I will see you later this afternoon when I am ready to take my leave."

"Of course you will." He peered closely at his friend's face. "You do look unwell."

"Just the results of a large breakfast on top of the excesses of a sleepless night of gaming and wenching. I'll be fine." Dante turned toward the door.

"Wenching, you say?" Lucien called after him. "You said nothing about wenching. Must we add another point to your total?"

Dante glanced back, one brow raised in sardonic humor. "Only if you add one to yours." Then he was gone.

Lucien stared after Dante even after his friend had

left the room. Had there been strain in Dante's eyes? Had his cheer seemed a bit forced at the end?

He made a mental note to be on hand when Dante was ready to leave for London. If his friend showed even the slightest hint that he was out of sorts, he would insist that Dante stay the night.

Except that Aveline was supposed to come to him again tonight.

Muttering a curse, he drummed his fingers on the table. He dared not request that she not come; she might think their bargain concluded. And he was far from finished with Aveline Stoddard.

Still, Dante was his best friend. Illegitimate as well, Dante made a perfect partner for Lucien's chosen licentious pursuits. And Lucien's popularity with the *ton*—or rather, his money's popularity with the *ton*—allowed Dante access to the sorts of high-stakes card games that allowed him to maintain his standard of living.

They understood each other, he and Dante. They were two of a kind. And no woman could ever come between them.

Not even Aveline.

Aveline couldn't get the stranger's face out of her mind all day. Every time there came a knock at the door, she was sure it was the unknown man from Thornsgate coming to expose her. But as the hours drifted by and no such event occurred, she began to relax. By the time she and her father had finished the evening meal, she had managed to convince herself that her fears were groundless.

After supper, as was her habit, she sat with her embroidery by the fire and listened to her father read to her from a novel. He changed his voice to reflect the dialogue of the various characters, and she giggled as he read a passage in a high-pitched, feminine voice.

How normal everything seems, she thought. If not for subtle aches in some private places, she might have believed that she had dreamed her night with Lucien DuFeron.

But it had happened. She had given her innocence to the most wicked rake in England. While she was grateful that he had made the experience a pleasurable one, she knew very well that if anyone ever found out, she would be ruined. She glanced at her father, who changed his voice yet again as a new character entered the scene. A small smile tugged at her lips.

It had been worth it.

Just then a servant opened the door to the parlor and announced, "Mr. Dante Wexford."

Aveline glanced up out of curiosity, then froze where she sat as the gentleman she had seen at Thornsgate that morning strolled into the room.

It was a question of who was more surprised, Aveline or Mr. Wexford. After the merest hitch in his confident stride and a quick, astonished glance in her direction, the gentleman regained his aplomb. He greeted her father with easy familiarity while Aveline stared blindly down at her embroidery, the men's friendly conversation fading in the face of her own confusion.

How had he found her? Surely Lucien hadn't given her away? Disappointment stabbed at her tender heart.

"And may I introduce my daughter, Aveline," her father said, bringing her attention back to the situation at hand. "My dear, this is Mr. Dante Wexford from London. We became acquainted at Melton's house party."

Melton's? Curious, Aveline raised her gaze to Mr. Wexford's as the gentleman bowed.

"A very great pleasure, Miss Stoddard," he said with a charming smile. But eyes gave away his true thoughts.

He knew.

She murmured some appropriate reply and dropped her panicked gaze to her embroidery in what she hoped looked like maidenly modesty.

"I had not expected to find such a vision of loveliness at Chestwick Manor," Mr. Wexford continued.

She heard the unspoken message. So, he had not known she would be here. That meant Lucien had at least not told this gentleman her name. Encouraged by the knowledge, she raised her gaze to his, and said, "And I did not expect to meet a man such as you here in my father's parlor, Mr. Wexford. It seems we are both surprised."

"Pleasantly, I hope." He cast a quick, admiring glance at her bosom. "Actually, I'm on my way back to London right now, though I'm frequently in the area to visit . . . friends."

She clutched her embroidery close to her heart before she was tempted to stab him with her needle. "Then I wish you good journey, Mr. Wexford."

"Why, thank you, Miss Stoddard." The mocking quirk of his lips told her he comprehended her unvoiced rejection. And didn't care a whit.

"If you intend to leave tonight, we had best conclude our business," her father said. "If you will excuse us, daughter, Mr. Wexford and I have business to conduct in my study."

Aveline rose. "Actually, I think I'll retire for the evening." She kissed her father lightly on the cheek. "Good night, Papa . . . Mr. Wexford."

"Good night, Miss Stoddard." Mr. Wexford favored her with a knowing look. "Pleasant dreams."

She held her head up high and ignored his subtle gibe. "Why, thank you, Mr. Wexford." Clenching her hands beneath the shelter of her embroidery, she exited the room. As she climbed the stairs to her bedchamber, she heard the two men move from the parlor to the study.

Business, was it? Papa had obviously lost money to Mr. Wexford at the gaming tables. And Mr. Wexford knew her secret, which made an already precarious situation even more dangerous.

Good Lord, what if he told her father? The baron would challenge Lucien to a duel, and Lucien would kill him. Not to mention that her reputation would be in tatters.

She had best find out more about Mr. Dante Wexford before he ruined everything. And the only one she could ask was Lucien.

Chapter 5

The second night began much as the first. Lucien once more had a meal waiting when Aveline stepped into the parlor. Dressed in black, he stood by the fireplace, the crackling flames casting flickering shadows on the walls. As Aveline pushed back the hood of her cloak, he turned to face her, lured by the whisper of the material as it slid away.

She hesitated near the doorway. He watched her with an intensity she couldn't name, the air suddenly too thick to breathe.

She feared she was falling in love with him.

It was the height of foolishness, to lose her heart to a scoundrel like Lucien DuFeron. She knew many women had fallen in love with him, that they had all fantasized about being the one woman who would claim his undying devotion. And no doubt he could barely remember their names.

She was no match for him; her tender maiden's heart could not hope to battle and win the scarred and hardened heart of a rogue. But oh, how she was tempted to try.

He came to her, his steps slow and measured. Her pulse skittered like pebbles scattered by stampeding horses. She knew what would happen now. She knew the taste of his kiss, the touch of his hand.

She *knew* what pleasures awaited her in the coming hours of the night.

"Haven't I frightened you yet?" He rubbed a lock of her hair between his fingers, a teasing note in his voice. "I thought surely you would not come back after last night's escapades."

Heat flooded her cheeks. "I'm not afraid of you, Lucien."

He chuckled. "Indeed?"

She raised her brows. "After last night, I doubt I will be shocked by anything you show me."

His mouth quirked in a knowing smile. "Are you certain?"

That smile sent a shiver of arousal through her. "Actually, I'm not certain of anything when it comes to you."

"Good." He tugged at the ties of her cloak and pushed the garment off her shoulders. "Because tonight I want you naked."

She bit back a gasp and tried for insouciance. "I've been naked with you already."

"All night." His dark, wicked eyes glittered. He

slid behind her and snatched open the laces and buttons of her dress with a speed that the best lady's maid would envy. "All night, Aveline," he whispered, his mouth nipping her ear, the heat of his breath tickling her neck. "Eating. Sleeping. Making love. Naked . . . all the time."

"Eating?" By some miracle she managed not to stutter.

"You'll dine naked." Her dress gaped at the bosom, and he took shameless advantage, reaching from behind her to cup her breasts through her thin chemise. "You'll sleep naked. You'll play chess naked."

"I . . . I don't know how to play chess." Her knees seemed to have melted. She sagged against him, eyes sliding half-closed in response to his caresses.

"I'll teach you." His lips pressed against her neck in a hot openmouthed kiss. "First move . . . knight takes queen."

He scooped her into his arms and carried her upstairs to his bed.

"Come, lover." Hours later, he flipped back the covers so her naked body was exposed. "I'll teach you to play chess."

Pink suffused her cheeks, whether at the endearment or embarrassment at her nakedness, he couldn't say. "Chess? I'd hardly think a man like you would think of chess at a time like this."

"Why not?" As she reached for the sheets to cover up again, he gave her a playful slap on the bottom. She yelped, and the wary look she sent him made him want to laugh. "Leave the covers be, impudent chit. Don't you recall my saying that you would do everything naked tonight?"

"But—" Her eyes widened as she realized he was serious. "I can't learn to play chess naked!"

"Of course you can." He gave her a playful leer. "Remember, I'm naked, too."

She glanced down at his lap, then seemed to realize what she was doing and jerked her gaze back to his face. "I thought you were joking."

He chuckled and threw back his own covers. "I never joke about bare flesh, my sweet."

He overrode her protests and soon had her seated across from him near the hearth, her smooth brow creased in concentration as she regarded the chessboard.

After her initial embarrassment, Aveline began to enjoy the glow of the fire flickering across his broad shoulders and well-muscled chest. His dark hair gleamed blue-black as he regarded the chessboard.

How quickly they had come to be at ease with each other, she mused. Had anyone told her two days ago that she would be sitting most comfortably in the presence of a man without a stitch on her body, she would have thought such a person insane.

Yet here she was, wicked wanton that she had become, learning to play chess with all her charms bared to his very interested gaze. And it didn't really bother her.

She should be blushing from head to toe. She should be protesting such shocking sensuality. But some part of her enjoyed the appreciative gleam in his eyes as his gaze swept her exposed flesh. She found herself subtly turning this way or that to tease him with glimpses of various parts of her body. He caught on to her game quickly, and with a knowing smile curving his lips, he found ways to touch her—his hand over hers as he demonstrated a move, his foot against hers under the tiny table where the chessboard rested, a soft kiss brushed casually over her fingers. By the time the game was done, her heart was pounding, and every inch of her skin tingled with what she had come to recognize as sexual awareness.

Yes, she had done this to save her father's life. But as Lucien won the game with a shout of victory . . . as he knocked over her king and stood, tipping over his chair in the process . . . as he scooped her over his shoulder and then tossed her on the rumpled bed, claiming her as the spoils of war, she knew there was more to it than that.

Some part of her had craved this knowledge, this contact with a man. She had thought to learn of such things from a husband. But now that she knew what it was all about, she couldn't imagine ever giving herself this way to any man but Lucien.

Even though he would be in her life for only one night longer.

Don't think about it. He kissed her, stretching her arms over her head like a conqueror, and she eagerly responded. She would take what he gave.

The hours sped by quickly. Again, he astonished her with his knowledge of the secrets of her own body. She had learned more about herself from him in these two nights than she had in the entire nineteen years of her existence.

But now she lay wrapped in his arms in the bed, her back snug against his front, and watched as a ray of early-morning light streaming through the window grew brighter and brighter with the increasing lateness of the hour.

She started to throw back the covers, but his big hand stayed hers. She glanced back at him, puzzled. He merely stared at her, his dark eyes intense with a churning variety of emotions that she couldn't name.

"I have to go," she whispered. "The sun is rising."

Still he said nothing, merely entwined his fingers with hers in silent entreaty. Her heart seemed to melt in her chest. What was he thinking? Why was he looking at her as if she held the key to some valuable secret?

"You know I can't stay," she said.

Still holding her gaze, he lifted her hand to his lips and pressed a kiss to her fingers. His eyes slid closed, his long lashes dark against his cheek in a moment of unexpected vulnerability.

Her breath caught. The tension swelled, an emotional net tightening around them, pulling them closer. Good God, what was happening? Where was the wicked rake she had known before?

She squeezed his fingers, and he opened his eyes to look at her. She could only gaze at him, her tongue tied by words she dared not say. Was afraid to say. She licked her lips. Maybe she *should* speak after all . . .

His expression flickered, and his gaze grew shuttered. He released her hand, then rolled from the bed, raising his eyebrows at her as he reached for his clothing. The moment was gone. The apathetic Lucien had returned in full force, the unguarded one gone as if he had never been.

With a sigh that mourned his loss, she, too, rose to dress.

Only later, as she rode home in the coach, did she remember that she had forgotten to ask him about Dante Wexford.

He missed her.

Lucien glanced at the clock. It was shortly after one o'clock in the afternoon, and Aveline would not come for many hours yet. And tonight was the last night she would come at all.

He could amend the bargain. Could demand more nights. A week. A month. However long it took him to tire of her.

He considered it, turned over the different options in his mind. He could make her do it, threaten to challenge her father.

And she would hate him.

Pulled up short by the utter ruthlessness of his thoughts, he rejected the idea. Aveline wasn't like other women. He wouldn't force her to continue their affair; he respected her too much for that.

Which amazed him to no end.

Scowling, he regarded the correspondence on his desk, no doubt the reason for his strange and vengeful mood. The letter was from his father's wife, Clarissa, the Duchess of Huntley, demanding his presence at a dinner party in his father's honor.

Clarissa rarely wrote to him; in fact, she hated his very existence. He was a living, breathing insult to her, but there was nothing she could do about it. He found her selfish and needlessly cruel. She thought him irreverent and a blot on the family reputation. Thus, they rubbed along in mutual loathing whenever they chanced to meet.

In a purely objective sort of way, he could almost understand her feelings toward him. She had only been married to his father for a year when the duke's former French mistress, Sophie DuFeron, had contacted the duke and offered to give him his five-year-old son in exchange for a certain amount of money. The duke, having no idea that he had even sired a child, immediately traveled to France to see the boy for himself.

Upon learning his date of birth, the Duke of Huntley had known immediately that Lucien was his. He had paid Sophie double her asking price on the condition that she disappear from the boy's life forever. She had immediately done so, and Lucien had never seen his mother again.

The duke had taken Lucien back to London, where he had installed him in the nursery at Huntley House, much to the horror of his young bride. Only the threat of being shut away for the rest of her life had stopped Clarissa from taking matters into her own hands to rid their lives of the lad. Her only consolation was that Lucien could never inherit the title; it would be her child, a legitimate heir, who would do so. And a year later she proudly presented that heir to the duke, their son Robert.

While Lucien had grown up well fed, educated, and elegantly clothed in ducal mansions, the cold personality of his father and the blistering hatred of his stepmother made his childhood an unhappy one. He had hoped to forge a bond with his half brother, Robert, but Clarissa made sure that her son adopted her hostile attitude toward Lucien.

The duke had always made it clear from the beginning that he had taken custody of Lucien merely out of a sense of responsibility, not because of any parental love he bore his child. Lucien's only comfort in this knowledge was that the duke didn't seem to favor Robert any more than he did his illegitimate son, leaving Lucien to deduce that his father was simply an apathetic man by nature. Though he lacked for paternal love, Lucien's material comforts had been seen to, and the duke had even arranged for Lucien's education at Eton.

On Lucien's twenty-first birthday, his father had presented him with a small sum of money to get him started in life. Through a series of shrewd investments, Lucien had quickly tripled the amount. Now at age twenty-five, his fortune rivaled Huntley's—a situation that never ceased to infuriate Clarissa. Lucien's "golden touch" and his connection to the duke had made him popular in London Society. His scandalous exploits had earned him the name Lucifer, and when he befriended Dante, the illegitimate son of an earl who would not acknowledge him, the two had been dubbed "Hell's Brethren."

Clarissa had *really* hated that. She remained icily tolerant of his existence every time they attended the same social function, her abhorrence of him unmistakable.

Which made it odd that she had invited him to an event in his father's honor. Knowing Clarissa, she would have excluded him if she could. No doubt his father had requested his presence, and Clarissa dared not defy the duke.

He made a note of the date—a fortnight hence—and moved on to his other correspondence. A glance at the clock showed it to be nearly a quarter past one.

Many hours had yet to pass before Aveline was due to arrive.

On their last night together, they didn't even make it to the bedchamber.

Lucien took her there, in the parlor, on the French settee, in a torrent of desperate passion that surprised both of them. Once she had regained her senses, Aveline was rather amazed the delicate-looking piece of furniture hadn't broken beneath them.

Later, he'd carried her upstairs—such a thrilling thing to be carried in a man's arms as if one weighed nothing—and started all over again.

At last they lay tangled in the bed, Aveline's softness warm against his side. Downstairs the clock chimed midnight.

Hours from now she would leave him, this time never to return.

He didn't like this weakness inside him. Why did he care that their liaison would soon be over? In the past his only concern had been that his mistresses satisfy him inside the bedchamber and remain complacent outside it.

Of course, Aveline wasn't his mistress. They had a bargain.

A bargain almost fulfilled.

She turned in his arms, her silky hair sweeping across his arm as she faced him. Her green eyes still glowed with lingering pleasure, and as he held her gaze, a blush crept across her cheeks.

He should be happy. Their bargain had turned into a successful and pleasurable interlude, with no tears or demands on either side. Aveline had acted with more honor than most men he knew, and he respected her for that.

He didn't want her to go. The peculiar feeling of attachment brought a frown to his face.

The gentle touch of her fingertips on his furrowed brow drew his attention. She smiled at him, a soft, teasing curve of the lips. "Have I displeased you, that you frown so?"

"Not at all." He drew on his infamous charm and traced his finger over her bare shoulder, flashing her the roguish grin that had crumbled many a maid's defenses. "You please me quite well. Our bargain is a success."

Her expression flickered, but her smile remained steadfast. "So it is."

Something tightened around his heart. He hadn't liked the look of uncertainty that flashed across her face. He didn't want anything to ruin their last night together, so he sought to tease her out of her melancholy.

Wrapping his arms around her, he nuzzled his beard-roughened cheek into her neck.

"Lucien!" she squealed, squirming in his embrace. "That tickles!"

"Does it?" He grabbed her flailing foot and bent over to rub his prickly chin against her arch.

She howled with laughter, flipping onto her stomach in her efforts to twist away from him.

"Well, now." Releasing her foot, he placed a hand on the small of her back to prevent her from turning over and ran his other hand over the soft globes of her bottom. "What have we here?"

"Lucien!" She tried to wiggle free, but he bent forward to brush a kiss over her spine. She gave a startled gasp and stopped struggling.

"Does this tickle?" He moved up her back, trailing kisses from her bottom to her nape.

"No," she whispered, her fingers clenching in the sheets.

He rose on his knees and slipped his hands beneath her, cupping her breasts. "And this?"

"No," she choked.

He slid one hand down along her belly, guiding her so that she knelt on all fours, then rubbed his erection against the softness of her buttocks. "And this?"

"Stop teasing me, Lucien," she begged.

"Very well." He positioned himself, then slipped easily inside her, closing his eyes in ecstasy as her body cradled him in her wet heat. Slowly he began to move, and she rocked with him, burying her face in the pillows as she mewed her enjoyment.

He held her hips in his hands, the softness of her derriere against his belly adding a sensual friction to their mating. All too soon the pleasure swelled within him. Caressing her buttocks, he thrust hard, giving a hoarse shout as he released his seed into her womb.

Aveline followed his climax a moment later, her body shuddering and sagging into the pillows, his name escaping her lips on a sweet sigh of satisfaction.

Dawn arrived all too soon.

With a heavy heart, Aveline slid from beneath Lucien's heavy arm and climbed from the bed where he slept. Pushing aside the curtains at the window, she stared at the faint orange glow on the horizon.

For the first time in her life, she resented the coming day.

How would their parting be? Would he turn cold and aloof? Would he casually pat her on the head or the bottom and thank her for a pleasant interlude? Would he have the carriage summoned, then leave her to her own devices while she vacated his life?

Her heart cried out in protest, and panic streaked through her. Dear Lord, it was too late. She had fallen in love with Lucien.

Foolish, foolish girl.

Tears stung her eyes, but she refused to shed them. She had known what she was getting into. No use crying because she had compounded her tumble from grace by falling in love with a man incapable of returning her feelings.

As she stared at the inevitable dawn, her life stretched out lonely and barren before her.

Lucien woke slowly, vaguely conscious that something was wrong. His bed felt cold, empty. When he opened his eyes, he saw Aveline standing by the window, the early rays of sunrise casting a rosy glow over her lovely flesh and turning her long blond hair a glittering sweep of dark gold. Her lush lower lip trembled. She bit down on it, then cast down her eyes and turned away from the sunrise as if she couldn't bear to look at it anymore.

Sunrise.

He sat up in bed. She was leaving. Their three nights were over.

The rustle of the sheets drew her attention, and she froze like a rabbit hearing the footstep of a hunter. Her eyes looked huge in her face, a variety of emotions rippling through them too quickly for him to identify.

His chest tightened, and he clenched his fists in the sheets. He wanted to yank her back in the bed and stop time, to keep her beside him and beneath him indefinitely. He didn't want her to go.

The strange notion gripped his attention and wouldn't release it. He didn't want her to leave, to return to her quiet life as the daughter of that gamester, Chestwick. She deserved better.

But was being the mistress of a notorious rake better than an honorable life as a wastrel's daughter?

Torn, he could only look at her, longing for something he could not name, ripped asunder by the simple truth that they had to part. She had to go back to her life and he to his. That was the bargain. It was right. It was honorable. As his mistress, she would be taken care of, but she would never be able to show her face in polite society again.

He had to let her go.

"A new day dawns," she whispered.

The words struck him like blows, and he wished he could stop the sun from rising. That time could stay motionless forever.

He couldn't stop time. But he could steal some of it.

He held out a hand to her. She hesitated, then ran back to the bed and tumbled into his arms. Their mouths met with heated desperation, every second ticking past bringing them closer to the moment when they would part forever.

He swept his hands over the body he had come to know so well, using his knowledge as a means to fuel her desire. He wanted her insane with need, screaming his name.

He wanted . . . everything.

She returned his every caress, using what he'd taught her to urge him to hard, aching arousal. Her mouth was everywhere, her small hands greedy as they stroked and smoothed his flesh. It was a contest of who could rouse the other more, each of them mad to give to the other.

Her soft lips closed around his erection, and his

eyes nearly rolled back in his head with the pleasure of it. Too much. Too soon. He let himself enjoy her ministrations for a moment or two, then reluctantly tangled his hand in her hair and tugged her mouth away before he exploded.

She slid a half-lidded glance his way, her lips pursed knowingly. Then she dipped down and gave him one last lick, sending a shudder through him.

"Wicked chit," he muttered, tugging her face to his. The smugness in her eyes was unmistakable. "Want to play, do you?"

She just smiled, a curve of the lips that must have made Adam take that damned apple from Eve.

Couldn't blame the poor bastard. Lucien was about ready to give her anything she asked as well. But the ticking of the blasted clock reminded him that there was no time for indulgence.

She might be leaving him, but he'd be hanged if she was going to forget him.

He rolled her onto her back, stretching her arms over her head, easily resisting her efforts to pull her hands free. Holding her small wrists in his much larger hand, he reached between her legs and stroked her.

She gave a small mewl of pleasure, and her knees fell open. He took advantage, settling quickly between her thighs but not taking her. He wanted to. The scent of her readiness intoxicated him, and he recognized that soft, pleading look in her eyes. But he wanted to make this last, make them both so insane with wanting each other that when he finally did take her, the pleasure would make them forget the world around them.

Make them forget that this was the last time.

He kissed her, his head spinning as she kissed him back the way he'd taught her, his fingers stroking her the way she liked. Her hips arched into his hand, a silent plea, but he knew what he was about. When he allowed her release, it would be something she would never forget.

Ever.

He nibbled her throat, her ear. "Say my name," he commanded.

"Lucien." A gasp escaped her throat as his mouth found her breast. "Dear God, Lucien."

"Tell me who's doing this to you," he murmured, some wickedness demanding that he make her admit it, make her *know* who it was that could make her feel this way. "Who's touching you? Who's kissing you?"

"Lucien," she panted. "Only you."

"Only me," he agreed. Her soft thigh brushed his aching erection, and he nearly lost control. He hissed in a sharp breath, calmed himself with clenched teeth and a reminder of what he was trying to do.

Damn it, he *would* do this. Would give both of them a memory to remember.

He nibbled at her breasts, and she arched her back, crying his name as he continued to stroke her closer and closer to climax. He felt a ripple against his fingers and stopped abruptly, not wanting her to find her pleasure too soon.

She gave a whimper of protest and moved her hips urgently against his hand.

"Not yet." With a wicked smile, he kissed her lips, stared down into her desire-clouded eyes. "Trust me."

She nodded, closing her eyes with a soft cry as he started caressing her again.

He brought her to the brink twice more, each occurrence stoking his own hunger until he could barely stand it. His heart pounded in his chest, sweat misting his back and forehead as his body trembled with the effort not to give in to release.

Finally, he couldn't bear it a moment longer. His body took over, seeking what it craved, whether he willed it or no.

He released her hands, and she clasped them around his neck. He scooped her knees over his elbows, pressing her legs up and wide, and tormented both of them a moment longer by rubbing himself against the hot, wet entrance to her body.

"Damn you, Lucien," she muttered. Her hands fisted in his hair, her eyes locking with his in hungry female demand. "Take me before I die from wanting you."

Her command broke the last of his control. He took her mouth and her body at the same moment, his greedy kiss mirroring his first powerful thrust.

She cried out and arched her back, so aroused that the first stroke sent her over the edge. Her body rippled around him as she climaxed, her fingers tightening in his hair.

He pressed her legs farther apart, allowing him-

self one satisfying moment to revel in her inner
convulsions. But his own pleasure nipped at him,
just out of reach, and he sought it recklessly.
Deeper. Harder. This way, that way. Fast strokes.
Slow ones. He wanted to climb inside her and wal-
low in pleasure.

Chanting his name, she moved her hips to meet
his thrusts, bringing him deeper and deeper, clenching her muscles around him. She bit his ear, kissed
him with openmouthed abandon, wrapped her
arms around him and dug her nails into his back as
she climaxed a second time.

He slipped over the edge. With a hoarse shout, he
emptied himself into her, the pleasure draining his
mind of anything but her.

"Aveline," he whispered, clasping her to him, still
shuddering inside her. "Aveline."

Chapter 6

Aveline was awakened by the call of one servant to another somewhere downstairs. For an instant she cuddled closer to the big warm body beside her, wrapping herself in the sheets and burying her nose in Lucien's throat. It was too early to get up. Too lovely right where she was . . .

Morning! Her eyes popped open, and she sat up with a jerk. Sunlight flooded the room. The jingle of a harness and the clop of a horse's hooves drifted up through the window from outside. Feet shuffled beyond the door to the bedroom as the servants walked the halls, performing their duties.

"Oh, no!" Panicked, she stumbled out of the bed, dragging some of the sheets with her in hasty covering as she made her way across the room to Lucien's bureau. With trembling fingers, she grabbed his pocket watch and flipped it open.

Dawn had come and gone more than an hour ago.

"If you are in need of funds, you need merely ask," Lucien drawled from the bed, his voice muffled by the pillow. "I'd rather keep my pocket watch, if it's all the same to you."

"I slept too long." She tossed the watch on the bureau and raced for her scattered clothes. "The sun is up. The servants are up. *My father* is probably up!" She dropped the sheet and grabbed her chemise from the floor, frantically turning it in her hands in search of the neck and armholes.

"The servants will say nothing if they value their positions." Lucien sat up and stretched, lazily unconcerned with his nudity. "And your father is probably yet at the tables."

"What a hateful thing to say!" She jerked the garment over her head and jabbed her arms through the sleeves.

He raised his brows in that mocking expression she had come to know so well. "My dear Aveline, might I remind you that it was your father's fondness for gaming that led you here?"

Smoothing the shift over her hips, she flipped her hair out of her face and glared at him. "I thought 'twas your fondness for dueling."

"Oh, no." He stood and walked over to the chair where he'd left his clothes. "We've come this far without lies, Aveline. Let's not start now."

"Lies?" She pulled her hair back from her face and tied it with the ribbon she found on the chess table.

"Let's do talk of lies, Lucien. What of your promise to tell no one of our liaison?"

He frowned as he tugged on his trousers. "And I've told no one."

"Then who is Mr. Dante Wexford?" She found her dress flung halfway behind a chair. "How was it he came to my home the other night and insinuated that he knew everything about us?"

"I have no idea what you're talking about."

"He came the night before last." She managed to get into the dress unaided, but then realized she couldn't reach the fastenings. "He apparently won some money from my father."

"Ah." With a smile, Lucien picked up his shirt. "That explains it then. His visit had nothing to do with us."

"It had everything to do with us!" Brandishing the slipper she had found tossed beneath the bed, she shook it at him with one hand while holding the edges of her dress closed with the other. "He flirted with me in a very suggestive manner. And the look in his eyes insinuated that he knows everything."

"Don't be ridiculous." He dodged the slipper she waved in his face and turned her around so he could do up the fastenings of her dress. "Dante flirts with all women. It's his nature."

"He saw me that morning," she reminded him.

Lucien sighed. "Yes, he did."

"Did he ask who I was? Did you tell him my name?"

"No, I didn't tell him your name!" Anger roughened his voice as he fastened the last hook and spun away from her. "You're being irrational. I told you our liaison would remain between us."

"Irrational?" She turned to face him. "He's your friend. Do you expect me to believe that you said nothing?"

"I said nothing. And damn you for doubting me." He took her by the shoulders. "You're upset at our parting. There's no need to conjure arguments to hide that."

"You arrogant prig!" She shrugged away from him. "I have no need to conjure anything. Look at the situation in which we find ourselves. Had you been an honorable man, you would not have demanded such a price for my father's life."

His features hardened, his eyes glittering with carefully restrained fury. "Had your father been an honorable man, there would never have been a challenge in the first place. You forget, he placed *my* honor in question."

"And the price for your honor was mine."

"Don't you dare try and blame me for what happened between us," he snapped. "*You* came to *me*. You accepted my terms."

"And *my* terms included complete secrecy. Your Mr. Wexford ruined that."

"Just as I've ruined you?" he mocked. "Grow up, Aveline. I didn't force you into my bed. You came of your own will."

A flush swept her cheeks, but she lifted her chin with pride. "I did. And I would do it again if it meant saving my father's life."

"Oh, well done!" He applauded, his face harsh with derision. "Do play the wronged innocent, sweet Aveline. Poor girl, her virginity sacrificed to the beast to save her dear father's life." He went to a small wooden chest on a nearby table. Flipping open the elegant box, he withdrew a handful of papers. "Here is what you sold yourself for, my dear. Your father's vowels—totaling just over three thousand pounds."

She clenched her hands at her sides, stung more than she cared to admit by his phrasing. "How could you say such a thing?"

"How could I speak the truth, you mean?" He laughed, the sound hard and jaded. "I've always known that everyone has a price, my dear, especially women." He came to her, caressed her face and throat with the papers clutched in his fist. "I thank you for being honest about your price, Aveline. Our time together has been—delightful."

Pain speared her tender heart. He made her sound like a harlot, like she had given him her body in exchange for money.

But hadn't she?

Her throat closed up as she fought back tears. She would not let him deride her, would not let him cheapen what she had done in order to save her father's life.

"You're a hateful, miserable man," she whispered.

"At last, the truth from your lips!" He leaned his face close to hers. "Take your father's vowels, Aveline. The bargain is complete."

Her spine stiff with controlled emotion, she plucked the papers from his hand. "Summon the coach."

He took a step back, then swept her a bow rife with scorn. "As my lady wishes."

Ignoring him, she turned away to seek her other slipper.

He didn't move for an instant, then suddenly stalked over to the door, yanked it open, and strode out of the room.

The slam of the door behind him released the tension that had held her emotions in check. With tears welling in her eyes and slipping down her cheeks, she carefully tucked away her father's markers and set about collecting her shoes and cloak.

Her heart was broken. But she would die before Lucien DuFeron would ever know that she had been foolish enough to fall in love with him.

From the window of an upstairs guest room, Lucien watched the coach pull away. He knew Aveline was in it, though he hadn't laid eyes on her again since he had slammed out of his bedroom. He hadn't trusted himself to face her again.

How could she have doubted him? How could she have accused him of breaking their agreement?

And since when did a woman's opinion of him matter?

He let his forehead rest against the window. Since Aveline.

Fool, fool, fool. This is what the softer emotions brought with them—nothing but betrayal and heartbreak. Weakness. He must have been mad to think even for a second that Aveline was different from other women. *She'd* come to *him*, hadn't she? She'd had a price just like everyone else. She'd offered her body in exchange for her father's life.

All right, so offering her body had been his idea. But he hadn't expected her to agree to it. And when she had—well, he was a man after all, and not one to ignore what was freely presented.

But he hadn't expected to care.

He straightened and absently rubbed at the ache in his chest, watching her coach disappear around the bend in the drive. She wasn't coming back.

Thornsgate suddenly loomed huge and cold around him. Empty. No longer would the halls echo with her laughter. Or that little gasping sound she made when he shocked her. Or the tiny mew of pleasure that escaped her lips when he slipped inside her.

He couldn't stay here.

He should go to London. Find Dante. Erase his memories of Aveline by losing himself in the arms of another woman. Ten other women.

But even as he left to give the orders to the servants, even as he mentally shuffled the names of possible paramours in his mind, he recognized the truth.

He would never forget Aveline.

Chapter 7

London
Two months later

London hadn't changed. It was still the most civilized of cities, rife with salacious entertainment for the most indulgent of souls. Though the Season wouldn't officially begin until the spring, there were those who had chosen to pass the Christmas holidays in Town, Lucien among them. But where others had ventured to London in these cold winter months to be close to family and friends, Lucien had lingered in the city after the holiday to do just the opposite.

He was trying to stay away from Aveline.

It was harder than he'd expected. He still didn't understand how one slip of a girl could so completely enthrall him. He'd known women more beautiful than she was, women more passionate, more stylish. But it was Aveline he craved in his arms at night, no matter how many clever courtesans he bedded. Aveline, whose laughter he wanted to hear ringing through the silent rooms of his London home. Aveline, whose innocent enthusiasm had made their time together more memorable than the most skilled of mistresses.

Aveline, who hadn't trusted him.

Sitting before the hearth, he watched the firelight gleam off the polished pieces set up on the chessboard. He remembered her blush as he had taught her to play chess—naked. Her determination to act sophisticated when he knew she was a sheltered innocent.

He reached over and picked up the white queen, rolling the piece between his fingers. Maybe there was some chance for them. Maybe he should see her, make sure she was all right.

He closed his eyes and clenched his fingers around the chess piece, as if to prevent the queen from escaping his grasp. Of course she was all right. She had her father to look after her, didn't she?

The day he'd left Cornwall, the baron had come to see him. He could still see it in his mind, the plump baron's face red with fury as he bellowed about honor and demanded satisfaction. Chestwick had found out about their affair when Aveline had come home that morning with his markers in her hand.

Lucien had refused to duel with him.

The baron had stared in disbelief as Lucien had

walked past him and into the carriage that would take him to London. Even Lucien could barely believe his own actions. He had never before walked away from a duel, especially one that assured victory. But no matter that he deserved the baron's ire, no matter that he didn't fear losing the match, he did not accept the challenge.

For Aveline.

Even if she didn't believe in his honor, *he* did. Their bargain had demanded three nights in his bed in exchange for her father's debts and his life. She had fulfilled her terms; he would fulfill his.

The ridges of the chess piece dug into his palm, bringing him back to the present. He tossed it back on the board. It rolled, knocking aside a pawn and toppling the black king.

Emmons, his London butler, entered the room and announced, "Mr. Dante Wexford."

With a dark look at the fallen chess pieces, he faced Dante as his friend swept into the room past the exiting butler.

"Gad, Lucien, you're not dressed." Himself garbed in elegant black evening wear, Dante sported a snowy cravat, impeccable white gloves, and a fashionable walking stick. A diamond stickpin sparkled at his throat. He arched his brows and indicated Lucien's more casual attire. "Certainly you don't intend to appear at Lady Presting's ball in *that*."

Lucien gave a weary sigh. "My apologies, Dante. I forgot all about it."

"Again? Lucien, do you realize that you have attended fewer than six events in the past two months? You, who used to appear at as many affairs in one *night*?"

"I know." Lucien reached out and scooped up the white queen again, contemplated it. "I find that I've lost my taste for London's social whirl."

"You've—" Clearly astounded, Dante stared. "You can't be serious."

"I am." He rose, slipping the chess piece into his pocket. "Brandy?"

"I don't want brandy." Dante followed as Lucien walked over to the decanter on a nearby table. "But there's bound to be some at Lady Presting's winter ball."

Lucien chuckled. "It's only one ball, Dante. There will be others."

"There have *been* others." Just as Lucien started to pour, Dante gripped his arm. Brandy sloshed over the table. "You've dismissed almost all of them."

Lucien cast an icy glance at Dante's hand on his sleeve. "You forget yourself."

"Don't speak to me in that tone of voice." Nonetheless, Dante stepped back, his hazel eyes hot with emotion. "You're no better than I am just because your father chose to acknowledge you."

"Will you cease harping on that?" Lucien set down the decanter with a loud clink. "I had no control over the matter. My father acknowledged that he was careless with his mistress and sired a son. That's all."

"You wouldn't say that if you stood outside Polite Society as I do."

Lucien rolled his eyes and took up his half-filled glass, turning back toward his chair. "This again, Dante?"

"Yes, *this again*." Dante stepped into his path, and Lucien halted, surprised by the naked frustration on his friend's face. "My father ignores my existence. I was not educated like you were. My only living is my talent at the card tables."

"I know." Sympathy heavy in his voice, Lucien stared down at his brandy, then sipped it.

"I don't want your pity, dammit!" Dante spun away, shoulders stiff. "Do you think I like having to depend on you for my very life? Without your entrée into Society, I would have no chance at all. It's fleecing the highborn that puts the food in my mouth and the clothes on my back."

"I know," Lucien said again, more quietly. "I'll go with you to Lady Presting's." He tossed back the rest of the brandy.

"Splendid!" All smiles again, Dante went to serve himself some of the fine French liquor.

With a weary glance at Dante's back, Lucien placed his own glass on a table, uncomfortable with the scene. Dante was his closest friend, but he never knew what to say to him when he got so emotional. The easiest tactic was just to give Dante what he wanted at the moment.

He had never been good at emotional entanglements. The debacle with Aveline had proven that.

"I shall be down directly."

Dante watched as Lucien left the room, his smile fading. His breath came out in a whoosh, and he withdrew his elegant handkerchief and mopped a bead of sweat from his brow. He had worried that Lucien would remain firm in his self-enforced solitude, that he would insist on staying home from Lady Presting's ball, no matter how Dante attempted to convince him. And that prospect would have been disastrous.

He tucked his handkerchief away and noted that his hands were shaking. Damn it all.

He went to the sideboard and poured himself more brandy. He had to remain calm. He didn't need Lucien suspecting anything. As the liquor slid down his throat, he closed his eyes, guilt weighing on him.

Could he do this? Was he capable of such an act? Lucien was his best friend, had always allowed Dante to follow on his coattails as he easily swept his way through the *ton*. Never had Lucien thought Dante inferior for the circumstances of his birth.

But a man had to survive. Dante gulped back the rest of his brandy. And Lucien had become the worst sort of hermit. How was a man to make a living if his best friend cut off his only means of reaching his goals?

Lucien's withdrawal from Society had resulted in Dante's pockets going to let. Without Lucien's cachet Dante had no way to gamble with the highborn. He hadn't lied when he said he depended on Lucien for his living.

But not anymore. No, never again.

He put down his glass and turned toward Lucien's desk to distract himself. Maybe his old friend had left a pound or two amongst the papers. Every shilling counted these days.

He ruffled the papers and searched the drawers but found nothing of value, no money left carelessly aside. Blast Lucien, but he had always been distressingly organized.

His eyes fell on a pile of letters sitting in a neat stack in the corner of the desk. He took up the first one and examined it. Unopened. It must be the day's post.

Pursing his lips, he flipped through the letters. Invitations by the boatload. Lucien really was the most selfish of friends not to have accepted some of them—and then asked Dante to accompany him, of course.

And then he found the letter.

He knew immediately it was from a woman, knew from the handwriting and the pretty paper. He sniffed the envelope—a delicate female cologne clung to it. He knew that scent. Where had he . . . lavender. That's what it was. The last time he had smelled lavender had been when he went to collect his winnings from Lord Chestwick.

Was this missive from the baron's lovely daughter?

He tapped the letter with his finger, traced the scrolling script that formed Lucien's name. Perhaps the little trollop wanted an assignation. She had been a ripe piece, lushly formed and beautiful. And no virgin if she had been leaving Lucien's home early in the morning.

He grinned. Perhaps he would find out the details of the rendezvous and go in Lucien's stead. Maybe he could turn her affection away from Lucien and onto himself.

The plan appealed more and more to him with every second that passed. Lucien hadn't been the same since he'd bedded the chit. Perhaps he'd formed a tendre for her. But once she took Dante as her lover and Lucien was reminded of how fickle a woman could be, maybe then he would forget her and go back to his old ways of scandalizing Society. Hell's Brethren would live again.

Maybe then Dante could turn away from the cold alternative he contemplated. Maybe things would get back to normal.

Enthused by the prospect, he ripped open the letter and prepared for a salacious reading of the contents. But after the first line, his jaw dropped. His hopes dissolved. There was no way that Lucien would ever return to his old ways after reading this. Hell's Brethren would die a quick, senseless death.

"Bloody hell, Luce," he muttered. "You should have known better."

He grabbed a piece of Lucien's stationery and scribbled a quick letter, just two lines. He thrust it into an envelope, addressed it to Cornwall, and buried it in the pile of correspondence waiting to be posted. Then he rose and deliberately threw Aveline Stoddard's note and envelope into the fire. As he watched the scented stationery curl and burn to ash, his heart grew heavier and heavier.

He no longer had a choice. He had to act before Lucien found out about Chestwick's daughter. The note he had penned would not hold her for long. Eventually, Lucien would find out. Eventually, he would go to her.

Dante couldn't have that. And he couldn't take the chance that the chit would come to London looking for Lucien and draw attention to things that should be kept in the shadows. The harsh words he had written should prevent that, but one never knew with young girls.

It had to be done. He had no choice.

"I'm ready," Lucien said, stepping into the room dressed in expensively tailored evening wear. "Come, Dante. The night awaits."

"That it does," Dante agreed, turning to face him with an insincere smile. "That it does."

Blackness swam before his eyes. The world tilted precariously, and Lucien moaned as his heavy head rocked with it. Where the devil was he? And why couldn't he see?

He forced his sluggish brain to think, but they'd clubbed him when they'd grabbed him, and the blow had clearly addled his senses. He sucked in a breath. Brine tainted the air, tangy on the tongue. The lapping of waves and the creak of sea-worn wood told Lucien he was on a ship. And his eyes were closed.

He wasn't blind, thank God.

With a hissed curse, he tried to rise from his face-down position, but a cruel hand between his shoulder blades shoved him back onto the hard, frozen deck.

His head throbbed, and he fought back nausea. Laughter and mockery jumbled in his spinning thoughts as his captors talked over his sprawled form. He fought for control. Whoever these brigands were, he would not give them the satisfaction of casting up his accounts in front of them.

He only hoped Dante had gotten safely away.

"And who have we here?" A booming voice silenced the others, and Lucien struggled to keep alert. This, then, must be their captain.

"A new cabin boy for ye, cap'n." One of the villains cackled as he swept a sack off Lucien's head. Lucien's skull thudded against the deck with the movement, and he couldn't suppress a groan. Bright spots flickered before his eyes as he slowly opened them.

"He's a big 'un." A meaty hand fisted in his hair, lifting his head so the scar-faced, red-bearded man could peer at him. "And dressed like a nabob. Someone doesn't like ye at all, laddie," he said to Lucien. "Someone wants ye all but dead, and that's the truth."

"Who?" Lucien whispered through dry lips.

The captain laughed and dropped Lucien's head against the deck again. Lucien closed his eyes against the waves of pain splitting his skull. "Someone, laddie. I don't ask who. I just take the money."

"Wasn't it some baron who had him fetched?" one of the men asked.

"The Prince Regent even," another chortled.

"Maybe 'twas Mad George himself!" another exclaimed, and the group dissolved into howling laughter.

With a rough shove of his boot, the captain turned Lucien onto his back. Lucien squinted and raised his hand against the flickering lights, which he now realized were torches on the deck. The captain stared down at him, studying his face. "He's not highborn, they said?"

"Nah. Wrong side of the blanket, he is," a one-eyed sailor sneered.

The captain grinned. "Then he's ours. My thanks to this baron. This 'un will make a fine addition to our crew."

The baron. Lucien winced as the crewmen dragged him to his feet. Chestwick. Had he arranged this as punishment for the affair with Aveline?

The captain laughed as Lucien swayed on his feet. "Ye've hit him too hard, laddies. It'll be at least a day before he'll be more than ballast!"

"I can pay you." Lucien's tongue felt huge in his mouth. "Let me go, and I will reward you handsomely."

"Is that so?" The captain sneered as his crew snickered. "We've been warned about ye, *Yer Lordship.* Yer a gamester and a liar with naught but the clothes on yer back."

"No." The deck pitched. Or was it him? "I have . . . I can pay you."

"Ye'll pay, all right. With yer back and yer brawn. Welcome aboard, laddie. Yer now part o' the *Sea Dragon's* crew."

Aveline clutched the letter in her hand and stared out the window, her eyes strangely dry. Perhaps she was numb. Perhaps she was in shock. She certainly should have been crying a flood of tears by now.

She had been well and truly cast off.

She looked down at the paper, spread the crumpled mass against the flat surface of her escritoire. The stark black handwriting was fancier than she had imagined Lucien's to be, but there was no misunderstanding its message.

Congratulations on your happy event. Please do not seek to contact me again regarding this matter.

How could he be so cold? So cruel? She laid a hand over her belly. How could he not *care*?

The door to her bedroom clicked open, and she swept the letter into her lap as her father appeared. He didn't know she had contacted Lucien, or even why. She had thought to give her father the news with Lucien at her side.

Stupid.

The baron stood silently in the doorway for a moment and regarded her with a somber expression that she knew boded ill. "What is it?" she asked. "What's happened?"

He hesitated, then said, "Lucien DuFeron is dead."

"What?" She clutched the letter tighter, her knuckles white. "What did you say?"

The baron sighed, sympathy softening his features. "He's dead. A footpad, they say. They found his body in a burned-down warehouse at the docks."

"No, that can't be." She rose to her feet. "There is a mistake."

"I don't think so. They couldn't . . ." He paused, clearly struggling to put things as gently as possible.

"The body was burned badly, but they found his pocket watch. It's DuFeron."

"No." She slowly sank back into her chair and stared blankly at him. "No."

"I'm sorry." Her father started to approach her, but she turned away from him to stare out the window. He stopped. But as moments ticked by, and she wouldn't look at him, he finally turned away and discreetly left the room.

A single tear dripped from her cheek to blur the writing on the letter she still clutched in her hand.

Part Two

After

Chapter 8

Cornwall, England
April 1816

He would have his revenge.

Lucien clenched callused hands around the reins of his stallion and stared down at Lord Chestwick's home from his vantage point on the hill.

It had taken him five years to come home to England. Four of those years had been spent as an impressed crewman aboard the smuggler ship *Sea Dragon* under the cruel hand of that bastard, Captain Sledge. He had passed the last year in slightly better circumstances as part of a pirate crew aboard the aptly named *Revenge*.

The *Sea Dragon's* destruction by the *Revenge* had been his salvation. And his year amongst the lucrative pirates had replenished—nay, doubled—the fortune that had once been his.

Dead was he? Hardly.

The burned body of the cutpurse who had nipped his pocket watch had been identified as Lucien DuFeron, and thus the London authorities had declared him dead and his will had been executed. His fortune was gone, his investments long ago paid out to the remaining investors. And his half brother Robert, curse his greed, had purchased Thornsgate but never deigned to step foot in it. The house stood empty and abandoned.

His father had died while Lucien served out his hell on the *Sea Dragon*, leaving Robert as the new Duke of Huntley. And when Lucien had appeared at Huntley House in London a few days ago, the servants had chased him from the door.

Only Dante had recognized him. The poor fellow had turned white as a sheet when Lucien arrived at his rooms, but he had quickly recovered himself and assisted Lucien in finding out what had happened in the time he'd been gone.

And what he'd found out had infuriated him. Father dead, house sold, fortune gone. Had he not done well for himself with the pirates, he'd be a pauper by now. But the injustice of it rankled, and he would not rest until his life had been restored to him.

He couldn't bring his father back, but he could reclaim the material trappings that had been stolen from him. And he could have his revenge on the man responsible for all of it—Chestwick.

He should have killed Chestwick all those years

ago when he'd had the opportunity. Had he resisted Aveline's beauty and just shot the man in a fair duel, then none of this would have happened. But no, he had been lured by her siren's face, by her sensuality and honor. He'd thought of her many times during his exile, and he couldn't help but wonder if she had known of her father's actions.

The mere thought of her brought a vision of her face into his mind, and he hardened his heart against the memory of her pleading green eyes. No matter how comely she was, no woman was worth losing what he had lost. Their blasted bargain had cost him everything.

But the nights they'd spent together hardly mattered anymore. She would have married already, probably provided her husband with an heir or two. Maybe she had grown haggish these past few years. Gotten plump. He doubted he would still find her attractive should they meet today.

But he wondered if she would find *him* attractive.

He glanced down at his gloved hands on the reins and flexed his fingers, seeing past the dark leather to the scars and calluses that covered his hands from years of working rough rope aboard ship. There were matching scars all over his body, most of which had been granted by the bite of Sledge's whip. Would the sight of them disgust a well-bred lady? Even the smaller scar beside his eye, which he had gotten from a seaman's careless blade, had been known to turn away a wench or two.

Would a woman like Aveline—a lady—want to spend three nights in his bed *now*? He looked little like the carefree Society scoundrel he had once been. He looked like what he was—a man who had survived Hell.

He realized where his thoughts were leading and stopped them short. There was no use in mourning the past; he had to concentrate on the task before him. He would confront the baron and kill him, as he should have done years ago. Perhaps then his haunted soul would at last find peace.

He kicked his stallion to a gallop and thundered toward the Chestwick home.

"Miss Stoddard, there's a gentleman asking to see your father."

Aveline sighed and put aside the bill she had just been perusing. The demands for payment had tripled in number over the past month. "Who is it, Mrs. Baines?"

"Not that Squire Lofton," the housekeeper replied with a disapproving sniff.

"And thank God for that. That man has been plaguing this house like a fly does the stables." Aveline rose and smoothed her hands down the skirt of her outdated pink morning dress. "Mrs. Baines, would you count how many candles we have left? I'd like to make them last as long as possible so I don't have to buy more this month. Then I can pay something to the apothecary."

"I'll do that." The housekeeper hesitated. "Would you like me to be there when you greet the gentleman?"

"That's not necessary." Aveline headed toward

the door. "It's probably just one of Papa's old gaming cronies come to express his condolences . . . and perhaps claim an old debt," she finished with a hint of sarcasm.

"Have a care," Mrs. Baines advised. "Sometimes a man who looks like a gentleman is nothing of the sort. I'll be about should you need me."

"Thank you for your concern, but I should be fine."

Lucien paced the length of the tiny parlor, impatience simmering beneath his thin veneer of control. Now that the time had come, he could barely contain his anticipation. Finally, vengeance.

Justice.

The door clicked open, and he looked up, prepared to face the man who had stolen his life from him.

Aveline stood frozen in the doorway, her green eyes wide with disbelief. She wasn't plump. She wasn't haggish. She looked as beautiful as he remembered her, with perhaps a more womanly fullness to her curves. But that minor change only made her look more the seductive siren and less the innocent girl of five years before.

Disbelief faded from her expression to be replaced by pure, radiant joy. "Lucien?" she whispered.

After all this time, the mere sound of his name on her lips still stirred him. Shaken by the warmth of her smile, the genuine welcome on her eyes, he almost went to her. Almost told her that he'd never forgotten her. But as he watched, her face grew as pale as the lace trim of her dress, and she clutched the door handle with white-knuckled fingers. Her happiness dissolved as if it had never existed. "You're alive," she said flatly.

"Surprised?" He concealed his disappointment by giving her the smile that had struck fear into the hearts of his fellow pirates. "I'm certainly surprised to see you. I asked for your father."

"My father is not receiving visitors."

"Not receiving?" His smile turned feral. "He'll receive *me*."

"He's seen no one for the past month." She took a tentative step into the room, watching him as if he were a ghost. "What do you want from him?"

"That's men's business, and I'll not discuss it with you. Where is he?" He made to move past her, but she remained stubbornly in his path, arms folded and a glint of determination shining through the tumult of emotion in her eyes.

He possessed the strength to push her out of the way with little effort, yet he hesitated. He didn't want to touch her. Even standing this close to her he could feel the heat rising between them. Distracting him.

"I was told you were dead."

The slight tremor in her voice bled through the armor of rage around his heart. His own weakness infuriated him. "A mistake, obviously."

His harsh reply made her blink, but then her eyes narrowed. "Obviously," she echoed, the bite in her tone equaling his.

"I would have thought you'd be glad of it." His temper spilled into the words, a tangled mess of frustration and anger and pain and need. "You seemed happy enough to be rid of me when we last met."

"I might say the same for you," she shot back. "You couldn't have been more clear that you were through with me, Lucien. But did you have to be so cruel?"

He gave a harsh laugh and took her chin in his hand. Her skin still felt like silk. "You have not yet seen cruel, my dove."

She jerked away. "You have no right to touch me."

"You never used to protest, sweet Aveline. As I recall, you used to beg for my touch."

Her face colored, but she met his gaze, hers glimmering with contempt. "That was a long time ago. Before you let the world think you were dead. Before—" She broke off and pressed her lips together as if to keep words from escaping.

"Before what?" When she remained silent, his anger swelled. "I've spent the past five years in Hell, Aveline. Don't test me."

"*You've* been in Hell?" Her voice rose with outrage. "What about me? What about the way you abandoned me?"

"Abandoned? Our parting was mutual, our bargain fulfilled. If you feel abandoned, blame your father. Five years ago, he had me abducted and impressed into service on a smuggling vessel."

"Impossible! He would never do such a thing!"

"Wouldn't he?" Lucien leaned closer, ignored the sweet smell of lavender that he'd always associated with her. "He found out about our affair. Don't even try to lie to me about that because he told me so himself."

She drew herself up, seemingly undisturbed by his nearness. "Why should I lie? He caught me coming in that morning with his markers in my hand. He knew what I had done."

"And he came to me, challenged me to a duel." He gave a laugh that held no humor. "I didn't accept the challenge, Aveline. I walked away—because of that blasted bargain we had."

She let out a long breath. "Thank you for that."

"Oh, don't thank me. I curse myself for being so bloody noble. Had I met your father in a duel of honor that day, I would not have lost everything."

"Is that what you want, Lucien? Revenge? Is that why you came here this morning?"

"Yes." He gave her a cold smile. "I've come to challenge your father to a duel."

Her eyes widened in horror. "You've come here to kill him!"

"To *duel* with him." He shrugged. "The outcome is up to fate."

"Do I look like a fool? Everyone knows you're a crack shot. 'Tis what got us into trouble five years ago."

"This is a matter of honor."

She inched backward toward the door. "You're mad."

"Indeed I am." His sharp look halted her stealthy retreat. "Mad with rage. My life was stolen from me. Revenge is my *right*."

She gave a bitter laugh. "I'm sorry for what happened to you, Lucien, but my father had nothing to do with it. No doubt it was some other victim of your selfishness who sought to dispatch you."

"I believe your father had everything to do with it."

"I don't care what you believe."

"Let's see what the good baron has to say about it." He pushed past her and stormed into the foyer. "What kind of man hides behind his daughter's skirts? Is his honor so lacking that he can't face me?"

She followed him out and propped her hands on her hips as he glanced into each of the rooms on the first floor. "I tell you, you've got the wrong man."

"I know what I'm about."

She gave a snort of disgust. "Leave an old man alone, and look to your own family for your villain. From what I hear, you've not endeared yourself to them any more than you have anyone else you've ever met."

"Have a care with that shrewish tongue, woman." He cast her a look of warning, but she didn't shrink away.

"What you're seeking is not here." She glared back at him, clearly as courageous now as she'd been five years earlier. "Leave us in peace and seek your vengeance elsewhere."

"Nothing you say will sway me." Damn, she was still so beautiful, still affected his senses like a potent liquor. But he had to remember that treachery often came very prettily packaged. She'd been upset the morning they parted because she'd feared discovery. Had his abduction been a scheme to silence the scandal? "Tell me, Aveline, are you going to produce your father, or shall I search the whole house and find him myself?"

Her lovely lips thinned into a line of displeasure. "You want to challenge my father to his face, Lucien? Fine. Come with me." Hands fisted in her skirts, she headed up the stairs.

At last, Lucien thought, hard on her heels. *At last*.

Aveline marched up the steps in front of him, her back stiff with displeasure, yet it was her softly rounded bottom that caught his attention. He remembered how many times he'd held that sweet derriere in his hands as they'd made love, the sensitivity of the flesh there.

She stopped at the top of the staircase and cast a look of loathing at him that curdled his burgeoning lust. He had no business thinking about bedding her anyway. Not when his vengeance was nearly within his grasp.

"This way." She walked down the hall and opened a door to one of the bedchambers. "Hello, Papa," he heard her say. "You have a visitor."

Lucien stepped forward, eager to confront the villain who'd tried to destroy him. Then he stopped in the doorway. Stared. "What fakery is this?"

"You asked to see my father." Her words dripped with disdain. "Here he is. Present your challenge."

"Have a care," he warned through gritted teeth. He spared her one glance, and what she saw in his face brought a hint of wariness to her eyes.

She'd ever been an intelligent female.

Then he looked back at his nemesis.

Seated by the window, Lord Chestwick stared out

at the sunny day. He wore a blue robe over his night-shirt and slippers on his bare feet. His graying hair stuck up in tufts on his balding head, and the prominent bones of his face indicated he'd lost a considerable amount of weight. His blue eyes fixed vacantly on some spot outside the window. As Lucien watched, a servant hurried forward to wipe a trail of drool from the baron's chin.

"What happened to him?" He squeezed the words from his tight throat.

"A wager with Lord Melton. Papa fell from a horse during their race. Days later he suffered some sort of spell and fainted. He's been like this ever since." Her face softened in compassion as she regarded her sire. "The doctor believes Papa hit his head when he fell and damaged his brain in some way."

"This can't be." Fists clenching at his sides, Lucien fought back the urge to howl with frustration at Fate's capricious sense of humor. Five years of hell and now his revenge had slipped through his fingers like smoke.

Chestwick was incapable of handling a pistol, much less firing one. And killing him outright, while tempting, would be murder . . . and much like drowning a puppy.

He wanted Chestwick to suffer as he had suffered. To lose everything—his honor, his possessions, his life. But that would never happen now . . .

He spun on his heel and stormed from the room, rage consuming him. Stopping near the staircase, he clutched the railing with both hands, fighting the instinct to roar his fury at the skies. He wanted to rip up the wood railing with his bare hands and fling it through the window. To shatter the glass. To tear apart the house one bit at a time until his anger was spent.

But his anger would never be spent. His soul would ever cry out for the vengeance denied him.

"I'm sorry," Aveline whispered from behind him.

"This is unacceptable." He pounded a fist on the railing.

"He has paid for any sin he ever committed," she said. "He can't move or speak or even feed himself. It will have to be enough for you, Lucien."

"Enough?" He turned to look at her, his body nearly shaking with black fury. "It will never be enough until he has suffered as I have suffered."

"What do you call that?" She flung a hand toward the bedroom. "His heart beats, his body breathes, but that man does not *live*." Her voice broke on the last word. "Leave now, Lucien. Take your threats and your vengeance and *leave us*."

"I haven't begun to make threats," he snarled. "When I do—"

She raised her chin in pride. "You've already done your worst to me, and I have survived."

"You call those three nights my worst?" He gave a cruel laugh and advanced on her.

She retreated until her back hit the wall, then she met his glare with one of her own. "We both know what kind of man you are, Lucien DuFeron."

He leaned close. "And what kind of man is that?"

"A rake," she threw at him. "A scoundrel. A selfish man who uses others like toys to amuse himself."

"Indeed?" He stared down into her eyes, ever conscious of her sweet breath brushing his chin, her soft lips so temptingly close to his. "Was my lovemaking so horrible? You seemed to like it well enough at the time. Seemed to relish it, as I recall."

She flushed, her eyes glittering with anger. "I'm certain you remember it that way. For me it was a chore to be endured in order to save my father's life."

"Oh, no you don't." He cupped her face, held it in place when she would have jerked away. "You won't lie about that, Aveline. To me or to yourself."

"Hateful man," she spat.

"Whatever your feelings toward me now, Aveline, I will not allow you to convince yourself that you didn't want me. That you don't still want me."

Her eyes widened in alarm. "I merely want to be rid of you!"

"Oh, yes. You still want me." His lips parted in a smile of pure male satisfaction. "Your pulse is pounding. Your breathing—" He glanced down at her breasts. "Your breathing is quite fast."

"Perhaps it's because I am overset by the madman who has entered my house with his wild accusations."

"Perhaps it's because you still want me."

"Only a man would think that."

"I *am* a man." He released her face and placing a hand on either side of her head, pinned her against the wall beneath his partially aroused body. "Or hadn't you noticed?"

"I notice that you must have been at sea for many months." She gave him a scathing look. "I'm no innocent girl any longer, Lucien."

"So I see." Rage was rapidly changing to hot lust. He looked down at her breasts where they plumped against his chest. "You have indeed grown into a woman, Aveline. Does your husband appreciate your spirit, I wonder?"

"I have no husband," she snapped. "Now please leave my home, Lucien, before I summon the constable."

He narrowed his eyes. "Brave words, Aveline. I will leave—for now. But I'm not finished with your father yet. Or you."

"I would not dare to think so." She met and held his gaze, her eyes simmering with anger and other, unnamed emotions.

He stepped back, gave a brief, almost insulting bow, and headed for the stairs.

Aveline gave a sigh of relief as she watched his retreating back, her knees nearly buckling from beneath her. Reaching out a shaking hand, she took hold of the back of a chair and eased herself into it. Lucien was alive. After all these years of thinking him dead, the knowledge stole the very strength from her body.

He still looked just as compelling as he always had, not quite handsome yet attractive in a basic sense that drew the female eye. He seemed bigger than before, stronger, more dangerous.

His black hair was unfashionably long but at the same time suited him in a barbaric sort of way. His sharpened features added to his aura of danger. A narrow white scar curled from his left eyebrow to his hairline, and his dark eyes burned with hot emotion.

He still took her breath away. And he wanted to destroy her father.

She let out a sigh of resignation. These past five years had been difficult, as her father had drifted more and more toward the gaming tables, despite his daughter's pleading. Aveline had received no offers of marriage, but many offers less honorable—especially from Squire Lofton. Her once-kindly neighbor had turned out to be the most relentless of the men who pursued her after her ruination became public.

As a girl she had dreamed of a handsome husband, but now she accepted the reality of the male gender with a weary bitterness that seemed tragic for a girl of her youth to experience. Once it had become common knowledge that she had shared a man's bed—indeed, it had only taken a few months before she could no longer hide the truth—men had regarded her differently. Gone was the deference owed a lady and in its place appeared a greedy glitter in male eyes, no matter how polite the words that tripped from their tongues. More than once she had dodged the groping hand of a former friend or eluded a lecherous admirer who thought to corner her alone.

She no longer trusted any word that passed a man's lips, no matter how innocuous. She had learned her lesson well, and would not be so gullible ever again.

And financial matters had gotten worse since her father's injury. Once word got out that he was incapacitated, the bill collectors had come banging on her door. She was granted no more credit at the village stores. She'd even had difficulty selling her embroidery because of the taint on her reputation. Eventually she had to tell the housekeeper to pass the work off as her own so they could sell it and keep food on the table.

No, Lucien could rant and threaten all he wanted. Nothing he could do now could compare with what she had already overcome.

A familiar voice drifted up the stairs, dispelling her worries and bringing a smile to her lips. The owner of that voice was the one bright spot in her life.

"Hello. Who are you?" the voice asked.

"I'm Lucien. And who are you?"

Alarmed, she jumped up from her chair and raced down the stairs, only to stop short halfway down, struck by the tableau before her.

Lucien crouched at the bottom of the stairs, his hat dangling from his fingers. As Aveline stumbled to a halt, two heads turned toward her; two identical pairs of dark eyes regarded her.

"Mama," her little girl said, "this is Lucien."

"I know, Chloe."

"Chloe, is it?" Lucien rose slowly, his eyes never leaving the child.

"I'm going to visit with Grandfather," Chloe said to Lucien, then tripped up the stairs to Aveline. "Mama, is Grandfather awake now?"

"Yes, poppet." Aveline looked down at her daughter and smiled, but her heart was pounding. She didn't dare look at Lucien. What did he think of his daughter?

She smoothed a hand through Chloe's ink black curls, so like her father's. And like Lucien, the child had dark eyes and even, regrettably, his black eyebrows. But Aveline liked to think that Chloe had her mouth and her stubborn chin.

"How old is Chloe, Aveline?"

Finally, she looked at him and was puzzled by the expression on his face. He looked as if someone had hit him over the head with a stewpot. "Chloe will be five this summer, won't you, poppet?"

Chloe nodded vigorously and held up four fingers.

"No, that's four, Chloe." Gently, Aveline straightened the child's bent thumb. "There you are. That's five."

Chloe proudly presented her new five fingers to Lucien.

"Yes, five. I see that." He nodded gravely to Chloe, but when he looked at Aveline, his eyes burned with fierce emotion. "We will talk about this when I return tomorrow."

"We're done talking, Lucien."

He gave a pointed glance at Chloe. "No, we're not." Raising his gaze back to hers, he clamped his hat on his head. "Tomorrow, Aveline." Then he stormed out of the house, slamming the door behind him.

He was a father.

Lucien mounted his horse with one smooth motion. He didn't dare look back at the house, was afraid of what he might do if he did. He merely turned the animal toward the inn where he was staying.

She would have let him walk out of there without ever mentioning the child.

He had no doubt the girl was his. Even if Chloe's age had not given the game away, her startling resemblance to him would have immediately told the tale. Aveline's claims of abandonment made sense now. Had she gone along with her father's wild plan in order to punish him for getting her with child?

Why hadn't she simply told him?

His body felt like an empty vessel, completely drained of all life. Or perhaps his emotions had grown so fierce, so complex, that he had simply stopped feeling them for fear of going mad.

First his vengeance against Chestwick had been stolen from him, then he had discovered that his lust for Aveline had never died. And that the lust in question had resulted in a child.

He had always taken precautions to prevent any of his lovers from becoming pregnant, but the uniqueness of their situation had so fascinated him that he had completely forgotten to do so with Aveline. And she, being an innocent at the time, had clearly not known to prevent conception on her own.

Now he had a daughter. What was he going to do about it? He wasn't about to abandon her. Having lived the life of an unwanted bastard, he had no wish to inflict it upon his little girl. Neither would he leave her there in Chestwick's house. Clearly financial matters had not improved for the baron, and even if they had, Lucien would walk over hot coals in hell before he left his daughter at the mercy of the man who had tried to destroy him.

And what of Aveline? Did she truly believe her father innocent of any wrongdoing, or was she merely protecting him? Either choice was possible, as she had always been a blindly loyal daughter.

And now he had a daughter of his own. The knowledge settled into his heart, warming it for the first time in his life. Now that he'd learned of Chloe's existence, he intended to be a good father to her.

He wasn't alone anymore.

Chapter 9

~~~GO~~~

Aveline was not at all surprised when Lucien returned early the following morning. She opened the door herself and blocked him with her body from entering the house. "Have you come to make more threats, Lucien?"

"I've come to talk about Chloe." He braced a hand on the doorjamb and leaned down, staring boldly into her eyes. "We can talk about it here on the doorstep for the world to overhear, or we can discuss it inside like civilized adults."

She wanted to shut the door in his face, but from the tone of his voice, he might simply tear it off the hinges to get his way. "Very well. This way." She left the door standing open—a petty rudeness—and led the way into the parlor.

He slammed the front door and followed her.

Closing that door as well, he threw his hat on the table. "I'm Chloe's father." His words rang with challenge.

"Of course you are." Accusation slipped into her tone despite her private vow to remain civilized. "She looks very much like you."

"Yes, she does." His dark eyes narrowed. "Were you ever going to tell me?"

She gaped at him. "I *did* tell you, you blackguard! I sent you a note in London."

"A note? I received no note." His disdainful glance swept her from head to toe. "What woman in her right mind would put such tidings in *a note*?"

"A nineteen-year-old girl who was scared to death." She made a sound of disgust. "How naive I was to think you'd come back to Cornwall and do right by me, by Chloe. I'm certain you have dozens of illegitimate offspring all over England."

"In that you are wrong." He clenched his fists at his sides, but kept his distance, as if he could barely control himself. "Never in my life have I ever sired an illegitimate child. Since I myself was one, I took great care never to inflict such a life on another babe."

"You obviously did not take such care with me."

He shook his head slowly. "I was forgetful. The passion between us burned hot, and the circumstances were unusual and stimulating. I was careless."

"And your response to my note? Was that careless?"

He frowned. "What response?"

"Oh, come now!" Finally able to vent her anger on

the proper target after all these years, the words spilled from her mouth unchecked. "I sent you a letter at your house in London and told you I was expecting your child. Your response was a two-line note that congratulated me on the happy event and bade me never contact you again."

His scowl deepened, his dark brows furrowing into a single line. "I never saw such a note, and I never sent any such reply."

"Then who did, Lucien?"

"I don't know. You might be making the whole story up."

She gave a snort of disbelief. "Do you have any idea what has happened to me over the years? I adore Chloe, but your abandonment ruined my life. I was ostracized. I never married because no decent man would come near me. The only proposals I received were the ones no proper lady should ever hear. Now my father is incapacitated, and I have no respectable way to survive. My daughter deserves better than that."

"Indeed she does. Which is why you're going to marry me."

"What?" She knew she gaped, but she couldn't seem to help herself.

"You're going to marry me, Aveline, and you and Chloe will come and live with me in London."

She narrowed her eyes at the certainty in his tone. He wasn't asking her to marry him; he was telling her. "You have such a romantic way about you, Lucien."

"Do you see a better solution?" He smiled, and for an instant he looked like the charming man she had known five years before. "If you marry me, Chloe will no longer be pitied or shunned for her lack of a father. With the power of my wealth behind her, the doors of Society will open for her, and she will be assured of a decent marriage. And the two of you will want for nothing."

"You paint a pretty picture." To give herself time to think, she walked to the other side of the room, toyed with the flowers arranged in a vase. "The offer would have been more welcome five years ago."

"You know what happened to me." His voice rumbled with anger. "I would have done the right thing for Chloe, had I been able."

She turned to face him. "You deny receiving my note."

"I never received any blasted note." He glared at her. "Aveline, you seem to be under the misconception that I am giving you a choice. I am not. You will marry me."

"And if I refuse?"

"Then Chloe will come with me anyway."

"You can't!" She took two steps toward him but stopped at the hard expression that sharpened his features. "I'm her mother!"

"Indeed you are, which is why I've offered marriage. Whatever your choice, Chloe will not grow up in this house. I assume the child will want her mother, and since I have wronged you—however inadvertently—I will do the honorable thing and make you my wife."

"How generous of you!" she snapped.

He shot her a look of warning. "Have a care, Aveline. I have both the money and the means to take Chloe away from you forever. She's my daughter, and I'll be damned if she will live here in the house of the man who tried to destroy me."

"What are you saying? That if I marry you, my father will remain here alone?"

"That's exactly what I'm saying." He clenched and unclenched his fists at his sides, though his eyes remained steady and cool. "You will marry me and come to London with Chloe. Your father will remain here. Alone. Robbed of his most valuable possessions—his family."

"I can't leave him," she whispered.

"Then I will take Chloe to London."

"You can't take my child!"

He raised his eyebrows at her outburst. "Indeed I can. As I said, I have wealth enough and power enough to do exactly that. Choose."

"You're asking me to make an impossible decision!"

"Nonetheless, you must do so."

"Who do you think you are, Lucien DuFeron?" she demanded. "How dare you come back into my life and tear it apart in such a way?"

"Cease your dramatics," he said with a dismissive wave. "I leave for London with Chloe today. If you are to come with us, tell me now so I can make arrangements for a special license."

She stared at this coldhearted stranger, reminded all too well of the selfish, womanizing rogue she'd met the night she'd come to beg for her father's life.

Did he really expect her to be able to choose between her father and her child? What kind of man demanded such a thing?

"Well?" He pulled out his pocket watch and noted the hour. "Time is passing quickly, Aveline."

"You expect me to be able to turn my back on my family without a second thought?"

"Just one member." He closed the watch and slipped it back into his waistcoat pocket. "Which member is up to you. Choose, Aveline. My coach is waiting."

"You haven't left me much choice at all," she said bitterly. "I will marry you."

He smiled with satisfaction. "A wise decision."

"But," she added, "the marriage will be in name only."

His smile faded. "You can't expect me to agree to that."

"And you can't expect me to share my body with a man who insists I abandon my invalid father."

He thrust a finger at the ceiling. "*That man* tried to ruin my life!"

"So *you* say. Have you any proof?"

"He had cause. He was furious when he found out we were lovers."

She rolled her eyes. "I'm surprised some other outraged father or husband hadn't come after you before then."

His lips twisted in a bitter smile. "Most of them didn't want to face me over dueling pistols."

"That's right, you make a habit of killing, don't you?"

He advanced on her with a suddenness that made her stumble as she scrambled to back away. Her legs bumped the back of the sofa, but still he came, crowding her and looming over her, surrounding her with his potent male presence. Anger and impatience shimmered in his eyes. "Every duel I ever fought was a matter of honor," he growled. "This was the only one I ever walked away from, and it nearly cost me my life."

She swallowed hard, unnerved by the waves of rage that vibrated from his big body. "You still have no proof that my father did what you claim."

"The villains who abducted me talked of a baron who had hired them to do the deed."

The blood drained from her cheeks. "Not my father."

"You've ever been a loyal daughter, but I can think of no other barons who bear me such enmity. Your father could not satisfy his honor when I refused to duel with him. Perhaps he sought to even the score another way." He took a step back and pulled forth his pocket watch to once more check the time. "I leave for London within the hour. I suggest you pack your things. And Chloe's."

"An hour is hardly enough time!"

"Have the servants pack a bag for each of you, and I'll send someone back for the rest. Or buy new."

"We only have a kitchen boy and the house-keeper," she snapped. "And Mrs. Baines can hardly be expected to—"

"Don't cross me, Aveline."

Warning underscored his words, and the hard

look he shot her way made her protests die unspoken. Five years earlier, Lucien had been a man no one had dared thwart. This new Lucien with his dark anger and physical scars seemed even more formidable.

"We haven't finished discussing our marriage," she said quietly.

"You want a marriage of convenience? Fine." He shrugged, impatience evident in every muscle. "I will leave you to your pristine bed until such a time that you request my attentions."

"That will never happen."

He raised mocking brows at her. "Never say never, my sweet. Marriage is forever. And forever is a long time." He moved to the door. "I will wait with the coach. Don't make me come after you, Aveline. Remember, Chloe is going with me today, whether or not you accompany her."

Aveline stared at the closed door long after Lucien had left. Her heart pounded; her eyes stung with tears. "Curse him," she whispered. "How can he be so cruel?"

Shaking, she sank down on the sofa. She clenched her fingers together to still their trembling and tried to force her chaotic thoughts into some kind of order.

How could he force such an unfeeling choice on her? Her daughter or her father. Naturally she couldn't let him take Chloe to London alone, and she knew he was right when he said he had the money and power to do that very thing. The best option was to go along. And by marrying him, it would benefit Chloe, something she could never deny her little girl. Lucien would provide Chloe with a splendid dowry and a bright future.

Much brighter than she would have had as the bastard child of a ruined lady.

But he'd seen her father, knew his state of health. How could he possibly expect her to turn her back on her parent, especially when it was so clear that her father could not provide for himself?

But why was she surprised? This was the man who had demanded her innocence in exchange for her father's life. The man who'd left her with child and then denied he'd known anything about it. And now he was obsessed with revenge, determined to see her father destroyed. How was she to trust such a husband?

In agitation she rubbed a hand over the arm of her chair, then paused, noting the worn pattern of the fabric. She glanced around the room and noticed the faded wallpaper and frayed draperies. She hadn't realized until this moment how close to destitute they really were.

Drat the man. Her fingers curled into a fist. Before her father's illness, she'd at least managed to keep food on the table and a roof over their heads, though just barely. And as things had worsened in the past few weeks, she had started to wonder how they would get on with the increased expense of Papa's medicine.

But now she was going to marry a wealthy man, who would see to her needs and to Chloe's. And since she doubted Lucien's generosity extended to her infirm father, she would continue to use her embroidery to pay for her sire's care, even if Lucien forbid her to ever see him. In fact, selling her work in London might even bring a better price.

She rubbed a hand over her face. So many emotions churned inside her. Anger at the past. Frustration with the things she could not change. Joy at the change in Chloe's circumstances. Agony at leaving her father behind. And beneath it all, to her everlasting shame, a perverse joy that Lucien DuFeron was alive.

As much as she wanted to hate him, as much as she despised the way he manipulated her, something inside of her had come back to life when she had seen him pacing in the parlor. Even after the shabby way he'd treated her, her body still reacted to his presence as if they had not been apart for the past five years.

And when he had mentioned marriage—well, her heart had nearly stopped. How long had she dreamed of that very thing?

But not like this.

Lucien had changed. He'd been a scoundrel five years ago, but she'd seen hints of vulnerability in him during their time together. She'd even foolishly fallen in love with him. But this man . . . this cold, vindictive man who thought nothing of tearing a young girl away from her mother or stripping an old man of his only family . . . She didn't know this man at all.

Yet she was about to marry him.

* * *

Lucien watched as the minute hand landed on the number twelve with a barely audible tick. He glanced at the still-closed door, his mouth thinning as he clicked the pocket watch closed. Aveline was testing his patience.

Wasn't it bad enough that he'd agreed to her ridiculous request for a chaste marriage? Did she have to challenge him at every turn?

Of course she did. She was Aveline.

The woman had ever tasked him, yet her stubbornness was one of the things he respected about her. She didn't allow people to dictate her actions, and when she decided she wanted to do something, she did it. Her unswerving loyalty to her father was another indication of her strong will. Unlike most men, he found passive women boring. Aveline had always stimulated him.

Which was how he came to be standing beside the coach waiting for her like some sort of servant.

He'd needed to put distance between them. It had taken everything he had to remain stoic during their conversation, and so he'd elected to wait outside rather than in the parlor as he normally would have done. The way she battled with him aroused him in a completely irrational way. By the time he'd had her pinned against the sofa, he wanted nothing more than to lay her out on it and make love to her until she screamed his name.

But she hated him right now. By making her leave her father behind, he'd assured that his future wife would detest the very sight of him. Still, it was the best solution. Her blind loyalty to her father wouldn't allow her to see the true villainy of the old man's machinations, villainy he could not allow to remain unpunished.

She should be thanking him for leaving her father alive, not refusing to share her future husband's bed.

The minute had ticked by. He stepped toward the house just as the door opened and the kitchen boy hauled a trunk out the door. Lucien gave a signal to his own footman to help the lad, then started toward the house.

As he came through the door, he noticed a couple of bandboxes stacked in the hallway. Satisfaction brought a small smile to his lips. So far it looked like Aveline intended to comply with his wishes.

All the rooms on the first floor were empty, so he climbed the stairs. He hadn't intended to come after her, but it was best for her to see that he would brook no disobedience. No doubt the mere sight of his displeasure would encourage her to hurry.

He glanced into two empty rooms on the second floor before he found himself standing before the slightly open door of the baron's room.

He didn't want to go in. He wanted to cling to his anger, not feel sorry for the man. But he *had* felt sorry when he had first seen him, and it infuriated him. Chestwick had attempted to kill him. He deserved everything that happened to him

The low murmur of voices had him pushing the door open, but he stopped in the doorway. Chloe stood beside the baron's chair, her tiny hand on his larger one where it rested on the arm of the chair. Aveline stood off to the side, watching with a sad, indulgent smile on her face.

". . . and Mama says we are going to live in London with my real papa. She says you have to stay here to keep Mrs. Baines company, but I promise I'll come visit you." Chloe bent forward and dropped a kiss on the baron's hand.

Lucien's heart clenched at the emotional tableau. Why had Aveline permitted this? Didn't she realize how difficult it was going to be for the child once she became aware that she would not be permitted to visit her grandfather?

As if she sensed his presence, Aveline caught sight of him. Her gaze held a challenge. *Go ahead. Tear your daughter away from her grandfather and tell her why she can't see him anymore.*

He narrowed his eyes at Aveline. Did she think he would hesitate to take the child away? "It's time to go."

Chloe jumped at the sound of his voice. Regarding Lucien warily, she backed away from her grandfather until her grasping hand found her mother's skirt. Aveline rested a reassuring hand upon her shoulder. "Is that him?" the little girl whispered loudly.

"Yes, Chloe." Aveline sent a challenging smile his way. "This is your papa."

Chloe narrowed her eyes at him in such an exact replica of his own suspicious scowl that a lump rose in his throat. Dear God, she was a DuFeron all right.

"The coach is ready to depart," he said, his voice harsher than he intended because of the emotions lodged there. "And my patience is at an end."

Aveline's mouth thinned at that, but she took Chloe's hand in hers without a word and marched toward him. She paused just in front of him, then glanced back at her father, who stared blindly out the window, oblivious. When she turned back to Lucien, her eyes shimmered with unshed tears. And accusation.

Without a word he stepped aside, and she swept past him, head held high, spine rigid with disapproval. Chloe glanced back at him as her mother led her down the stairs, her innocent face reflecting her confusion as she picked up on the heightened emotions of the adults around her.

Something that felt like guilt trickled through the ever-present fury he carried, and impatiently he swept it away. Striding into the room, he stopped before the baron and looked down at his nemesis.

He should be feeling some sort of satisfaction, or at least a calming of the restless rage that constantly consumed him. Yet he felt nothing but a small stirring of pity as he looked at the broken shell of a man who was Lord Chestwick.

He wanted to say something. To leave Aveline's father with some dramatic parting speech that would haunt him in his loneliness. But he could think of nothing and finally settled for a brief, mocking bow before he quit the room.

London—and his future bride—awaited.

Chapter 10

After three days of traveling by coach with a four-year-old child, the clean and prosperous Duckworth Inn looked like heaven to Aveline. As she washed the dust of the road from her face in the small chamber she shared with her daughter, she could hear Lucien moving around in the room next to them. The curious intimacy of it unnerved her. Only when she heard his door close and his footsteps disappear down the hall did her heartbeat return to normal.

He'd tried his best to forge a relationship with Chloe, and the child was slowly opening up to him. Aveline's heart had melted more than once during the trip as she noted Lucien's many furtive glances at Chloe, the astonished pleasure glimmering in his eyes as if he couldn't believe he was the father of this

145

precious child. At one point Chloe had been seated next to Lucien, and she'd drifted off to sleep, curled up on the seat with her head resting on her father's thigh. Aveline herself pretended to nap and watched with choked emotion as Lucien went to smooth the child's curls, then hesitated, his hand hovering over her, before he pulled back. The look on his face reflected his uncertainty.

Aveline couldn't help but be touched by this obvious evidence that he cared for their child. After all, Chloe needed a father, and the fact that he was trying to fill the role only softened some of her resentment.

But she could never forgive him for making her leave her own father behind.

Seated on the bed, Chloe gave a big yawn.

"Are you tired, poppet?" Aveline asked, drying her hands with the towel beside the basin.

"Hungry," Chloe said, then yawned again.

The poor thing. Lucien had kept a steady yet moderate pace over the past few days, but Chloe was unused to travel. No doubt she needed a hot meal and warm bed in short order.

As if in answer to the thought, a knock came at the door. Aveline opened it to find a young woman holding a tray.

"Good evenin', miss," the girl said. "My name's Jen, and my father's the innkeeper. Mr. DuFeron sent me here with a plate of something for the little one."

"Bless you," Aveline said, and reached for the tray.

The brunette moved the tray out of her reach with a cheerful smile. "Oh, no, miss. Mr. DuFeron told me to bring this straightaway and to watch over the little miss while you dined with him in the private parlor."

Aveline propped her hands on her hips. "Did he now?"

"Oh, yes, miss. Never you fear about the little one. I've three younger sisters and know what I'm about when it comes to that. I'll just make sure the darlin' eats up, then goes straight to bed. I'll even sing her to sleep like I do my sisters."

Despite her misgivings, Aveline smiled. "I think she'd like that. And her name is Chloe."

Aveline stepped aside so that the innkeeper's daughter could enter the room. Jen proved as able as she claimed when it came to children and soon had Chloe giggling as she ate her soup.

"Go on now, miss," Jen said with a shooing motion toward the door. "Enjoy your supper and don't fret about Miss Chloe. I'll have her fed and in bed in a thrice."

"Very well." Aveline hesitated only a moment in the doorway, then made her way downstairs, Chloe's muffled laughter following her.

Nerves tangled in her stomach as she obtained the direction of the private dining room. For the past three days, Chloe had acted as unknowing chaperone, assuring that Aveline and Lucien were never really alone. Yet now he waited to dine with her behind closed doors, and she found herself trembling like a debutante at her first ball.

Impatient with herself, she shook off her anxiety. If she could handle him five years ago over the course of those three incredible nights in his bed, she'd deal well enough with him now. She was hardly a green girl anymore, and the man was going to be her husband. Despite all they had between them, how hard could it be to share a simple meal with him?

She opened the door and stepped into the room before she could change her mind. Lucien stood looking into the fire, but he turned as she entered.

For an instant she was thrown back in time to their first night together. Now, as then, he wore black, which emphasized his sheer size and dark coloring. The firelight flickered over his features, throwing his bold nose into sharp relief against his deep-set eyes and thick eyebrows. His mouth looked soft and tempting, and for one wild moment she remembered what that mouth could do to her.

The scar beside his eye and his long hair gave him an air of danger that struck her as remarkably erotic.

"How's Chloe?" he asked after a moment, and she realized she'd been staring at him.

"She's having supper. The innkeeper's daughter has a way with her."

"Good." He swept a hand at the table set for two. "Please, make yourself comfortable. I've ordered a dinner of roast duck, the specialty of the house."

"It sounds delicious." So civilized was their conversation. But as she approached the table, and he didn't move, she realized that there was nothing at all civilized about this situation. The air nearly crackled with tension.

Lucien held the chair for her. Gingerly she seated

herself, more than aware of the nearness of him. Then she caught a whiff of his scent.

Her eyes slid closed as her celibate body woke with a vengeance. Dear Lord, how often had the smell of sandalwood reminded her of their decadent lovemaking? More than once she'd taken a whiff of the scent while in the perfume shop, then furtively put the bottle back, as if hiding a guilty secret.

And wasn't she? Despite all he'd done, her body still craved his attentions.

Lucien stepped away and reached for a bottle sitting on the table. "Wine?" he asked.

She shook her head. The last thing she wanted was her senses addled. Already her heart pounded so loudly she was surprised he couldn't hear it.

He shrugged and poured himself a portion, then lifted it, swirling the liquor around before bringing the glass to his lips. His strong throat moved as he swallowed, and he slid his tongue once over his lips to catch the last droplets that clung there. He placed the goblet on the table, his large fingers a contrast to the delicate glassware.

She tried not to remember how those hands had felt on her skin.

"I wanted to speak to you," he said. "Tomorrow we will reach London. And tomorrow morning, before we leave here, we will be married."

She jerked her gaze away from his hands. "So soon?"

"I've obtained a special license."

She raised her brows, his practical words helping

to suppress the throbbing of her traitorous body. "That was quick work."

He shrugged. "I'm a man of means and influence. Anything can be done if the proper amount of money is offered."

She gave an indelicate snort. "I think you really believe that."

"It has always been so." He smiled with a great deal of charm. "Once you are my wife, you will see for yourself."

"I doubt it." She wished now that she had accepted the wine, if only to have something to do with her hands. "Money doesn't buy everything, Lucien, and I feel sorry that you believe it does."

"Don't feel sorry for me." He swirled his wine. "Despite what happened, I came back to England richer than before I left."

"A cold comfort."

"Do you think me cold, then?"

The soft words sent a tingle down her spine. Yet she met his gaze, her own giving nothing away. "I think your heart is empty, and that's a sad thing."

"Perhaps I need a wife to warm it." He smiled at her with enough charm to start a melting sensation in the pit of her belly. "We're going to be married, Aveline, and I don't look forward to a polite yet hollow relationship. We have a child together, and I'd like us to be a real family."

Had she imagined it, or was there a hint of wistfulness in his voice?

"Well," she mused, "you haven't exactly endeared yourself to me with your recent actions."

"I'm aware of that, but certainly you can understand my position."

"And certainly you can understand mine."

He chuckled. "You always challenge me, Aveline. It's one of the things I like about you."

"How gratifying," she said with a sarcastic flutter of her eyelashes.

"I deserved that." He gave a sigh. "I cannot relent on this. Your father must pay for what he's done, and this is the only punishment both you and I can live with. Be grateful I left him in his own home. My first instinct was to have him committed to Bedlam, but I didn't want my wife to hate me. This is my compromise."

"Dear Lord." Aveline rested a hand over her pounding heart, sick over what might have been her father's fate. "You're right. I would have hated you."

He put down his glass, then moved close to her chair, sliding his hand along her shoulder. "I don't want you to hate me, Aveline. Do you remember how good it was between us?"

His fingers brushed her collarbone, and her body burst to life as if it recognized its master. "I remember."

"I never forgot you." He caressed the nape of her neck, trailed his finger down her spine. "Even when I lived in Hell, I thought of you, remembered our time together." He bent down, brushed a kiss over her sensitive nape, startling a gasp from her. "I never wanted to let you go," he whispered.

She clenched her fingers until they hurt. "Then why did you? Why did you send that letter?"

"I didn't." He cupped her chin, turned her face up to his. "I swear to you I didn't. If I had known you were with child, I would have come straightaway."

She closed her eyes against the imploring expression on his face. Dear Lord, she wanted to believe him, but she'd learned not to believe in pretty declarations. He'd left her once, long before she'd known she was with child, and she wasn't about to trust him with her heart this time. "If it wasn't you, then who was it?"

"I don't know. But obviously forces were working to keep us apart. The letter. My abduction. Perhaps I am right, and your father intercepted the letter. I can't think of anyone else with the motive to do such a thing."

She shook her head and pushed his caressing hand away. "It wasn't my father's handwriting. The letter aside, you still let me leave at the end of our three nights together. Why did you do that if you wanted me to stay?"

"We had a bargain," he said roughly.

"We did," she agreed in a soft voice.

He stroked his hand down her arm. "Haven't you thought about us. Even once?"

"Yes," she admitted. "How could I not?"

"How could you not?" he echoed. He untangled her fingers and tugged her to her feet. "You were big with my child." He splayed his hand over her belly. "I'd like to get you with child again."

She swallowed hard, fighting to keep her anger alive even as her body melted beneath his touch. "I've already said this will be a marriage in name only, Lucien. I will not lie with a man I cannot trust."

His brows flew up at that. "You can trust me, Aveline."

She sent him a skeptical look.

"Do you really think the two of us can live together as man and wife and not share a bed?" He took her hand, shocked her by pressing her fluttering fingers against his rock-hard erection. "This is reality, my dove. This is what you do to me. And this—" He stroked a thumb over one of her nipples, satisfaction turning up the corners of his mouth as the tiny bud hardened instantly. "This is what I do to you."

"Sex," she asserted, jerking away so they were no longer touching. Her fingers still tingled from the intimate contact, and she clenched her hand into a fist. "There is no love. There is no respect. 'Tis just animal attraction, nothing more."

"Don't you want more children?"

She closed her eyes against a wave of longing. How did the man know exactly what to say to so deeply affect her? "I would love more children. But you forced me to choose between my father and my daughter, and I cannot—*will not*—act the proper bride with that between us."

"You must admit that the evidence—"

"You have no evidence but a comment made by brigands," she interrupted. "But think about this— it takes money to arrange for the elaborate abduction of a man of your consequence. *And my father had no money*. How was he to arrange such a thing when we barely had funds with which to buy food?

And in London, no less? He hasn't left Cornwall in years."

Lucien's mouth tightened. "Perhaps he had a partner of some sort."

She gave a bitter laugh. "Oh, yes, that's it. Who else hated you enough to do away with you? Perhaps you should look to your own family for this 'partner.'"

"Perhaps I should."

"Do it then." She raised her chin and held his gaze with pride. "Save your soft words and your seduction. I'll marry you for Chloe's sake. I'll bear your name and manage your household. But that's all."

He said nothing for a moment, then gave her a rueful smile. "That's too bad. I admit I was looking forward to a traditional wedding night."

"How disappointing for you." She gave a careless shrug, hoping he didn't see how much she would have enjoyed such a night as well.

"We'll be married in the local church before we leave here for London."

"This mockery of a wedding hardly matches my girlish dreams. I don't have a wedding dress or flowers. And my father isn't here to offer me in marriage." Her voice broke on the last, and she turned away to hide the tears that she could no longer restrain. "What you have done has damaged any relationship that still existed between us," she whispered.

Lucien stared at her back with a feeling of helplessness that fit about as well as a badly tailored coat. He knew she was crying, had seen the gleam of moisture in her eyes before she looked away. He wanted to reach out and fold her into his arms, to comfort her. But he didn't know how. After all, he was the reason her father wouldn't attend her wedding, and he had no intention of changing that. The die was cast, and Chestwick would pay for his sins.

But he hated to see Aveline unhappy.

Since he had come back into her life, the puzzling feelings from five years ago had flooded him all over again. No longer did he feel empty, but now there was so much emotion that he had no idea what to do with it all.

Aveline was right; money wouldn't help him in this case.

He swiped a hand over his face, uncertain how one handled a weeping fiancée, especially when one was the cad who had caused the tears. She didn't seem to want his comfort, and he was at a loss as to what else he could do.

Seduction he could handle. But this . . . ?

He put down his wineglass. Started to go to her, if only to do *something*. He opened his mouth to speak, but no words came forth. Stunned, he stopped in his tracks.

How could he not know what to say? Wasn't he still Lucien DuFeron? Still Lucifer, the most scandalous, charming rake in London? Had he been gone so long that he'd forgotten how to talk to a woman? The devil knew he'd bungled everything with Aveline since he'd returned. How could it be that he couldn't summon the right words to his lips now, the correct tone, the proper smile?

Was he still the Lucien he'd always been, or had he become someone else?

Damn it all. In the space of a single moment, he realized the extent of what had truly been stolen from him. More than money. More than property or even family. Somehow the very essence of who he was had been taken from him, just like his material possessions.

How was it he could not charm his own betrothed?

A knock came at the door, a welcome interruption, and Aveline swiped surreptitiously at her eyes as he went to answer it. The smiling innkeeper entered the room trailed by two lads, all of them carrying platters of food that smelled delicious. As the boys arranged the food on the table, the innkeeper spent a moment or two gushing how pleased he was to have Lucien in his humble establishment. Lucien responded to the man's comments, but all the while his attention never left Aveline.

When the innkeeper and his assistants finally left, Lucien went to the table and poured himself another glass of wine. The soft trickle of the liquid hitting the goblet rippled through the tense silence.

"Would you care for some wine now?" he asked.

"Yes," she whispered, then subtly wiped the corners of her eyes. "Yes, I think I would."

Lucien poured a second glass, not looking at Aveline as she approached the table. He didn't want to see her tear-reddened eyes or the sad slump to her shoulders. Didn't want to know what his revenge was costing her.

"Eat," he said. "I'm sure we're both overly emotional because of hunger."

"Yes." She sounded about as convinced as he was, but he had to admire her willingness to shelve their disagreements for another time. "Perhaps you're right."

They ate in silence, the distance between them far more than the simple length of a table.

Their wedding day dawned bright and cheerful, though the same could not be said of the bride. Aveline rose from her bed that morning with a knot of dread in her stomach. Was she making a mistake? It wasn't too late to turn back.

She washed her face at the basin and stared into the looking glass on the wall, at the reflection of the child still slumbering in the bed behind her. Was she doing the right thing for Chloe? Yes, Lucien was her father, but he was also a ruthless man who resented being vulnerable. Would he have the patience to raise a child of Chloe's sensitivity?

Would he be a good husband, or would he shame her with indiscreet affairs all over London?

She frowned. Where had that thought come from? Men had mistresses all the time, and since his wife refused to share his bed, a man of Lucien's strong appetites was bound to find female companionship elsewhere. As long as he did right by Chloe, Aveline resolved to say nothing of any indiscretions she might hear about.

But another layer of despair encircled her heart.

Wiping her hands dry, she turned to her small trunk to decide which of the two dresses she had hurriedly packed would be her wedding dress. The pink, perhaps. It brought out the color in her cheeks, and she wanted to look her best on her wedding day, even if she was marrying a rogue.

A quick knock sounded at the door, and before Aveline could even bid the visitor enter, the door opened and Jen came into the room. "Miss!" she exclaimed, a wide, excited smile on her face. "Look who's come! 'Tis Mrs. Tibbs, the dressmaker!"

A tall, well-rounded woman entered the room, her lips pursed with concentration. A pencil stuck out of her brown hair where it was piled atop her head. "This is the bride then?"

"Jen, what—"

"Never you worry, miss," the dressmaker interrupted. "I've just the thing for you, and we'll have it fitted in a thrice." She snapped her fingers, and two young women scurried into the room, both of them holding armfuls of gorgeous peach silk.

Aveline gaped as one assistant unfolded a beautiful dress. "Mrs. Tibbs, please, what is this about?"

"Your future husband's bought you a wedding dress. And the little one, too." All business, Mrs. Tibbs took the towel from Aveline's numb fingers. "Hold still now, so I can get exact measurements."

Aveline stood still out of pure astonishment while the dressmaker measured her. "Yes, he was very close," she said with a chuckle. "Your fiancé gave me some approximate measurements, and he was quite nearly exact. When we are finished, this dress will fit you perfectly."

"We've this for your daughter, miss," one of the dressmaker's assistants said. She held out a smaller version of the dress in the same pale peach color.

"We will do the child when the mother is done." Mrs. Tibbs snapped again, and the second assistant stepped forward with Aveline's dress. "Let's put this on and make the alterations. There will be a wedding this morning!"

Aveline stood stupefied in the midst of the activity as Mrs. Tibbs pinned the dress to fit exactly, then slipped it off Aveline and handed it to one of her assistants, who immediately sat down with a needle and thread to make the adjustments.

They woke Chloe, who was beside herself with excitement that she was getting a wedding dress, too. By the time they had Chloe measured properly (a slow process thanks to the child's ecstatic fidgeting), the young seamstress had finished the modifications to Aveline's dress. Aveline allowed the modiste to fit the dress to her, awestruck at the beauty of the peach silk.

"Such a beautiful bride," Mrs. Tibbs murmured, as they all stared at Aveline in the mirror.

"Would you allow me to do your hair?" Jen asked. "I always do my sisters' hair for the local dances."

She couldn't resist the eagerness in the girl's eyes. "Of course, Jen. I'd be grateful."

As Jen ran off to get her hair accessories, Aveline smoothed her hand once more over the silk of her skirt and wondered what other surprises awaited her from her future husband.

Lucien stood at the bottom of the inn's staircase and watched as Aveline and Chloe descended. Aveline took his breath away; the peach silk brought out her green eyes and blond hair and made her skin look like fresh cream. It clung to her body like a lover, sweeping around her legs with a soft swish as she reached the last step. She wore a wreath of flowers in her upswept hair. At his inquiring glance, she touched it and smiled a bit self-consciously. "Jen insisted."

"You look beautiful." He glanced down at Chloe. "You both do."

"Do you like my flower, Papa?" Chloe asked, touching the white wildflower mixed in with her dark curls.

Lucien's heart stopped when she called him Papa. Then he took a shuddering breath and touched her cheek. "I like it very much. In fact, I like it so much that I have more for you in the coach."

"Yay!" Chloe bounced up and down with glee.

"Flowers?" Aveline asked.

He shrugged when she continued to stare at him in astonishment. "We're getting married. We need flowers, don't we?"

She gave him a small smile. "Indeed we do."

"That's it then." Uncomfortable with the conversation, he turned to Chloe. "Are we ready?"

"Ready!" Chloe sang.

"Then let's get married."

Chapter 11

I t was his wedding night.

Shirtless and in his stocking feet, Lucien stared into the fire, a glass of brandy in his hand. They'd reached his London town house late that afternoon, and he'd dreaded each hour that brought them closer to this moment. He could hear Aveline moving about her bedchamber on the other side of the connecting door, and he wondered what she was doing. Was she changing her clothes? Brushing her hair? Or was she simply as restless as he was?

He should be in there making love to her, not brooding in his own bedroom. But she'd made it clear that she would refuse his advances if he tried to exercise his rights as a husband, and he didn't relish putting more obstacles between them by insisting she do her wifely duty.

She thought him ruthless. Heartless even. Selfish. Cold. But there was nothing cold about his feelings for her. He wanted her badly, hot and willing beneath him, but that would never happen with the specter of her father between them.

And she didn't trust him. That stung most of all.

He looked down at his arm, at the scar that coiled like a snake from his wrist to his elbow. He remembered the day he'd gotten it, when he'd rebelled against Sledge and his cruelty. The bastard had put him to the whip for the third day in a row, just for sport, and Lucien's rage had exploded. He'd grabbed the whip, ignoring the sting, and let it wrap around his arm like a serpent; then he yanked on the weapon and sent Sledge sprawling, much to the amusement of the crew.

He'd paid for that one. Sledge had tied him with his belly flush against the mast and put the cat to him, ripping his back to ribbons with the nine-tailed whip. Then he'd splashed a bucket of seawater over the wounds and beaten him again as Lucien nearly passed out from the pain. He'd later learned he'd been tied to that mast for two days without food or water, and every couple of hours Sledge would come back and lay another few lashes on him, then soak the new wounds with salt water. It was a miracle he'd survived.

He'd lived in that Hell for four long years until the pirates had rescued him.

Could Aveline possibly comprehend the extent of his suffering? Was there any way she could understand the brutality of it, that the only thing keeping him alive on that ship had been thoughts of revenge?

Maybe she was right not to trust him. But he had spared her father's life, which was more than he'd intended when he'd first come seeking the man. Taking away the baron's family, forcing him to live in loneliness and isolation, was the only vengeance he could take without making Aveline despise the sight of him.

He deserved justice for what had been stolen from him.

A cry of alarm sounded from the other room, followed by a crash. Lucien put down his brandy, then raced to the connecting door and opened it. Aveline lay on the floor, a small table and a smashed vase next to her. She pushed herself to her hands and knees as he reached her. "What happened?" he demanded, assisting her to her feet.

"Nothing of consequence." Already her cheeks blazed with embarrassment. "My nightdress caught the corner of the table as I walked by, and it fell over and tripped me."

"Are you injured?" He ran his hands down her arms, searching for broken bones.

"No, I'm fine. Really." She pushed his hands away. "It was just a silly accident."

Someone pounded on the door. "Mrs. DuFeron, are you all right?" her maid asked.

"Oh dear." She pinkened further. "I feel so foolish."

"Don't move." Lucien strode to the door and cracked it open an inch. "It's all right, Peggy. My wife tripped, that's all."

The maid's eyes widened at his presence in Aveline's room, but she immediately dropped her gaze and bobbed a curtsey. "Very well then, sir."

When she was gone, he closed the door and turned to face Aveline. Words of reassurance died on his tongue at the look on her face. She had paled, her eyes wide and lips parted as if in shock. He hurried to her and took her by the shoulders so he could peer at her pupils. They looked normal. "Aveline, are you certain you're all right? Did you hit your head?"

"No." She glanced down at his hand gripping her shoulder, then slowly traced a trembling finger along the scar curling around his forearm.

His entire body tensed, both from reaction to her touch and the realization that he had turned his back to her when he went to speak with the maid.

She'd seen the scars.

"Did this happen while you were gone?" she asked, her gaze fixed on his arm.

"Yes." He couldn't take his eyes from her pale finger tracing along his darker skin. That scar ended, but another started close by, and so she followed the new one along the curve of his shoulder.

"May I see the rest?"

He closed his eyes and nodded, anxiety clenching his gut. Before her outright refusal to share his bed, he'd hoped to ease her into the knowledge of what his body had become, perhaps by making love to her in the dark at first, then gradually revealing his physical flaws to her once he'd reminded her of the delights they could share.

Too late.

She moved behind him, the fragrance of lavender lingering in her wake. He kept his eyes closed, trembling like a stallion scenting a mare as her soft fingers followed the lines that crisscrossed his back. There were many of them, some curling over his shoulder, others coiling around his waist and ribs, some dipping beneath the waistband of his trousers. She touched them all.

Little did she know that each stroke of her fingertips fired his hunger for her.

By the time she came back around to face him, he was hard, sweaty, and nearly shaking with need. She brushed the hair from his forehead and touched the scar along his temple.

He opened his eyes and grabbed her wrist. "Don't."

She froze, glancing at him with a hint of alarm. "What's the matter?"

"Just don't. Unless you've changed your mind about sharing my bed." He released her wrist, and her hand dropped to her side. Was she disgusted by his appearance? He couldn't tell.

She took a step back from him. "I'm sorry. I was just curious."

"Consider your curiosity satisfied."

"Perhaps it's not. May I ask you something?"

He shrugged, uncertainty and desire knotting his insides.

"This is what happened to you while you were away? This is what you believe my father responsible for?"

"Yes." He met her gaze now with fierce pride.

She nodded, as if she hadn't expected anything

different. "Whether or not Papa is to blame, I cannot say. I think it *unlikely*, though it is certainly not impossible. But the man I know could not have done so cruel a thing."

"You look at him with the eyes of a beloved daughter. I see him as just a man, and a weak one at that."

Her cheeks flushed with temper. "I take offense at that."

"Take offense if you will, but we are talking about a man so obsessed with gaming that his daughter had to struggle to survive when she should have been living a comfortable life. A man so deluded that he thought to accuse me of cheating because he had wagered more than he could pay."

"Because of your ordeal, I choose to ignore your remarks," she said.

"Just as you've ignored your father's behavior."

"That is quite enough! Whatever he has or hasn't done, he is still my father, and I will not malign him!"

The grief in her voice halted the bitter words he would have uttered. "You're right," he said quietly. "I apologize."

"I can understand that you hate him for what you think he's done, but please realize that I cannot do so."

"You're a loyal daughter, but you're also my wife. How long do you think you can keep this between us?"

"Are you asking me to choose again, Lucien? But this time to choose between my father and my husband?"

"There comes a time when every daughter must stand by her husband and leave her childhood behind."

"This is not a matter of childhood." She hugged herself as if she were cold. "What stands between us is much more than that."

"Agreed." Her wedding ring caught his eye as it glittered in the candlelight. "You're no longer a child, Aveline. I, more than anyone, know that."

"You want me in your bed."

The blunt words surprised him, but he seized the change of topic with nearly humiliating eagerness. "I do, yes. I'm no different from any other bridegroom."

"Do you think I've made this decision to punish you? Do you think it's easy for me, knowing I'm starting this marriage on the wrong foot?"

"I have no idea what you're thinking."

She shook her head, her blond hair rippling over her shoulders. "As your wife, I owe you my loyalty, and that you have. I understand why you're doing this—truly, I do. But I owe my father loyalty, too. I've married you as I said I would. I'll be your hostess and run your household. I'll always be the mother of your child. But I cannot in good conscience share my body with you knowing that you have left my father to die alone. Even," she rushed to add before he could speak, "if I understand why you did it."

"A pretty speech." Still hungry for her, still stung by the possibility of rejection, he dragged her into his arms, pulling her hard against his aroused body so she could not doubt his intent. "But I think you're lying to yourself. What if I brought your father to London right now? Could you then bear my touch?"

She froze and raised her eyes to his, hope shining in them. She parted her lips as if to speak, but then hesitated.

He gave her a grim smile. "You may be angry at me about your father, but I don't think that's the real reason you refuse to share my bed."

"Believe what you want," she snapped, recovering.

He laughed. "There's no mystery between us as with other newly married couples. You know what pleasure I can give you. Are you certain you can live with me day after day, year after year, and still resist the temptation?"

She pushed against his chest, but he held her fast. "There is more to a marriage than the bedchamber."

"Indeed, but without it, the other things mean little."

"You'll say anything to get what you want."

He shoved her away. "You think much of yourself. When you decide to act like a woman instead of a little girl, let me know. I might still be interested." He turned his back on her shocked expression and returned to his own room, slamming the connecting door behind him. Then he sagged against it.

How much of her refusal to lie with him was due to her emotions, and how much was due to his maimed body? She hadn't seemed disgusted when she'd touched his scars, but she hadn't responded when he'd embraced her either. She'd seemed . . . indifferent.

Once it would have taken only the touch of his hand to turn her into an eager lover. Instead . . .

He slammed a fist against the door behind him. Curse Chestwick! So much damage done. Four years of hell. His daughter's illegitimacy. Now he faced rejection from the only woman he'd never been able to forget.

He hoped the baron lived a long life of misery, suffering with the knowledge of what his actions had wrought.

Shoving away from the door, Lucien went to search out his brandy.

Aveline jumped at the thud of a fist on the door, and she watched the portal warily, waiting for Lucien to storm back in and claim his rights as her husband. But he didn't come.

Who was this man she had married?

He looked like the Lucien she had once known, but his words and actions this evening had revealed to her a man in torment. How could she not have realized the impact his suffering had had on him?

She traced her fingers along the palm of her hand, as if once more feeling the puckered flesh of his back. The scars had crisscrossed each other, one upon the other, some two or three scars blending into one. She could only imagine the pain he must have experienced, though it seemed from his words to her that there were deeper marks no one would ever see. The scars on his soul.

Her heart broke for him. His abduction had affected all their lives, leaving something standing between them that could never be made right. And her refusal to share his bed was only making a bad situation worse. But what choice did she have?

It wasn't easy for her to resist Lucien's advances, for she remembered well the pleasure to be found in his arms. And now that she understood the torment he'd suffered, she wanted more than ever to hold him and comfort him.

But this was the man who had taken shameless advantage of her situation five years earlier. The man who'd turned his back on her when she was expecting his child. The man who'd given her no choice but to abandon her father when he needed her the most.

How was she supposed to give him a wife's loyalty and affection when he'd never done the right thing in all the time she'd known him?

She understood his rage at her father, for the only clue he had to the identity of the one who had arranged his abduction had been a chance remark about "the baron" from one of the brigands. No doubt he had clung to that through the years of torture, using that one statement as a focal point that would get him through each day, dreaming of revenge.

Still, a casual statement made by an untrustworthy villain was hardly enough evidence to deem her father guilty. Yes, Papa had been enraged when she'd come home that morning with his vowels clutched in her hand. He'd realized immediately what must have happened, especially knowing Lucien's reputation. And yes, he had stormed off to challenge Lucien to a duel, which Lucien had refused.

Or had he? What if he'd had a good night at the tables and hired a press gang? No, that was unlikely, as her father had never been able to conceal a winning streak from anyone.

Or had he participated in some crazy scheme to get rid of the man who had defiled his daughter, especially since he had not yet known she was with child? Had he known *that*, nothing would have done but to make Lucien marry her.

Plausible explanations all, but until undeniable proof was produced to prove his guilt, she would remain loyal to her parent.

And until Lucien gave her reason to trust him, until she was certain he would not abandon her again, she would continue on the solitary path she'd chosen.

With a last, longing glance at the door connecting her bedroom to her husband's, she climbed into her lonely bed.

Chapter 12

⟨ ─∞─ ⟩

The day after one's wedding was supposed to be bright with glowing memories of the night before. All Lucien could recall, however, was the bottom of his brandy bottle. He sat alone at the breakfast table, head in his hands. Never since he had been a green boy just home from school had he ever overindulged in such a manner.

But enforced abstinence tended to do that to a man.

"Mr. Dante Wexford."

Lucien looked up just in time to see Elton, his new London butler, leave the room and Dante enter it.

"I see you're back from your mysterious trip to the country," Dante said, seating himself uninvited at the table with the ease of long acquaintance. "Have you discovered a new investment? I vow, your man Fenworthy will be in transports. He's been going to church every Sunday to thank God for your deliverance."

"How gratifying to know I've been missed, even if it was only by my man of business."

"Now, now, Lucien." Dante helped himself to an orange and began to peel it, a cheerful grin on his face. "You know I missed you, too."

"You must have, for what other reason could you have for coming to call so early in the morning? What is it, ten o'clock? I vow you don't usually rise until two."

"To tell the truth, I haven't been to bed yet." With a chuckle, Dante took a bite of an orange section. "But I knew you would be back in Town, so I came straight-away to see you. Am I not the best of friends?"

"You mean your curiosity could not keep you away." Still grinning, Lucien took a sip of hot, black coffee. "Congratulate me, Dante. I'm a married man."

Dante choked on the piece of fruit he'd just bitten. "Did I hear you aright? Did you just say *married*?"

"I did indeed."

"Well that was fast work. And who is the lovely lady?"

"Someone I knew long ago. Aveline Stoddard."

"Chestwick's daughter?" Casually, Dante rose and poured himself some coffee. "I met her once. Charming creature."

"I thought so, too."

"Does that mean you have no intention of attend-ing the Portworthys' ball this evening?" Dante sipped his coffee, made a face, and reached for the sugar. "Old Portworthy's launching his youngest daughter. Face like a horse and a fortune like Midas. 'Tis said to be the crush of the Season."

"And naturally you will be there."

Dante raised a brow and reached for the cream. "Naturally."

"I have to say, old friend, that I'm pleased to see you moving more easily in Society these days. Who is your benefactor?"

Dante bobbled the creamer, nearly spilling cream all over the table. "Fellow named Adminton took me under his wing, got me an entrée into the polite world."

"A good thing he did, considering I wasn't there to do so."

"Yes." Dante stirred his coffee, tapped the spoon on the rim of the cup. "The connection with Adminton was quite fortuitous."

"Perhaps I will look in on Portworthy's ball tonight. It might be a good way to introduce Aveline to Society."

"So soon? You've only been gone a week, so you can't have been wed very long. Surely you're not going out in Society already?"

"Why not?" Lucien sipped his coffee again, then looked up at a movement in the doorway. Aveline hovered there, clearly uncertain as to whether or not she should enter. By the devil's own luck, she looked amazingly beautiful in a pale pink dress with tiny flowers all over it, her blond hair upswept in some fetching creation held precariously in place with a pink ribbon. Desire woke and curled around his loins like a noose, reminding him of everything he couldn't have. "Ah, here is my lovely bride now," he drawled, rising to his feet.

Flushing at the bite in his voice, she entered the room, watching him from the corner of her eye as one would a wolf about to pounce.

She'd always been intelligent.

Dante had also risen when Aveline entered the room, and now he bowed. "Dante Wexford at your service, madam. I was acquainted with your father."

Aveline gave a polite curtsey. "I remember you, Mr. Wexford."

"I'm humbled." He pulled out a chair for her. "Please do join us."

"Thank you." She took the seat Dante offered— the one right next to her husband, curse his friend's meddling soul.

"Good morning, Lucien," she said, as both gentlemen sat down again.

He couldn't answer, distracted by the scent of lavender that teased his senses. As his wife turned her attention to the fruit bowl, gently cupping this orange or that bunch of grapes as she made her selection, it was all he could do not to take her little hands and put them in more interesting places. The beast inside him jerked at the leash and howled.

Dante sent him a look of amusement, and he realized he was staring at his wife like a starving man. He assumed a bland expression and sipped his coffee, though it was her flesh he wanted to taste.

"Please don't let me interrupt your conversation," she said into the silence.

"We were discussing the Portworthys' ball this evening," Dante offered, ever attentive to a pretty face. "Your madman of a husband thinks to attend tonight when he should be on his honeymoon."

"Does he?" She took a bunch of grapes from the bowl and began to pluck the plump fruits from their vine to her plate, her gaze fastened to her task. "I'm certain Lucien knows what he is about."

Lucien smirked. "See that, Dante? Every man should have so loyal a wife."

She glanced up at the hint of sarcasm in his tone. For a long moment they stared at each other, her eyes swirling with emotions he couldn't identify. He knew he was acting the boor, but he couldn't seem to help himself.

"Loyal and beautiful," Dante said with that damned cocksure grin of his.

"Quite so." Lucien tore his gaze from his wife and turned his attention to his breakfast. "I assume you have something suitable to wear to the ball, my dear?"

Aveline gasped. "You mean I am to go, too?"

"Of course you're to go." Lucien sliced his ham into bite-sized pieces. "Do you think me a complete clunch to leave my new bride home alone so soon after we are wed?"

"I didn't know what your plans were."

He stabbed a piece of ham and lifted it to his lips. "Now you do."

Aveline fingered a grape, tempted to forget her manners and throw it at her husband's arrogant head. What possessed him to act so obnoxious this morning?

"Do you have an appropriate dress?" he asked again, completely oblivious to the impropriety of discussing such things in front of company.

She flicked an embarrassed glance toward Dante, then replied, "Most of my clothes have yet to arrive, *husband*."

His eyes narrowed. "Then you must visit the modiste today, *wife*, and obtain something to wear to the ball."

"Certainly there's not enough time—"

"Pay extra for it to be ready today." He glanced away as he spoke, and they might have been discussing the sale of cattle or the repair of a barouche for all the attention he paid the subject. Was he still sulking because she'd refused him last night?

Her own temper smoldering, Aveline turned to Dante. She didn't trust Lucien's friend and never had, not since he'd made those innuendoes to her five years ago. Still, her hardheaded husband clearly wasn't about to assist her. "Mr. Wexford, I have lived most of my life in the country. Would you happen to know the name of the most fashionable modiste in London these days?"

"Madame Foussard, without a doubt." Dante smiled with both calculation and charm. "She's all the rage with the smart set."

"Thank you, Mr. Wexford." She gave him a gracious nod. "I shall visit her today."

"I would be pleased to accompany you and show you the delights of London." Dante popped a slice of orange in his mouth. "If your husband permits, of course."

"Dante, stop flirting with my wife," Lucien said before she could speak. He scowled at her. "*I'll* accompany you, my dear. This scoundrel has other appointments, I'm certain."

"Pray, don't upset your schedule on my account." With an angry toss of her head, Aveline rose to help herself to some ham from the sideboard.

"Oh, it's no trouble." Lucien leaned back in his chair, tracing the design of the cutlery as he watched her, his dark eyes unreadable.

"I'm certain you have business to attend to, especially since you've been gone from town nearly a week." Having acquired several slices of ham and a cup of tea, Aveline took her plate back to the table and pretended she didn't notice her husband's growing irritation. "I can manage perfectly well, though I thank you, Mr. Wexford, for the kind offer."

Dante inclined his head. "A pleasure."

Lucien picked up his knife and tapped it idly on the table. "Dante, the offerings of my table do not include my wife."

"So you've said." Dante sat back in his chair and sipped his coffee, clearly amused. "I was only being polite."

"Of course you were. Really, Lucien," she scolded. "Mr. Wexford was only trying to help."

Lucien leaned forward. "Mr. Wexford is a known

rake, my dear, and I advise you to be wary of him."

"Is he?" She raised her brows with delicate sarcasm. "I've heard the same said of you."

Her husband's face grew stormy, and Dante chuckled. "She's got you there, Luce old man. But they do say reformed rakes make the best husbands."

Aveline regarded Lucien innocently over the rim of her tea cup. "Yes, though I've not had time enough to decide if the adage is true."

"There's always tonight," Lucien answered with a smile that was mostly teeth.

Aveline's cheeks pinkened as Dante whooped with laughter. "But tonight we're to attend the Portworthys' ball, aren't we?" she replied with sweet sarcasm.

"But after the ball, you come home with *me*." Lucien jabbed a piece of ham with his fork, then slipped it into his mouth.

"Glad to see marriage hasn't dulled your wit, Lucien." Wiping tears of mirth from his eyes, Dante rose. "If you will excuse me, I'd best get some sleep, else I won't make the Portworthys' ball. The gathering should prove most entertaining."

"Indeed," Lucien murmured.

Aveline ignored the warning in the muttered word, though every inch of her body tingled with awareness. "Thank you for coming to call, Mr. Wexford."

"Congratulations to both of you on your marriage." With a bow, Dante left the room, the servants trailing behind him with empty platters, leaving Aveline and Lucien alone.

"Well," Aveline said into the tense silence, "he

seems somewhat more agreeable than the last time we met."

"And when was that?"

Lucien's lazy purr didn't fool her. "Five years ago when he came to collect a debt from my father."

"Ah yes, I remember."

Reluctant to pursue the topic of her father, Aveline pushed away her breakfast plate and rose. "I believe I will search out my abigail to accompany me to the modiste."

"Aveline." She paused. Danger lurked in his gaze and in the stillness of his body. "Don't think that because you and I do not share a bed that I would condone an affair with another man."

She stared in shock. "I would never indulge in any such affairs, and I resent you implying otherwise."

He raised his brows. "I'm merely warning you, wife. Don't test my temper by flirting with other men, especially Dante."

"Fine." She folded her arms across her chest. "And don't *you* test *my* temper by flirting with other women!"

He chuckled. "Jealous, are you?"

"Ha!" She flattened her hands on the table and leaned forward. "You and I are caught together in this mess, Lucien. Let's not muddy the waters with others."

His gaze dipped down to her bosom and lingered, and she realized that her bent-over position had her breasts practically exploding from her bodice. With anyone else, she would have immediately straightened. But when he looked at her with a question in his eyes, when he lifted his hand to slowly stroke a finger down the swell of her cleavage, she didn't move. Didn't stop him. Didn't say a word.

His hand paused over her heartbeat, and desire swept across his features, his eyes darkening with unmistakable heat. "You're right, Aveline. This is between us alone."

She swallowed hard, her pulse skipping wildly as he traced along the edge of her bodice with his finger, then brushed a thumb over her already erect nipple. With a soft moan, she closed her eyes as pleasure washed over her.

She heard the scrape of a chair, a low growl of need. Then she was in his arms, his mouth hard and hungry on hers. His hand cupped her breast through her clothing, and for just one moment she allowed herself to forget the obstacles, forget the higher morals that kept them apart. For just one moment she allowed herself to be a woman starved for the carnal delights this man could bring her.

He tasted like orange and coffee and pure, hot sex. The very scent of him cast her back in time to those three nights of sin they'd shared. The heat. The dark. The passion. The hunger.

Eagerly she swept her hands over his broad shoulders, groaned as he pressed her urgently against his hard body. She tangled her hands in his hair and bit his bottom lip, her body singing as he sat her on the edge of the table, his hands gripping her thighs.

For one fleeting instant, she thought he'd toss up

her skirts and take her right there amongst the breakfast dishes.

She clung to him, one hand tugging loose his cravat. Then she buried her face in his throat, nibbling the sensitive column of his neck. A tremor shook him, and his hands clenched on her thighs. He muttered something beneath his breath, and she slipped her fingers beneath the collar of his shirt, seeking warm, smooth skin.

Her fingertips encountered puckered flesh instead.

Scars. Like a dash of cold water, her principles rose up to berate her. Her father. Lucien's accusations. What was she *doing*?

She jerked away from him. "Lucien, stop."

He followed her when she strained away from him, his mouth sliding down the expanse of her throat to caress the slope of one breast. Despair welled up as she pushed at his chest with both hands. Dear Lord, it *hurt* to push him away.

She wanted more than anything to feel his body join with hers, to revel in the fierce possession she remembered even five years later. But she couldn't. No matter how much she wanted to, she *couldn't*.

"Stop, Lucien. I said *stop*!" She accompanied the last demand with a sharp shove that actually set him back a pace.

He blinked in confusion, dark eyes heavy with lust, lips still moist from their kisses. One hand still caressed her nipple. "What?"

She shoved his hand away from her breast and hopped down off the table, though this new position put her right up against him—and the unmistakable bulge in his trousers. He made a purring sound in the back of his throat and pressed against her, trapping her between the table and his aroused body.

"We have to stop this." She nearly moaned the words. "Right now, Lucien."

"We're married." He bent to nibble her ear, rubbing his chest against her breasts, his hardness against her belly.

Deliberately she curled her hand around his neck and slipped her fingers beneath his collar to find the rippling flesh of his scars. The reminder gave her courage.

"I won't share a bed with you, Lucien," she panted. "Nothing has changed."

He froze. Very slowly, he took her arm from around his neck and lowered it to her side. His face looked carved from granite, his eyes diamond hard and just as cold. He stepped back from her. "My apologies if I have misinterpreted your interest," he said icily.

She took a deep, shuddering breath, cheeks burning. "I apologize if I misled you. It won't happen again."

He gave a brief nod. "Understood. But I meant what I said. If I find out about another man—"

"I've told you already that I have no intention—"

"You already know I'm a crack shot," he interrupted. He gave her a menacing smile that made her explanations fade on her lips. "And I'm not nearly as forgiving as I used to be."

"Clearly." She rubbed her hands over her arms, cold without his warm embrace.

"Don't make me prove it." He stormed from the room, leaving her alone and trembling in his wake.

Lucien stalked down the London street with no particular destination in mind. Ever since his captivity, he'd learned to appreciate the freedom of being able to walk wherever he wanted, and he found it often soothed him to do so. Just then, however, he also needed the physical activity to counteract the sexual craving that clawed at his insides, begging to be set free on his pretty little wife.

Damn her. And damn himself for being so stupid. How could he have misinterpreted her posture for anything more than it was? He knew Aveline didn't possess a hint of guile. Had he been so hungry for her, so desperate, that he would grab at any excuse to make advances?

His lips curled in disgust. What was the matter with him? He rutted after his wife like an animal in heat. Had he no pride? No dignity? He'd not begged or groveled during his years as a captive on the *Sea Dragon*, and he'd be drawn and quartered before he started. Especially for the affections of a woman.

Five years ago, females rich and poor had avidly pursued him as a lover. Had fought over him, begged for his attentions. Wasn't he Lucifer, the most infamous rake in London?

He'd be damned if he was going to sniff after Aveline like a hound on a bitch, begging for a crumb of affection. He'd survived years of torment under Sledge's whip, and he'd conquer this, too. He'd had plenty of experience in the art of seduction—some would even call him an expert. It was time he put those skills to good use. Some women needed to be pursued. Others needed to be coaxed. And some . . . He grinned. Some women needed patience.

He would simply wait her out.

He knew how to satisfy a woman, and he also knew Aveline remembered his talents in the bedroom. Sooner or later their enforced closeness would get to her. The tension would build until neither of them could be in the same room without stripping the other one naked. When desire stalked her every waking moment, *she* would come to *him*.

And he would be waiting.

Aveline had expected to make the trip to Madame Foussard's alone, so she was quite surprised when Lucien climbed into the carriage across from her.

"You're coming with me?" she blurted out.

Stretching out his long legs, he sent her a challenging look. "I said I would."

"I thought . . ." She trailed off.

"Yes?"

"You weren't here," she said quietly. "I thought you'd decided against coming."

"I keep my promises, Aveline."

She raised her brows. "Do you?"

His lips quirked in a sardonic smile. "You might remember a certain bargain from several years ago. I adhered to it to the letter."

"Yes, you did," she agreed. "Right up to the part where you sent me away after the third night."

"It was what you wanted."

She gave a harsh little laugh. "You never knew what I wanted."

"Tell me what you want now." At her sharp look, he smiled with the innocence of a boy, belied by the wicked gleam in his eyes. "At the dressmaker's."

She rolled her eyes and ignored his soft chuckle as the carriage made its way to the modiste's.

Madame Foussard greeted Lucien like a long-lost son.

"Monsieur DuFeron!" She clasped her hands together in joy, a smile stretching across her somewhat homely face. "How wonderful that the rumors of your death were untrue!"

Lucien smiled with genuine warmth. "Quite untrue, madame."

The modiste went on in a spate of French too fast for Aveline to follow, but Lucien chuckled and answered in the same tongue. Catching sight of Aveline's puzzled expression, he switched back to English. "Madame, we have come on a most urgent matter. My wife is in desperate need of an evening dress."

"Your wife?" The plump Frenchwoman looked Aveline up and down with a practiced eye, then nodded. "It is my pleasure to dress you, Madame DuFeron," she said in heavily accented English. "Your husband, he is a longtime customer of my establishment."

"Really?" Aveline cast an arch look Lucien's way, but the rogue merely grinned without repentance. "Do you have anything appropriate for this evening, madame?"

"This evening?" Madame Foussard clasped a hand to her bosom. "So soon? *Impossible!*"

Lucien stepped forward. "As always, I will make it worth your while, madame. Pray tell me you have something ready."

"To create a dress in mere hours . . . something worthy of your wife's beauty—"

"I'll double your price," Lucien said.

The modiste blinked, then stuck her head through the curtains into the back room. "Yvette! Marie! Monique! *Venez-vous ici! Vite, vite!*" She turned back to them and smiled ingratiatingly. "Please come this way. We must measure Madame DuFeron."

Lucien chuckled as the dark-haired woman disappeared into the next room, shouting orders at her seamstresses in rapid French. He offered his arm to Aveline. "Behold the power of money."

"When it comes to a dress," she said with a scoff. She laid her hand on his forearm and walked with him toward the back room.

"I'm well aware money can't buy everything," he said. He stopped and held aside the curtain for her. "You, for instance."

"Quite true." She slipped past him, their bodies nearly brushing, the scent of him making her head spin. Then reality came crashing back as he also stepped into the small fitting room. "What are you doing? You can't come in here!"

"Of course I can." He gave her a wicked smile. "I'm your husband, and I'm paying the bill."

"Monsieur," the dressmaker called, indicating a chair. "Do sit here. You must tell us your opinion."

"See?" Lucien chuckled at Aveline's shocked expression, then sauntered over and sat where the modiste bade him.

"Madame, he cannot . . . I cannot . . ."

"A woman dresses for a man, Madame DuFeron," the dressmaker said, herding her toward some standing mirrors mere paces away from her husband. "We must make certain your husband is pleased with your purchases."

"Yes, Aveline." Lucien met her eyes in the mirror, a hungry gleam in his. "You must please me."

"You must tell me at once if there is something you do not like, Monsieur," the modiste continued.

Lucien gave a grave nod. "Of course I will, Madame."

"Yvette! Marie!" Madame Foussard called. Then she sighed and threw up her hands. "These girls, they are so slow! I must do the measuring myself. Undress, Madame DuFeron."

"I beg your pardon?"

"Undress, Madame!" The modiste collected a measuring tape and a pencil and paper. "I must have the most exact measurements in order to do my work."

"But—"

"You heard Madame Foussard, Aveline," Lucien said softly. "Undress."

He glanced over her body as if he could already see her naked. Her breath caught, and she lowered her lashes, afraid he would see the answering attraction in her eyes. He was already too confident, and any indication of surrender would start something she was not ready to finish.

"Ah, you are shy." The modiste clucked her tongue. "To the chemise, *c'est bien.*" The woman put down her materials and began to unfasten Aveline's dress.

One of the seamstresses entered the room, and Aveline didn't dare look at Lucien as the dressmaker stripped the gown away and handed it to her assistant with a snapped order in French. The young girl laid the dress aside, then took up the paper and pencil as Madame Foussard snatched up the measuring tape and whipped it around Aveline's waist. She barked out numbers in French as she measured various areas of Aveline's body, which the girl scribbled down.

"Your wife is a beautiful woman, Monsieur," the modiste said. She took Aveline's chin in her hand and turned her face so she could see it in the mirror. "And such green eyes! I have the perfect material for her." She shot a command to her assistant in her native tongue, and the girl scurried from the room.

Aveline met Lucien's eyes in the mirror. He made no effort to disguise the appreciation in his expression, his gaze touching on her nearly exposed breasts with an intensity that made her nipples harden in response. A blush rose in her cheeks as the rest of her body responded with a flood of warmth.

A small smile of satisfaction touched his mouth, and he pointedly shifted in his chair.

She cast down her gaze, breath shuddering from between her parted lips. If she could feel his desire with the room between them, what would happen if he touched her?

She cast a quick glance back at him. He was the most starkly sensual man she had ever seen, and she knew only too well what sorcery he could work on her body. Inside the boudoir, he exceeded her greatest expectations.

But outside it, he failed them.

She took a deep breath, strengthening her resolve. She refused to give herself to a man who could not be trusted once his desire had been satisfied. He'd left her shattered once before. It wouldn't happen again.

The assistant hurried back into the room, her arms overflowing with delicate green silk.

"Here is the dress, monsieur, madame. *Ravissant, n'est-ce pas?*" Madame Foussard shook out the half-finished gown and held it up against Aveline. "The lady who ordered this, she says it is not her color. But on Madame DuFeron—*alors, c'est incroyable!*"

Aveline couldn't prevent a gasp of delight as she beheld the evening dress. The seafoam green silk shimmered with iridescent flashes of soft blue and pink whenever the material rippled. Though the neckline seemed lower than she normally dared to wear, she couldn't help but notice how the color flattered her. Her green eyes looked almost catlike, her skin creamy smooth and her hair soft gold. She reached out a wondering hand to caress the delicate fabric.

"Madame, you have done it again," Lucien said hoarsely. He cleared his throat and stood abruptly. "Such a gorgeous creation needs appropriate accessories. I shall see to the matter."

"But, monsieur, you would leave now?" the modiste exclaimed.

"I'm afraid I must." He glanced at Aveline in the mirror. Fierce, primal lust heated his gaze. "I'll be back for you."

And in this case, she knew that was a promise he would keep.

Chapter 13

The new gown made her feel like a princess.

Lucien had sent the carriage back to Madame Foussard's that afternoon to bring her home, though he himself had not accompanied it, and she'd not seen him at dinner. But as she descended the stairs that evening, he waited for her at the base of the staircase, looking devastating in basic black evening wear. He'd cut his hair, and while it was still long, it looked less savage and more à la mode. Even the scar near his eye couldn't detract from his elegance.

"Good evening, my dear," he said, as she reached the last step. He lifted her hand and brushed a kiss against it. "You look breathtaking. I shall be the envy of every man at the ball."

"Th-thank you." She pulled her hand from his

grasp, unnerved by the heat that tingled along her fingers.

"I've taken the liberty of obtaining a small token for you." He reached for a black velvet case on a nearby table and flipped it open. She gasped at the contents. "A husband's prerogative," he added.

Against the black velvet lining glittered a necklace of diamonds and pearls. She reached out to touch one matching earring, then hesitated, as if by doing so the gorgeous jewelry would disappear into her fantasies. With a small smile of amusement, Lucien scooped up the necklace, then set the box back on the table.

"If you would allow me . . . ?"

She closed her eyes and nodded, presenting him with her back. She felt the heat of him as he stepped up behind her, the cool touch of the gems against her bare skin as he draped the necklace around her throat. His fingers brushed the nape of her neck as he fastened the clasp, and she couldn't suppress a shiver as her nerve endings tingled in reaction.

He paused for a moment, hands resting against the slope of her shoulders. Then he swept a finger along her spine, stopping where bare skin ended. She made a soft sound, unable to conceal her reaction. He stepped away, and she heard him getting one of the earrings out of the box.

He came around in front of her, and she glanced at his face. The same hunger that tormented her was reflected in his taut features. Drawing out the action, he fastened the jewels to first one ear, then the other.

"There," he said, taking a step back to admire her.

A possessive smile touched his lips. "That's how my wife should look."

Something deep inside her melted at the way he said "my wife," and she had to fight the instinct to step into his arms. Her husband could be entirely too charming when he set his mind to it.

He chuckled as if he could read her thoughts. "Come, my sweet," he said, offering her his arm. "The *ton* awaits."

"Mr. and Mrs. DuFeron!"

At the Portworthys' ball, they paused in the doorway to the ballroom. Whispers rippled through the crowd and became a dull roar. Their hostess had all but swooned when she'd realized that her daughter's come-out ball was the first social appearance of the newly married couple, and now Aveline knew why. The presence of the resurrected Lucien DuFeron and his mysterious new bride guaranteed the event's success.

Aveline clung to Lucien's arm as he led her into the sea of humanity. People swarmed around them, offering congratulations and pressing for introductions to his new wife. Aveline found it all a bit overwhelming and stayed close to her husband. Lucien swept through the throng with experienced aplomb, expertly sidestepping well-wishers until the crowd gradually began to disperse.

"Well," Aveline said when they finally escaped the throng, "you're certainly a popular man."

"My money is popular," Lucien replied with typical cynicism. "That and my skill for profitable investing."

"Surely you have *some* friends who like you for yourself."

"Except for Dante, I have no friends." He stopped at the edge of the dance floor. "Would you care to dance?"

"I haven't danced much in public," she began. Then she noticed the shuttered expression that swept across his face. "I'd love to dance with you," she qualified. "I'm just not very good at it."

The shadows fled from his eyes, and he gave her the first genuine smile she'd seen in days. "I am."

She couldn't help but respond to his good humor. "I shall trust you," she teased, "but when your toes grow sore from my constant treading upon them, you have only yourself to blame."

"I'll take the risk," he said gravely, then led her into the next set for a country dance.

Her husband was indeed an excellent dancer. Aveline found it easy to match his movements as they turned and stepped and came together and parted. It was almost like making love, she thought, the way their bodies seemed to anticipate each other's rhythm. Advance, retreat, step, turn. She met his gaze as they stepped toward each other, then held it as they retreated. She turned, but cast a glance back at him. Came around close enough for her skirt to brush his legs.

His eyes narrowed, his face taking on the intent look of a predator. Aveline let her gaze slide away, then felt compelled to glance back. Her heart sped up, and her cheeks heated at the way he looked at her. They performed the dance in perfect harmony,

Aveline following Lucien's lead, achingly aware of the tension rising between them.

He took her hand, and his touch sent a quiver through her. He let her go, and she longed for the moment when they would touch again. The crowded ballroom fell away. The orchestra faded into a dream. Nothing existed but she and Lucien and the heartbeat thundering in her ears.

The music stopped, and the gentlemen bowed to the ladies. Only Aveline noticed Lucien's hesitation before he followed suit. As she curtseyed back to him, she realized that he had been as caught up in their mutual attraction as she.

Lucien took her arm in a possessive grip and led her from the dance floor. She noted that his breathing seemed a bit labored. From the dance? Or from something else?

He dipped his head low to her ear. A thrill spiked through her as his breath brushed her skin.

"Would you care for a glass of punch?"

She blinked, excitement fading as the passionate words she anticipated proved no more than a mundane question. "Ah . . . yes, I would. Thank you."

He stopped by a potted palm and gave her a brief, polite bow. "Wait here. I'll be but a moment."

She might as well have *been* the dratted palm tree for all the notice he gave of her charms. She didn't understand it. He seemed to have changed from ardent lover to distantly polite husband in the space of mere moments. Had he already found a mistress?

Despair flooded her as she watched him disappear into the crowd. She was married to the most desirable man in England, and because of some rotten circumstances, she couldn't even enjoy it.

"A lovers' spat?" Dante appeared by her side as if from nowhere, a smirk playing about his lips. "Tell me it isn't so."

"Of course not, Mr. Wexford." Aveline glanced over the crowd, hoping to catch Lucien's eye. "Nothing of the sort."

"That's not what I observed." He made a tsking sound and shook his head. "How tragic."

She sent him a look of annoyance. "I thought you were Lucien's friend."

"I am."

"Then why do you mock us?" Aveline faced him, snapping open her fan. "Are you so bored with your own life that you can think of nothing else to do but jeer at your friends?"

He stiffened. "You know nothing of me or of life in Town, my dear Mrs. DuFeron. There are jackals all around us much worse than I. Have a care one of *them* does not start rumors about your marriage."

"There are no rumors to start."

"Aren't there?"

She waved her fan faster in an attempt to conceal her alarm at his knowing tone. "What are you implying, Mr. Wexford?"

"I remember the first time I saw you, dear lady."

"When we met in my father's study. I remember as well."

"No." He plucked the fan from her fingers, ceasing her agitated fluttering. "It was morning. You were in Lucien's coach, leaving his house, having spent the night."

She snatched back her fan and glared at him. "I don't know what you're talking about."

He met her gaze, held it. "You were so beautiful. I had just won a small sum from your father at the tables. If he didn't have the money to pay me, I was going to ask for you instead."

Her mouth fell open, and she instinctively took a step backward. "My father would never have agreed to such a thing!"

He shrugged. "It seemed to work for Lucien."

With difficulty, Aveline pulled her dignity around her and stared him down with a confidence she didn't feel. "Whatever happened all those years ago no longer matters, Mr. Wexford. I'm Lucien's wife now. Marriage has a way of erasing one's sins."

A superior smile curved his lips. "Nothing can erase Lucien's." He gave her a brief bow and disappeared into the crowd an instant before Lucien returned.

"Was that Dante just now?" he asked, handing her a glass of punch.

"Yes, he stopped to say hello." She sipped the insipid drink, hoping it would settle her nerves. Something about Dante Wexford set her on edge. The man was a snake, always looking to manipulate the weaknesses in others.

"I'm surprised he took himself off so quickly." He gave her a searching look that hinted of distrust. "He must have a lady waiting for him."

"I wouldn't know." She shrugged, scanning the

crowded ballroom with casual disinterest. "I barely know the man."

"Remember what I told you."

His low warning kindled her temper. Glaring, she shoved the glass of punch into his hand, uncaring that it splashed over his white cuff. "I'd like to know what I've done to give you the impression I'm contemplating an affair."

He took her by the arm and pulled her closer to the potted palm. "Keep your voice down before you cause a scene."

"You started it," she snapped in a harsh whisper. "You and your unfounded insinuations."

"This is *not* the time."

"I really don't care." She kept her voice down, but her anger burned hot. "What makes you think I'm looking for a lover? I've done everything you wanted."

"Not everything," he muttered through his clenched teeth.

She rolled her eyes. "Is that *all* you ever think about?"

"Only when you deny me." Concealed behind the palm tree, he slid a hand along her hip, over her buttock. "Only when you taunt me with your beauty, tease me with your kisses, then walk away."

She colored. "I don't mean to . . . to tease you. I just get . . . you just . . . stop that!" She took a step back, forcing him to stop caressing her bottom. "Do you think it's easy to resist you?"

He looked startled, then calculating. "Isn't it?"

She was saved from answering.

"Lucien, I've heard the most dreadful rumor—" A beautiful woman suddenly appeared beside them, her words casual but cutting. She stopped short upon seeing him, distaste creeping across her elegant features. "Good God, what happened to your face?"

Lucien stiffened. "A consequence of my time away from England."

"Dear Lord." A young blond man standing slightly behind the woman, stared at Lucien's scar, horror dawning in his blue eyes. "What the devil have you been at now, Lucien?"

"Robert, hush," his companion commanded. The young man—clearly he could not be more than Aveline's own age—bristled, but did not speak again.

Aveline glanced at Lucien, expecting him to set these people on their ears as he did with anyone else who dared speak down to him. Instead he only stared defiantly at the two, every muscle in his body tensed.

Who were these people? And what hold did they have over her husband that he restrained himself so unnaturally?

At least he did not face them alone. She reached out to him and gently slipped her hand into the crook of his arm. Though he never looked at her, he laid his over hers with a possessiveness that deepened the glowers of the newcomers.

"Aveline," he said with polite formality, "this is the Duchess of Huntley, my father's wife, and the Duke of Huntley, my half brother. Madam, Robert, this is Aveline DuFeron—my wife."

This was Lucien's family? This coldly arrogant woman and her wet-behind-the-ears son?

"Wife?" the young duke scoffed. He glanced down at her belly with insulting speculation.

"Well," the duchess drawled, following her son's glance, "she doesn't look to be breeding, but time will tell."

Aveline's cheeks burned, and Lucien's face took on a look of cold calculation. "Madam," he said, "that was in bad taste even for you."

"It's a fair question," Robert spluttered.

Lucien turned on his half brother with a ferocity that had the man stepping backward. "Insult me all you like, Robert. You've a right to your enmity. But never speak of my wife in any but the most respectful of tones. She's a lady and should be treated as one."

"You expect others to grant your lady courtesy and respect," the duke retorted, tensing as if for battle, "but I have yet to see you do the same. How ironic you are, Lucien."

"Enough." The duchess laid a hand on Robert's arm, silencing him, then cast Lucien a look of malicious amusement. "What else do you expect people to think, Lucien? You've only just returned to England, and suddenly you are married. Why else the hasty wedding?"

"That is my affair and no one else's." Lucien sent a hard look to his half brother. "If anyone asks, you may tell them that Aveline and I had an understanding before my . . . departure. Once I returned, I merely followed through with our agreement."

The duchess curled her lip. "It will do as well as any explanation. Once again, Lucien, you bring scandal to the family."

"How can it be scandalous to fulfill a promise?" Aveline asked. The three of them glanced at her, startled, as if they had forgotten her existence. "My husband has done nothing to cause talk."

"My dear girl, anything Lucien does causes talk." The duke gave her the indulgent smile one might bestow on the slow-witted. "As you will soon learn after a few weeks in London."

"I don't doubt it," she returned. "But perhaps if he had the support of his family, the rumors wouldn't fly so quickly."

The duke's blue eyes widened in astonishment at the set-down, and the duchess gave Aveline a look that froze her to her toes. But before either one could say a word, Lucien spoke.

"My wife and I are expected at another affair." He gave the briefest of bows to his family, and Aveline hastily followed suit to dip a curtsey. "Kindly excuse us."

He led Aveline away before either one could reply, his long strides forcing her to hurry to keep up with him. She cast an anxious glance at him, but his stony expression revealed nothing. She hoped her plain speaking hadn't angered him, but she hadn't been able to hold back once she'd seen the disdain with which his family treated him.

He called for his carriage and handed her into it. She thought she noticed a stiffness to his posture, but before she could look more closely he swung into the seat opposite her. The footman closed the door with a sharp click, and the coachman clucked to the horses. The carriage pulled away.

Darkness wrapped around them. She twisted her fingers together in her lap and wondered how badly she'd erred. She'd always been taught to show the utmost respect to the peerage, but something about the duchess's superiority and the duke's patronizing tone had pricked her temper. What if her smart retort had only made matters worse between Lucien and his family?

The silence dragged on between them. Unable to stand it a moment longer, she said, "I'm sorry, Lucien."

"Sorry?" His voice gave her no clue to his mood. "What have you to be sorry about?"

"I shouldn't have been rude to your family."

"Indeed, insulting a duke is not the most intelligent path to social acceptance."

"I know." She sighed with frustration. "I just didn't like the way they talked to you, as if you are somehow less than they are."

"I'm a bastard, Aveline. Their attitude is quite common."

"That doesn't make it right."

"Quite true." To her surprise, he chuckled. "Dear Lord, did you see Clarissa's face? It was priceless."

She squinted to see him, but the shadows of the coach prevented her from reading his expression. "Does that mean you're not angry with me?"

"Angry? Dear girl, no one in my entire life has ever defended me to my family." He leaned forward in the seat, and the passing lights from outside revealed his lips curled in amusement. "Who would have ever thought it would be my sweet and gentle wife?"

She let out a long breath. "I was worried I had ruined things for you."

"With them?" He shrugged. "My relationship with them has been strained since the day I went to live with my father. I doubt it will ever change."

"You were raised in your father's house?"

"Yes. My mother was once his mistress, and when my father discovered he had a son, he acknowledged me and brought me home to England."

"What happened to your mother?"

"She's still in France, I suppose. She took the money my father gave her and disappeared. I never saw her again."

Appalled, she asked, "How old were you?"

"About Chloe's age."

"How awful!"

"Not really. I was raised as the son of a duke, even if I can't inherit the title. I was fed, clothed, and educated, though Robert was lauded as the heir when he came along a year later." He chuckled. "I thought Clarissa would take to her bed with apoplexy when I reached my majority and made my fortune so quickly."

"I noticed you don't get on with the duchess."

"Not at all. She's always resented me, you see. Always considered me a living insult to her. I think the fact that my father raised me in the same house as his legitimate son made her hate me all the more."

"What about your brother?"

"Half brother," he corrected. "Robert didn't like me any better than his mother did. And we had a falling-out a few years ago that hasn't improved matters."

"Did no one ever love you, Lucien?" she whispered.

For an instant she thought she saw a flash of emotion in his eyes—something that might have been longing or loneliness. Then he gave her a cocky grin, banishing the brief impression of vulnerability. "Of course. Women have always loved me."

Inexplicably disappointed in his answer, she muttered, "Arrogant man," and turned her attention to the dark buildings of London passing outside her window.

Her husband gave a wicked chuckle. "Have you ever made love in a carriage, my sweet?"

"What?" she squeaked.

With a smooth move that betrayed his vast experience, he crossed to the seat beside her, crowding her into the corner of the carriage with an arm on either side of her head as he leaned close. "I asked," he murmured, "if you have ever made love in a carriage."

"You know well enough I haven't!"

He raised his brows. "But that would indicate that I've been your only lover."

Hot color flooded her cheeks, and she was glad that the night hid her embarrassment. "I've never made any secret of that."

"But until this moment, I never realized." He bent and pressed his mouth to the base of her throat, touching his tongue to the pulse there. "I'm the only man ever to touch you."

She closed her eyes, letting her head fall back as her flesh rippled in reaction. "Lucien, you are a rogue."

He chuckled against her neck, dropping feather-light kisses beneath her ear. "I thought you knew that already."

"We can't . . ." She cleared her throat and pushed against his shoulders. "Lucien, we're almost home."

"Shall I have John Coachman drive around London?" He hooked a finger in her low-cut bodice and pulled. One breast popped free of confinement. He shifted closer and closed his mouth around her burgeoning nipple.

"Dear Lord in Heaven," she whispered, tangling her fingers in his hair as desire swept through her. He knew just how to touch her, and the story of his childhood had softened her heart toward him. No doubt he knew it, the scoundrel.

He drew back from her breast, tugging the nipple in his teeth for an instant before giving it a last lick. Then he kissed her.

A moan slipped past her lips as he fed on her mouth, nibbling at her lips, teasing her as if he had all the time in the world. At the same time, he slid his hand beneath her skirt, slowly pushing it up her leg until it bunched near her thigh. Another few inches, and he'd have her all but naked.

The carriage jolted, and the coachman swore as one wheel banged into a pothole. Lucien muttered a curse and grasped her thigh to keep them both from tumbling to the floor. The coach lurched again, then the ride leveled.

All at once she remembered where she was. "Lucien, stop."

"Are you certain you want me to?" He traced her inner thigh.

She shoved his hand away. "We can't do this, especially not with the coachman sitting right there."

"I assure you, we're not the first ones to ever couple in a carriage."

She tugged up her bodice. "No, Lucien. Nothing has changed."

With a wicked laugh, her husband moved back in his own seat. "Something has indeed changed."

"What?" she snapped, shoving down her skirts.

"You showed me loyalty in front of my family."

"They treat you abominably."

His smile flashed white through the darkness. "Your affection is overwhelming. I hope you will soon extend that loyalty to my bed."

"I doubt it."

"I don't." And with a confident chuckle, he settled back in his seat, once more hidden in the shadows.

Chapter 14

The next morning, the baggage from Cornwall arrived.

Aveline knelt before her embroidery trunk and regarded the contents. Despite the distraction of the previous night's ball, the trunk, and the letter from Mrs. Baines that accompanied it, reminded her all too well of her complicated situation.

According to her letter, the housekeeper had successfully sold some of the completed pieces and accumulated enough money to keep the household going for the next month. Her father was well, and she wasn't to worry.

She tossed the letter on a nearby table. How could she *not* worry? Her father was ill, she was married to a man who hated him, and she had been forced by circumstance to creep about like a thief to provide money for her parent's living expenses because her husband wished him dead. Such a situation promoted worry.

Aveline took a skein of royal blue thread from the trunk and toyed with one frayed end. She would sell the remaining pieces as needed. At least the leeway of a month would give her enough time to create more, and she could do so in plain sight of everyone, even Lucien. Who would suspect her motives, when embroidery was so well accepted as a gentle lady's pastime?

But she hated the deception.

With a frustrated huff, she tossed the thread back into the trunk. Pretense was not her nature, and all this secretive planning left her tense as a harp string. Why must she be caught in the middle of Lucien's argument with her father?

After meeting Lucien's family last night and hearing some of his background, she understood a little better why he didn't seem to understand relationships. He'd expected her to accept his decision about her father without a murmur and to join him in his bed, leaving everything behind. He couldn't understand her ongoing loyalty to her father, or her reluctance to trust him with her heart. Couldn't comprehend how she managed to resist him even though the attraction between the two of them continued to burn hot.

He'd obviously never truly been part of a family. He'd never had anyone care about him. How could he possibly understand the bonds of family love?

Bonds that sustained a person through the worst of times. Bonds that held fast when everything else collapsed around one.

Bonds that could be trusted and understood.

There had been plenty of times when she'd been certain her world was about to collapse around her. She had dealt over and again with the sometimes devastating results of her father's incessant gambling. Many nights she had wondered if he'd finally managed to gamble them into poverty, but each time she'd managed to find a way to triumph over the adversity. Somehow, she'd fixed it.

She'd fix this, too. Somehow.

She sorted through the colorful materials in her trunk, pondering her next project, when her fingers encountered a folded paper jammed into the bottom corner of the trunk. Frowning, she picked it up and unfolded it.

Congratulations on your happy event. Please do not—

She gasped and dropped the paper as if it burned her. Lucien's note! Good heavens, she must have hidden it away inside her trunk after she'd heard of his death.

Slowly she reached for the missive and unfolded it again, spreading it flat on her lap. She stared at the words that had once burned a hole in her heart, yet the hurtful rejection didn't devastate her as it had then. But something about the letter disturbed her.

Tracing the slanting script with her finger, she pondered why something seemed *wrong* about it. The handwriting looked quite ordinary . . . rather neat actually. She might almost have written it herself.

Then she realized.

The writing looked neat and ordinary because *it was*. She outlined the slanting cursive and remembered the day she had married Lucien. She'd watched him sign the register—with his *left* hand.

Lucien was left-handed, his writing bold and *slanted in the opposite direction*. Whoever had written this letter had been right-handed.

Lucien hadn't written it.

Stunned, she slumped back into a sitting position right there on the floor. Lucien had told the truth. He hadn't written this letter. Yes, he might have had a secretary do it, but she doubted it. Something this delicate needed to be tended to personally, and Lucien was not a man to let another handle his intimate affairs.

He hadn't known about Chloe. He hadn't willingly abandoned her . . . at least, not that time.

The rage she'd nourished over the years drained out of her with a suddenness that left her weak. Except for the way he'd coolly ended their liaison, every nasty thing she'd believed about Lucien had been a lie. He'd never received her note, never had the opportunity to do the right thing. Until now.

She closed her eyes against the devastating truth. Someone had deliberately tried to keep them apart. No, more than tried. *Succeeded*. That person had sent her this hurtful letter to get rid of an unfortunate complication. No doubt the same person had arranged for Lucien's abduction and subsequent years of torment.

It hadn't been her father. Doubts she hadn't realized she possessed faded away to be replaced by heart-warming relief. The note wasn't in his handwriting either.

Then who? Who had taken their lives in his hands five years ago and left them both in misery? And why had he done it?

Perhaps Lucien would know. She glanced down at the letter crushed between her fingers. Maybe this would be enough proof for him to realize that her father was not the enemy he sought. Maybe now they could forge some sort of relationship out of the tattered remnants of their marriage.

Maybe now she and Lucien could look for the *real* culprit.

Shoving the note into her pocket, she hurried downstairs to find her husband.

Lucien had gone out and wasn't expected back until dinner. Disconcerted, Aveline sat in the parlor and poked her needle through her new embroidery project with a hint more force than necessary. In her pocket, the note practically burned like a hot coal. When she heard someone approach the parlor, she glanced up eagerly, but her enthusiasm faded when she saw it was just Elton.

"The Duke of Huntley," the butler said, then departed.

Lucien's half brother strode into the room. Aveline

frowned, setting aside her embroidery. As she stood and curtseyed to the duke, she reached into her pocket and tucked the note a bit deeper. "Good afternoon, Your Grace."

"Good afternoon." He gave her an uncertain smile, once more reminding her how very young he was to bear such a weighty title. "I must say, I expected you to have your man eject me from the house as soon as I was announced."

"There's still time," she pointed out.

He chuckled. "Indeed there is. I shall have a care then."

They stood there for a moment in awkward silence. "Do sit down," she said finally, remembering her manners.

"Thank you." He settled on the sofa across from her. "I take it Lucien is not at home?"

"No, he's not."

"Oh. I'd hoped to see him, but I also wanted to speak to you."

"To me?"

"Yes." He paused. "Did you enjoy the Portworthys' ball last night?"

"Yes, I did."

He waited, as if expecting her to say more. When she didn't, a hint of impatience flickered across his features. "Are you enjoying London?"

"Yes, I am. Your Grace, is there something I can do for you?"

"Well, that's right to the point, isn't it?"

She shrugged and picked up her needlework.

"After last night, I don't see any need for subtlety. You made your disdain for my husband—and for me—quite clear."

"Lucien and I ... well, there is history between us." He shifted, clearly uncomfortable. "Then there was the shock of your marriage. First we believed Lucien dead, then suddenly he's alive. Then we discover he's taken a wife."

"A common enough occurrence."

"Taking a wife, yes. The fact that he still lived, no."

Frowning, Aveline lowered her needlework to her lap. "Your Grace, are you telling me that last night was the first time you've seen Lucien since he returned?"

"It is." A faint flush settled along his lean cheekbones. "I told you there was history between us. I must say, his appearance rather shocked me."

"He looks different," she agreed, "but he is hardly disfigured."

"Of course not. It was just ... he didn't look the way I'd remembered." He gave her a weak smile. "I'm told he attempted to call on me when he first came home, but the servants didn't recognize him and sent him away."

"How awful!" She shook her head, her heart aching for her husband.

"I didn't find out about it until later. I looked for him, but he was difficult to find. When he rented this town house I came to see him, but he'd already left for Cornwall."

"I see." She concentrated on her stitches. The

young duke seemed almost sincere. She didn't know what to make of it. And what was this history he kept referring to?

"Mrs. DuFeron—"

"Oh, please." She sent him an exasperated look. "Your Grace, please call me Aveline. I am, after all, your half brother's wife."

He seemed to relax perceptibly. "Then you must call me Robert."

"Very well . . . Robert."

"Aveline," he began again. "I'm sure you're aware by now that my family has never completely . . . accepted . . . Lucien. It's not something in which I take pride."

"Hmmm." She kept her eyes on her sewing, though she hung on his every word. "Do go on, Robert."

"I'm in a position to change that attitude," he continued, determination fierce in his blue eyes. "Despite the problems in our past, I'd like to get to know my brother, and I believe you might be the key to that."

"Indeed?" She tied off a thread and snipped it with tiny scissors. "How refreshing."

He stiffened. "Do you doubt me?"

"Quite frankly, yes." She met his gaze squarely, still put out with him for his shameful behavior toward the two of them the night before. "Lucien has been through an experience that would have broken most men. I will not see him hurt again."

Robert's face reddened, and anger sparked in his eyes. For an instant he resembled Lucien very much, especially in the glower he lowered upon her. "How dare you suggest that I would cause harm to my brother. I am the Duke of Huntley, madam!"

"I'm certain you will forgive my impertinence, Your Grace," she replied. "However, given your history with my husband, even you must admit that this turn of face appears most suspect."

"What I must admit is that I doubt the character of the woman my half brother has married." He stood, and she followed suit.

"So now he is 'half brother' when before he was simply 'brother'? It must be quite convenient to distance yourself with that distinction whenever you are displeased."

He looked down his nose at her. "I came here with the intention of fostering peace with Lucien. But now—"

"Mama!" The duke spluttered into silence as Chloe raced into the room. The child threw her arms around her mother's legs, burying her face in Aveline's skirt. "Mama, the mean lady sticked me with a pin!"

Very much aware of Robert's shocked expression, Aveline ran a soothing hand over Chloe's curls. "Now, Chloe, I'm certain it was an accident."

A maid appeared in the doorway, red-faced and breathless. Her eyes widened in embarrassment as she took in the scene; then she bobbed a quick curtsey. "I'm sorry, Mrs. DuFeron. She took off so quickly, and I couldn't catch her!"

Aveline laughed. "Believe me, Martha, I'm aware of how fast my poppet can run. Take a moment to catch your breath before you take her back to the nursery."

"Thank you, madam."

Steeling herself for the inevitable disapproval, Aveline turned her attention back to the duke. He glanced from her to Chloe and back again with a puzzled frown. "Forgive the interruption, Your Grace," she explained. "My daughter is being fitted for some new dresses, and apparently we had a mishap with the modiste."

"Your daughter? Were you a widow then?"

She refused to look away as she answered, "No, I was not."

"I see."

She noticed the harsh judgment settling across his features, but she refused to let it bother her. Instead, she bent to Chloe and disengaged the child's hands from her skirts. "Chloe, this is the Duke of Huntley. Come and make your curtsey."

Chloe turned her head within her mother's skirts and sent the duke a suspicious, one-eyed look. Then she submitted to her mother's urging and faced him completely, carefully executing her somewhat shaky curtsey.

Robert sucked in a breath as he got a good look at Chloe's face. "But she looks just like—"

"She looks just like her father," Aveline said, lifting her chin with pride.

"How old is she?"

"Almost five."

Chloe nodded in agreement and displayed her five fingers.

"Hello, Chloe," the duke said. "I'm your uncle Robert."

Before the child could respond, Aveline signaled to the maid. "Go with Martha, Chloe. I'll come up in a few minutes to help with your fittings."

"Promise?" Chloe asked, slipping her hand into Martha's.

Aveline cupped Chloe's cheek. "I promise."

Robert stared after the little girl as she left with the maid. Only when the child was gone, did Aveline turn her attention back to her brother-in-law. "What did you mean by telling her that?"

He flinched, clearly startled by her demanding tone. "Telling her what? That I am her uncle?"

"You seem to claim your family only when it's convenient, Your Grace."

"I told you to call me Robert."

"I reserve that privilege for close family and friends, and you are neither," she said. "I will not have Chloe confused. You cannot seem to decide if you want to claim Lucien as your brother or not, and until you make up your mind, Chloe will only know you as the Duke of Huntley."

Sulky arrogance settled over his handsome features. "Her social consequence would increase should I claim her as my niece."

"She's too young to worry about social standing yet, thank goodness."

"But you aren't."

She stiffened at his soft, knowing tone. "I beg your pardon?"

"Don't you worry about Chloe's future? I have eyes, dear sister-in-law, and I can clearly see that Lucien is the child's father. Since the two of you married only recently, she must have been born out of wedlock. And I am certain I am not the only one who will make the distinction."

"That is not your concern, Your Grace."

The finality in her tone paused him for only a moment. "You're quite plainspoken for a woman."

"I believe in saying what I mean."

"Actually, I find that rather refreshing. One grows tired of the hidden messages people mask in polite conversation."

"You will always know where you stand with me, Your Grace. That much I can promise you. Now if you will excuse me, I must attend to my daughter. Elton will show you out."

She left him standing there and went to save Chloe from the dressmaker's pins.

Lucien shrugged off his coat and loosened his cravat. He'd ended up dining with some business associates and so had returned home later than expected. He glanced at the connecting door between his room and his wife's and wondered if she'd missed him.

Stokes, his valet, bustled about the room, putting his discarded coat away and assisting him with the removal of his boots. When the little man went to remove his waistcoat, he waved him away and unbuttoned it himself.

"That will be all for this evening, Stokes," he said, shedding the waistcoat and handing it to him.

"Very good, sir." The balding valet put the garment away, then gave a quick bow and slipped out of the room.

Lucien glanced again at the connecting door. Elton had informed him that his half brother had come to call and had spent nearly thirty minutes with Aveline before taking his leave. What had Robert wanted? He almost never called, and when he did it was usually to ring a peal over Lucien's head for some scandal or other. But Lucien hadn't scandalized anyone in quite some time. In fact, he'd done the opposite. He'd *married* the mother of his illegitimate child.

He made out the rustlings of Aveline moving around in her room, the soft murmur of voices as she spoke to her maid. He'd wait until the maid left, then he'd go visit his wife, ostensibly to ask about his half brother's visit.

He unbuttoned the collar of his shirt, a smile playing about his lips. Nothing stirred sexual desire like seeing one's mate clad in nightclothes. He would go into her room in his shirtsleeves and inquire about Robert's call, all the while pretending that he didn't notice the intimacy of the situation. Nothing drove a woman mad like a man who did not appear to notice her charms.

He heard the click of a latch, and Aveline slipped through the connecting door. She halted when she saw him, eyes widening as she pulled her wrapper more tightly around her scantily clad form.

"Lucien," she whispered, "I thought you were still downstairs."

He raised his brows. "Then you expected to find someone else in this chamber?"

"I had intended to wait—" She stammered to a stop when he grinned. "Oh, you're teasing me, aren't you?"

"A little." He shrugged and turned away from her, if only to gain control of his own awakening lust. With her curling blond hair tumbling down her back and her sweetly curved body barely covered by that frippery of lace and silk she wore, she all but begged for a tumble. *Would* beg for a tumble, if he had anything to say about it.

He searched out his brandy decanter as a distraction. "I understand the Duke of Huntley came to call today."

"How did . . . oh, of course. The servants would have told you."

"Of course." He faced her with a full glass, feeling more in control as he took his first swallow. "What did he want?"

"I'm not certain of his purpose, but he did tell me that he hadn't known that the servants turned you away when you first returned home."

"I suppose I should take comfort in the fact that my relations didn't instruct the staff to eject me." He swilled the brandy, then raised mocking brows. "Did he at least bring a wedding gift?"

"Of course not," she scolded. "Really, Lucien."

He shrugged. "You'd think my half brother the

duke would at least have the decency to present us with a wedding gift." He came toward her, his lips curving as she edged back a step. "Unfortunately even the highborn sometimes forget their manners."

"He tried to be polite. He's very young, isn't he?" Her gaze dropped to his mouth as he took another drink of brandy. Just for fun he licked his lower lip, as if savoring the liquor. She quickly looked away. "He said he'd come to make peace with you. Something about forgiving past history."

"Did he? An interesting development. And you're right; he is young for his office. He's five-and-twenty, in possession of an old and respected title with a fortune at his feet, yet the boy still lets his mother guide his life."

She moved toward the low fire that burned in the grate. "He was not very complimentary once he saw Chloe and ascertained that you were her father."

He scowled. "He'd best hold his tongue about Chloe."

"He seems more concerned with her social standing, probably because it will affect him." She sighed and looked back at him, her skin gilded by the flickering firelight. "I know he's your half brother, but I don't trust him. I don't like the way he treats you."

He shrugged. "He's the duke."

"That's no excuse."

Lucien sipped his brandy again. Aveline remained by the fireplace, the light from the flame silhouetting her curves against the fragile silk nightclothes. Lucien tightened his fingers around his goblet to stop himself from taking what he wanted. "Is there some reason you were looking for me, wife?" Even he heard the lust that roughened his tone.

Her head came up, and she spun to face him. With the fire behind her, her eyes looked huge in her face, lips parted, her knuckles white as she held her wrapper closed with one hand. He took in the stillness of her body, the increased pace of her breathing. Awareness vibrated between them.

She wasn't indifferent to him.

"There was a reason." Her voice sounded raspy, and she cleared her throat. "I found the letter I received. The one I thought was from you."

Distracted by the shape of her breasts beneath the flimsy silk, he almost missed the import of her words. Then it hit him, and he jerked his gaze to hers, desire forgotten. "You still have it?"

"Right here." She held out the wrinkled and folded piece of paper she had been concealing in her hand. "It was packed in one of my trunks."

He put down his brandy and opened the letter carefully, half-afraid of what he might find inside. Then he realized what she'd said. "The letter you *thought* was from me?"

"I know now that you didn't write it." Honesty shone from her open expression and echoed in her steady voice. "Look at the handwriting, Lucien. You're left-handed. This was written by someone right-handed."

His fingers shook as he opened the note, and he

hoped she didn't notice. This letter was the first real clue as to why he had been abducted. "You're right," he said, scrutinizing the looping script. "I didn't write this."

"And you knew nothing about it?"

He frowned. "Nothing. Though I can certainly see why you thought I had abandoned you." He scratched his chin. "This writing looks familiar."

"It does?" She hurried over to him. The scent of lavender drifted up from her hair as she leaned in to see the note, innocently pressing her breasts against his arm. "Where have you seen it before?"

"I'm trying to remember." Trying to think at all.

"You do realize what this means, don't you? Someone deliberately tried to separate us."

"Someone succeeded."

"Someone," she said pointedly, "who was not my father. This isn't his handwriting either."

"We've already agreed that your father probably had a wealthy partner." Unable to concentrate with her so close, he moved toward the fire, acting as if he were trying to see the words better. "Perhaps that's who wrote the note."

"Stubborn man. Can't you admit that you may have been wrong about my father?"

"Maybe." *Where* had he seen that writing before? "But you have presented me no proof of his innocence."

"And you've presented me with no proof of his guilt." Her nightgown swished against her legs as she came over to him and laid a hand on his arm.

"Lucien, you must keep an open mind about this."

"Must I? I want a real marriage, Aveline." And wouldn't Dante and the rest of London Society howl with laughter if they knew. He cupped her cheek with his free hand, grateful that his bride was too inexperienced to realize the power she had over him. "But I can't forget what happened to me. I can't let the culprit go unpunished."

"How can I trust a man committed to revenge?" she whispered, laying her hand over his. "Let your anger go and *live your life*."

"I can't." He pulled away, curling his hand into a fist. "You don't know. You can't understand."

"Can't I?" She touched the scar on his wrist. "I can see what's been done to you, and it breaks my heart."

He jerked away. "What if it was your father who turned my life to Hell, Aveline? What then? Do we live separate lives as husband and wife because you can't understand the concept of justice?"

"Justice and revenge aren't the same."

"They are to me. And might I remind you, dear wife, I showed restraint in the case of your father. I haven't truly exacted revenge; the baron still lives. Had it been any other man who had done this thing to me, I would have killed him."

"Dear Lord." She clasped a hand to her bosom, her eyes wide with shock.

"I apologize if it disturbs you; however, you seem to think I can simply turn my back on this. I can't."

"You're consumed by it," she whispered. "Hatred and revenge. Do you have any room in your heart for anything else? What about Chloe?"

"I will not neglect my daughter."

"Someday she'll be old enough to understand why she never sees her grandfather. What will you tell her?"

"Perhaps I won't have to tell her anything." He paused, hoping he wouldn't have to say the words.

"You're hoping he dies first." The flat tone of her voice echoed the horror dawning in her eyes. "Which leaves us right back where we started."

"A marriage of convenience. Is that what you really want?"

"Of course not." She twisted her fingers together, distress flickering across her features. "But I'm caught between both of you, Lucien. I love my father, and I . . . you are my husband."

"Is there no middle ground?" He set the letter aside. "Is there nothing about our marriage that makes you want to fight for it?"

"Of course there is. But my father—"

"Grow up, Aveline," he snarled. "Your father is just a man, not some untarnished white knight. And I'm just a man. Neither of us is infallible."

"I never said he was—"

"You can't protect him anymore. Not from this."

"Will you let me finish one sentence?" she cried.

"No." He moved in on her, driven by anger and frustration and nearly strangling desire. He crowded her against the small chess table beside the fire. The pieces fell over and rolled off the chessboard and onto the floor. "Someone tried to ruin our lives, and we must consider all the suspects. Even the ones we don't want to consider."

She closed her eyes. "I can't believe he'd do something so awful, Lucien. I just can't."

"Someone is trying to destroy us. And someone is succeeding."

Her eyes popped open. "What do you mean by that?"

"This thing festers between us like an unhealed wound. It affects our marriage and even our daughter. Don't you see, Aveline? He's winning. We're helping him win by giving in to doubt and suspicion."

"I'm not the only one guilty of that. You suspect my father with hardly any evidence."

"And you withhold yourself from our bed—from our marriage—in defense of him."

"Must we go over this every time we talk?"

"Until we come to an understanding."

"You mean until I agree to share your bed." She pushed him away, and he allowed her to, even though the feel of her hands against his chest made his heart beat faster. "It's not just about my father, Lucien."

"Then what is it? Tell me what I have to do to make our marriage real, because I grow weary of an empty bed."

She stiffened. "Use the letter. Find out who's behind this. Because until we know for certain, we'll never be able to make this marriage work."

"So once I prove your father guilty, you'll be a true wife to me."

"Oh, Lucien." She shook her head sadly. "I keep telling you, it's not about whether or not Papa is guilty. That's just a symptom of the real problem—your preoccupation with vengeance."

"The guilty must be punished."

"Perhaps. But 'tis God's place to judge, not yours." With a disappointed sigh, she walked over to the connecting door, then stopped there and glanced back at him. "You could bring my father here tomorrow, Lucien, and I would still not share your bed. Because what you did to Papa has only clarified for me the reason I can't share myself with you."

"And what reason is that, if not loyalty to your father?"

"Trust," she whispered. "How can I trust a man who puts revenge above everything—even his wife and child?" With a sad smile, she slipped away to her own room.

He watched her go, wrestling with the desire to bring her back and show her what there could be between them. But he refused to beg. He hadn't groveled for Sledge, and he wasn't about to do so for his young wife.

And just what did she mean, he'd put revenge before his wife and child? He'd married her, hadn't he? Claimed Chloe as his own and made an honest woman of Aveline. Was this some woman's trickery to get him to send for her father?

He rubbed a hand over his face in confusion. He wasn't certain when he'd started wanting their marriage to become real. Originally he'd just wed her out of duty to give Chloe a name. But as the days passed, it became more and more evident that the mighty Lucifer had fallen, and into the delicate hands of a twenty-four-year-old innocent from the country at that.

He could almost hear Dante laughing. No doubt his friend would thoroughly enjoy watching the wickedest rake in London panting after his own wife. He'd probably set wagers all over Town as to the outcome . . .

A hazy memory surfaced, and he snatched up the note, focusing on the handwriting. He'd indeed seen that almost effeminate script before, and the realization nearly choked him.

Dante.

Chapter 15

"The Duchess of Huntley."

Aveline smoothed her skirt as the duchess appeared in the doorway. She'd been in the nursery when the butler had sent a maid to inform her that the duchess's carriage had pulled up in front of the house. She'd had mere moments to ascertain that her appearance was acceptable and to race downstairs to the drawing room to greet the closest thing to a mother-in-law that she had.

The elegant blond woman swept into the drawing room, dressed all the crack in a becoming shade of sapphire that brought out her ice-blue eyes and creamy skin. Her sharp cheekbones and pointed chin gave her an ethereal appearance that was spoiled only by the discontented purse of her lips. The duchess had undoubtedly been a great beauty in her youth—indeed, still was a most attractive woman—but Aveline could not forget her incredible rudeness at their first meeting. As the duchess's disapproving gaze settled upon her, Aveline dipped a curtsey. "What an unexpected pleasure, Your Grace."

"Indeed." Clarissa wrinkled her nose and glanced around the elegantly furnished drawing room as if seeking the source of a bad smell. As Aveline rose from her curtsey, she firmly reminded herself that it was bad form to be rude to her husband's family, no matter how much they might deserve it.

"Please sit down," she said, indicating the sofa. "I can ring for refreshments if you like."

"Not necessary." The duchess carefully perched on the very edge of the sofa. "I assume Lucien is not at home?"

"No. I'm certain if he had known you were coming to call—"

"Well, that's neither here nor there," the duchess interrupted. "I shan't be here very long. I only came to inform you both that I am holding a small dinner party in your honor this Thursday."

"Thursday? But that's the day after tomorrow."

A faint smile played about the woman's lips. "I did say it would be small."

Aveline folded her hands tightly in her lap and forced her lips to curve in a semblance of courtesy. "How lovely, Your Grace. Thank you."

Clarissa gave a regal nod. "It is, of course, the least I can do to welcome you to the family. An invitation will arrive today with the mundane details."

"You are kindness itself to inform us in person, Your Grace."

"Indeed." Clarissa's cold, critical gaze swept over her. Despite the comfort of knowing that her gown had been created by the most fashionable modiste in London, Aveline still felt like a country bumpkin next to the duchess's effortless elegance. "I assume you have an appropriate wardrobe," the woman said.

"I do."

"Good. I am told you have a daughter."

"We do. Her name is Chloe."

"An illegitimate daughter." A hint of delighted malice slipped into Clarissa's tone.

Aveline stiffened. "Lucien is her father."

"How redeeming of him to make an honest woman of you." The duchess stood, and good manners prompted Aveline to follow suit. "Well, it's too late to undo the thing. I expect I shall see you on Thursday."

Without waiting for a proper farewell, the duchess took her leave. Aveline stared after her, shaken. Lucien's stepmother had been polite, but the courteous words masked haughty disdain for anything having to do with Lucien.

Not for the first time, she considered that Lucien had grown up in the same house as that woman. How had he endured all those years living with people he knew detested his very existence? Apparently his father had been a responsible parent—he had, after all, arranged for Lucien to live with him and took care of his daily needs and education—but Aveline got the distinct impression that the old duke had not been particularly loving toward his son. And his legitimate wife and child had made Lucien's life as difficult as possible.

No wonder her husband had such difficulty understanding her devotion to her father. He had nothing with which to compare it.

Lucien hesitated outside the door, torn by the emotions that warred within him. Then he raised his fist and pounded. He kept pounding until he heard the click of the lock. The door cracked open, and Dante peered out, eyes bleary with sleep.

"Luce, what the devil do you want? It's the middle of the night."

"It's ten o'clock in the morning." Lucien shoved open the door, sending his friend stumbling backward with the portal. "I need to talk to you."

"Gad, man." Squinting against the bright sunlight, Dante hurried to close the door. "This is not an hour for civilized people."

Lucien looked at his friend. Dante's hair was mussed, his eyes reddened from a night of dissipation. He hadn't even undressed for bed; his shirt hung pulled out over his trousers, wrinkled from the mattress. His stockinged feet curled against the floor.

"What is it, Lucien?" he asked with a yawn. "Only the gravest of circumstances would bring you here at such an hour."

Lucien swallowed back the bitter taste of betrayal. This was his friend, his comrade in arms. Where there was Lucifer, there was Dante. Hell's Brethren, scandalizing Society together, watching each other's back.

Or stabbing it.

"I want to ask you something." His throat tight, he pulled forth the letter and handed it to Dante. "Why did you write this?"

Dante gave his usual cocky grin as he unfolded the missive. "What's this, some love letter from a former mistress?"

Lucien watched Dante's face closely as he read the note. Had he not been watching for it, he would have missed the flicker of alarm that flashed through Dante's eyes. But by the time his friend looked at him, he appeared as calm and composed as ever he had at a card table.

Indeed, Dante was brilliant at cards. No one could ever tell what he was thinking. And it was the same thing now.

"What does this mean, Luce? Where'd you get it?"

"You know where I got it."

"I don't understand." Despite his polite expression, some of the confidence had left his tone. "Is this supposed to mean something to me?"

"Don't mistake me for one of your marks, Dante," Lucien warned. "I've known you too long. You know very well what that letter means. I want to know why."

"Why what?" Dante flashed a puzzled smile. "I still don't—"

Lucien grabbed Dante by the front of his shirt and shoved him up against the door. "Don't toy with me,

Dante. I know you wrote this. Now tell me why."

"By the devil, have you lost your mind?" Dante tugged at one of Lucien's hands.

"Talk." He leaned in until they were practically nose to nose. "Don't force a challenge, Dante. You know the outcome."

"All right, blast you!" Dante sagged back against the door. "I wrote the note. I sent it to Aveline as if it were from you. Is that what you wanted to hear?"

He'd known of Dante's guilt, but hearing him admit it still staggered him. "Why?" he choked out.

"I was desperate." Dante tried to smile, but his eyes reflected his panic. "Dammit, Luce, remember how things were! After you came back from Cornwall, you were different. That girl had some sort of hold on you. I thought she wanted money."

"So you sought to protect me? How noble," he sneered. "You're lying, Dante."

Sweat misted on Dante's forehead. "All right, that was only part of it."

"Tell me the rest." He locked eyes with the man who had claimed to be his friend. "The truth this time."

"After you came back from Thornsgate, you didn't want to attend any of the events in Town. I depended on you to do so. My living depended on it."

"Ah, now I begin to see." Lucien stepped back, allowed Dante to take a deep breath. "This was all about money."

"Partly. I did want to protect you, Luce. I know how careful you are not to get a woman with child.

How could this chit from Cornwall be telling the truth?"

"You overstepped your bounds and interfered in my personal affairs."

"It all turned out well enough. You married the girl."

Lucien shoved him away. "I married the girl—years too late for my daughter to be considered legitimate."

"She's a female. Settle a proper dowry on her, and her suitors won't care if she was born before or after the vows."

"That's not the point." Sickened by what he'd learned, Lucien turned away. "You interfered where you had no right. Because of you, my daughter bears our curse of illegitimacy."

"Dammit, Lucien, don't you think I've agonized over that?" Dante came forward and grabbed Lucien's arm. "I sent that note the night we were set upon by footpads. The night you disappeared. Don't you think I've suffered these past five years with that knowledge?"

"Doing it a bit too brown, aren't you?" Lucien shook off Dante's hold. "What you did was wrong, even by your standards."

"We've been friends for many years. Can't you forgive a friend one mistake?"

"I've forgiven you many things over the years, Dante. I don't know if I can forgive this." Lucien brushed past him and opened the door. "I find the timing of your act very interesting as well. If I ever find out you had anything to do with my abduction—"

"Are you mad? I was attacked that night, too."

Lucien cast him an icy glare. "If I ever find out you were involved in *that*, my *friend*, there will be no hole in which you can hide, no excuse that will sway me. I *will* kill you."

He stepped out of Dante's rooms, slamming the door behind him.

"Mama, is your tea too hot?"

Aveline pushed away the memory of the duchess's disturbing visit and lifted the tiny teacup to pretend to sip the nonexistent tea. "Delicious, my dear Chloe."

"And how is your tea, Lady Rose?" Chloe turned to one of her dolls, who sat in the chair beside her at the tiny table, and fluffed her dress.

Aveline watched her daughter, love nearly squeezing the breath from her lungs. Chloe had settled comfortably into her new life. She had a governess, Miss Edgerton, who had this afternoon free from her duties. Miss Edgerton was the impoverished spinster daughter of an old and respected family, and she seemed to be of a cheerful disposition as well as good breeding and education. Already Chloe had started to mimic some of the woman's more attractive mannerisms.

Aveline enjoyed it when Miss Edgerton took her weekly free afternoon, for it allowed her to spend time with Chloe as they had before Lucien had come back into her life. There had been times when she cursed that day, but as she watched Chloe now, she couldn't regret her choice, even though the issue of her father yet pained her.

A movement at the nursery door drew her eye. Lucien hovered there, and the look on his face as he watched Chloe nearly stopped Aveline's heart. Wonderment. Baffled pride. Longing. Why did he linger in the doorway? Why didn't he come in?

He started to turn away, and their gazes met. He paused. Utter loneliness lurked in the shadows of his eyes. It called to her. Chloe looked up to see what had claimed her attention.

"Papa!" The child leaped up from the table and raced over to her father. Taking his hand, she tugged him into the room. "Papa, come have tea with us."

Pleasure and uncertainty warred on Lucien's face. "I wouldn't want to intrude."

"You're not intruding," Aveline assured him, warmed by his endearing hesitation. "In fact, I do believe Lady Rose has another appointment."

"You have another 'pointment," Chloe told her doll, then removed her from the chair. "Sit here, Papa."

Lucien looked down at the child-sized chair with skepticism. "I believe I'll stand, Chloe. I'm likely to break it otherwise."

Chloe pursed her rosebud lips and glanced from her father to the chair. Then she nodded in agreement and poured imaginary tea into a cup. "Here you are, Papa."

Lucien took the cup, balancing the fragile china in his large, masculine hand. "Thank you, Chloe." He glanced at Aveline, who mimed sipping her tea. He followed suit. " 'Tis quite delicious."

"Try these cakes, Papa." Chloe held up a plate. "Cook made them."

He hesitated, puzzlement flickering across his face as he regarded the empty dish.

"You're supposed to pretend to take a cake," Aveline whispered to him.

"Ah." Confusion cleared, and he picked up an imaginary piece of cake. "Thank you so much, Chloe. It's my favorite."

With a dimpled smile, Chloe turned to the other doll still seated at the table and offered her the cake platter.

Aveline leaned closer to Lucien. "Have you never played pretend, Lucien?" she whispered.

He shook his head, awkwardly balancing the teacup and his "cake," then elected to place the cake plate on the table. "My tutor would never allow such a thing." He frowned. "Should we instruct Miss Edgerton to focus more attention on Chloe's lessons?"

"Of course not." Genuinely surprised, she sipped her own pretend tea when she saw Chloe frowning at her. "All children need to play, Lucien. 'Tis natural."

"I never played." He stared down at the child-sized teapot on the table, brow furrowed in thought. "I didn't have any other children to play with."

"Not even your half brother?"

"Especially not him."

"Papa," Chloe interrupted, "you can play with *me*."

His features softened as he smiled. "Why thank you, Chloe."

The little girl dipped her head near her doll as if listening, then added, "Miss Margaret says you can play with her, too."

Lucien made a small bow. "And my thanks to you, Miss Margaret."

Chloe giggled. Lucien grinned back at the little girl, the first genuine smile Aveline had seen him wear since he'd first appeared on her doorstep. Warmth squeezed her heart. He was trying to be a good father, even though he clearly had no example to use as guidance.

"If you didn't play as a child, what did you do, Lucien?"

"I studied." He obligingly picked up the teapot and poured as Chloe held up Miss Margaret's cup. "My father respected knowledge, so I tried my best to excel at my lessons. To make myself worthy of being his son."

Poor lonely boy. "The duchess came to call today," she said, remembering. "She's having a dinner party for us on Thursday to celebrate our marriage."

"Celebrate?" His dark brows peaked with skepticism. "It's probably more truthful to say she must do the correct thing or else be gossiped about."

"Probably." She sighed.

"As much as I'd enjoy flouting Clarissa's will in this, I fear we must attend." He gave her a rueful smile. "Else it will be the two of us who suffer the brunt of flapping tongues. And we must do our best to stay in Society's good graces." His gaze drifted to Chloe. "For several reasons."

"Society seems to have accepted our marriage," she

murmured. "Perhaps it will be an enjoyable evening."

"Peppered with Clarissa's sly remarks and Robert's bursts of jealous anger? I doubt it."

"As bad as that? Certainly they won't cause a scene. They're your family."

"No." He stroked a hand over Chloe's dark curls. "I have a real family now."

The child looked up and smiled at him, and for an instant Aveline felt left out. The two of them seemed to be forming a strong attachment, which was exactly what she'd hoped; but at the same time she longed to be part of the little family that was slowly developing. She herself had built the wall that now separated her from the family unit, and even though Lucien had made overtures to include her, she dared not tear that wall down.

She couldn't. Because she herself had once been a little girl with an adored papa, and she dared not turn her back on him now when he needed her the most.

But oh, it was so tempting . . .

Miss Edgerton returned at dinnertime and took over the care of Chloe with her usual brisk efficiency. Since dinner would not be served for another hour, her husband had taken himself off to his study to work on business matters. Aveline had opted for a walk in the tiny garden.

The sun was setting over London, casting a pink glow over the cream-colored roses and marble statues. She reached out a hand to touch one velvety bloom, recalling Lucien's face as he'd played with

Chloe for the first time. His uncertainty had struck her as precious, and with her newfound knowledge of his childhood, she was beginning to develop a soft spot for the emotionally neglected, complicated man who was her husband.

"May I join you?" As if she had conjured him, Lucien stepped through the French doors and into the garden.

"I thought you had business to attend to."

"It can wait." He came toward her, looking more relaxed than she had ever seen him. "In this light, you look incredibly lovely. Like one of these goddesses come to life."

She glanced at the nearby statue of Aphrodite. "Do you imply that I'm made of stone, sir?" she teased.

His lips curved in a smile of genuine warmth. "On the contrary."

"Good." She held out a hand to him. "Come walk with me, Lucien. Enjoy the evening." ·

His startled expression settled into one of pleasure, and he took her hand. Twining his fingers with hers, they strolled down one of the paths, a curious peace between them.

"Chloe was thrilled that you played with her today," Aveline said after a few moments of companionable silence.

He laughed. "I never realized it was permitted."

"Of course it's permitted!" She shook her head, chuckling. "Lucien, you're her father. You can play with her or take her on outings or feed her berry tarts for breakfast if you've a mind to."

"Really? Berry tarts?"

She sent him an amused glance. "Well, if you do that, I'm afraid I shall have something to say about it. But you get the general idea."

"I do." He stared down at their clasped hands, then met her gaze, his candid and strangely vulnerable. "I've never had a family, you know. Not a real one where people cared."

Tenderness nearly choked her, and she squeezed his hand. "I know."

"So I don't know how it's done—this family business. You and Chloe will have to be patient with me." He gave her a crooked smile that reminded her of a boy who'd gotten caught tracking mud into the house, and her heart melted.

"Of course, we'll teach you. She's already happier than I've ever seen her."

"I'm glad." They stopped near a bush of blood red roses. "I'm trying to be a good father, Aveline. And a good husband."

"I know." She bit her lip. "I wish I could be a better wife to you, but—"

"Shhh." He touched a finger to her lips to silence her. "Let's not talk about that now. Let's just enjoy this fine evening—and each other's company."

She gave a hesitant nod. "I'd like that."

"Whatever problems we have will still be there tomorrow."

"Yes." She smiled. "I do enjoy your company, Lucien. When you're not trying to seduce me, that is."

He flashed her a wicked grin and began walking again. "Nonsense, madam. We both know you enjoy that as well."

She blushed and refused to reply. His roguish laughter echoed throughout the garden as they strolled along, their problems set aside as they discovered the pleasure of each other's company in the soft spring evening.

Chapter 16

Dante stepped out of the gaming hell, squinting his eyes against the bright sunlight. He'd been at the tables since the wee hours of the morning, losing steadily. He smelled of liquor and cigar smoke, and the daylight stung his reddened eyes. All he wanted was the oblivion of sleep. But he hadn't been able to sleep since the previous morning. Lucien's visit haunted him.

Who could have known that he'd marry the girl? That she'd save the note and actually show it to him? The crushing guilt from his long-ago actions weighed on him, making it hard for him to breathe. Lucien had been his best friend. The only person who'd ever accepted him without question.

And he'd betrayed him.

He stumbled down the crowded street, frantically

pushing his way through the crowd as if he could outrun his own emotions. His eyes teared. From the sunlight, he thought. The damned sunlight always made his eyes sting after a night of dissipation.

As he reached the street corner, a glossy black coach, curtains drawn, jerked to a halt in front of him. The crest on the door was covered. But he knew what coat of arms hid behind it.

The door opened. "Get in."

He knew that voice, should have expected this. Swallowing hard, he hauled himself into the coach.

The door shut, and the coach started forward with a lurch. Dante held on tight, his head spinning from lack of sleep and too much drink, and forced himself to meet the narrowed blue eyes of the other passenger. "Your Grace, I—"

"Be quiet."

He pressed his lips together in instant compliance.

"I'm displeased by recent events, Dante. You told me Lucien was dead."

Dante managed a sickly smile. "I thought he was. I was certain the brigands had done away with him."

"I paid for an assassination, not a mere kidnapping."

"We were cheated," he said, trying to work indignation into his voice.

"Were we?" The two words held such menace that Dante would have fled had he not been trapped in the coach.

"O-of course we were."

"Why don't I believe you?"

He tried to summon a convincing smile. "Why would I betray you? We had a bargain."

"So we did. Entrée into society for you, Lucien dead for me. But Lucien is not dead."

"An oversight."

"One I intend to rectify."

"W-what?"

"I've taken matters into my own hands." His partner smiled. "Since you clearly do not have the stomach to kill him, I've hired someone to make sure it gets done."

"Who?"

One brow arched over blue eyes that glittered with distrust. "I'm not so foolish as to tell you that. But I do have a task for you." The speaker leaned forward, blond hair gleaming in the dim interior of the coach. "And if you fail in this task, my next step will be to send the assassin after *you*."

Dante gulped and nodded. "Understood."

"Good." Satisfaction underscored the word. "Tonight is the dinner party at my home, and I expect you to attend. Now, this is what you will do . . ."

Aveline stepped into the Duke of Huntley's London mansion with some trepidation. Garbed in an enchanting silk evening dress of ivory threaded with gold that bared a daring amount of décolletage, she knew she looked the part of a wealthy man's wife, especially with diamonds glittering at her ears and throat. Yet she still felt much like a moth wandering into the web of a spider.

Only Lucien's presence beside her kept her head high and a smile on her lips. Their accord in the garden the night before had given her hope that they might yet find some compromise in their marriage. Tonight he looked devastating in simple black evening wear with a blood red ruby stickpin at his throat. Together, they made a striking couple, and she was proud to be by his side.

As they were announced to the people gathered in the drawing room, she noticed that the duke, too, was dressed in traditional black evening clothes, but his aristocratic blond good looks faded when compared to Lucien's dark, sensuous features. Of the two men, Lucien seemed more powerful, more dangerous. Robert still struck her as a boy playing at being a man.

Robert came forward to greet them with polite formality, as did his mother. The duchess wore an evening dress with an even lower neckline than Aveline's, which somehow managed to be scandalous and elegant all at once. She had her hand on the arm of an older, distinguished gentleman she introduced as Lord Adminton.

"We've kept the party small," she informed Lucien with an insincere smile. "Only twenty-four people. I do believe you know everyone."

"Yes." Lucien's eyes narrowed as he noticed something across the room. Following his gaze, Aveline saw nothing to provoke such a stare, only Dante near the mantel in conversation with a beautiful dark-haired woman about Lucien's age. "I do indeed know everyone."

"Wexford came with me," Adminton said, his voice gruff. He had a large bushy mustache that twitched when he spoke. "Knew the two of you were thick as thieves. Thought you might want him here."

"Indeed." Lucien smiled politely. "Quite considerate of you, my lord."

"We'll be going in to dinner shortly," the duchess said, "now that the guests of honor have finally arrived." She walked away with the earl, leaving them alone with Robert.

"Pay no attention to my mother," the young duke said. "She's a stickler for punctuality."

"As well I know," Lucien replied with a wry grimace.

"Perhaps you might want to introduce your bride to everyone," Robert continued. He gave his half brother an uncertain smile. "I'm glad you came, Lucien."

Lucien granted his brother a sardonic look in return. "How could I not attend a party in my honor?"

The young duke nearly flinched. "Nevertheless, I'm glad you did. Please excuse me while I see to my guests." He walked across the room to join an older couple and their pretty young daughter in conversation.

"I think he means it," Aveline murmured. "Whatever bad blood exists between you, I think he truly wants to make amends."

Lucien gave a snort of laughter. "Let this be your first lesson. Never trust the *ton*, my dear. Especially not the Huntleys."

"I trust *you*." She smiled at his obvious surprise. "At least I trust you to get me through this gathering. I do admit to being intimidated."

"Don't be." He lifted her hand to his lips, brushed a kiss across her fingers. "You're the daughter of a baron and the bride of one of the richest men in London. No one belongs here more than you do."

She gave a nervous laugh. "Just stay beside me."

His fingers tightened around hers, and he placed her hand back on his arm. "I will."

Lucien escorted Aveline around the room at a leisurely pace and introduced her to the other guests. He had hoped that dinner would be announced before they reached Dante and his companion, but luck was not with him. Despite his dawdling, he soon found himself standing before the couple.

"Luce! There you are, old man." Dante looked like he'd spent the night in a bottle, but he grinned at Lucien, clearly hoping their encounter the other morning had been forgotten.

Lucien nodded, the barest of civil responses. "Dante."

Dante's smile faltered, and Lucien could feel Aveline's questioning gaze on him. He ignored both and turned to Dante's companion. "Good evening, Lady Turnbottom. May I introduce my wife, Aveline DuFeron?"

The stunning brunette glanced at Aveline. "How do you do?"

"I'm pleased to make your acquaintance, Lady Turnbottom," Aveline replied politely.

Leticia, Lady Turnbottom, immediately fixed her slumberous dark eyes back on Lucien. "It's been a long time, Lucien. I was pleased to hear of your resurrection."

She rolled the r's in the word like the purring of a cat. At one time he had found her husky voice—and her shapely body—desirable. Now he just found them obvious.

Dante smirked, and he felt Aveline stiffen at his side as Leticia's interest in him became apparent even to his country-bred wife. "It has been a long time. How is Lord Turnbottom?"

"Dead." She gave him a slow, intimate smile as if Aveline and Dante didn't exist. "I'm a widow now."

"I'm sorry for your loss."

She gave a throaty chuckle. "I'm not."

Dante chuckled. Aveline gave a little gasp at the woman's blatant lack of sorrow over her husband's demise, and Lucien agreed with her unspoken horror. At one time he would have found the woman's comment amusing. Now, as a husband himself, he hoped instead that Aveline never spoke of his death with such callous disregard. The fact that he once would have laughed with Dante and Lady Turnbottom shamed him.

He turned to Aveline, and just looking into her pretty green eyes, honesty shining from them, made him feel better. He wasn't the man he had once been.

A day or so ago that had concerned him. Now he realized that the person he was becoming was someone he might like a whole lot more.

"If you will excuse us," he said, "I would like to introduce my wife to the rest of the guests before we are called to dinner." He gave Leticia the briefest of bows before steering Aveline away from the couple.

"Have you and Dante quarreled?" she asked softly as they approached the next group of people. "You seemed angry at him."

"Angry" was hardly the word to describe the roiling sense of betrayal that churned inside him. "We had a disagreement."

"It seemed more than that."

He flashed her a look of impatience. "Not now, Aveline."

"All right." She set her chin in that mulish way of hers and slanted him a meaningful look. "But you and I will talk about this later."

"Perhaps." He bit back a chuckle at the annoyance that flashed across her face, then led her to the next group of people.

The dinner party seemed interminable.

Aveline sat across from Lucien at the meal and was forced to watch Lady Turnbottom, who was seated beside him, flirt with him all evening long. The brunette was obviously the sort of female with whom Lucien had associated on a regular basis, a soulless widow who did not even pretend, out of simple courtesy, to mourn her husband's death.

Instead, she whispered to Lucien and cast him alluring glances. Turned her body this way and that to tempt him with her lush bosom, half-bared by her outrageously low-cut gown. Leaned in close to him and trailed her fingers along his hand when she thought no one would notice.

Aveline noticed. And it made her want to stab the woman with her fork.

Shocked at her own violent reaction, Aveline turned her attention away from the flirtation. After all, she had refused to share Lucien's bed. Every member of Society would sympathize completely with her husband and condone any affair he chose to conduct. She really had no claim to jealousy over his flirtation with another woman when she herself had refused him his husbandly rights.

Nevertheless, he could have the dignity not to conduct his affairs beneath her very nose.

Finally, the long, elaborate meal ended, and Aveline gratefully rose with the rest of the ladies. The men lingered behind to drink their port and smoke their cigars. Lucien cast her an inquiring look, but she pretended not to see it as she followed the duchess into the drawing room.

She wished she could be alone, but as one of the guests of honor everyone wanted a word with her. Most of the ladies appeared very kind as they spoke with her, but she was very much aware of Lady Turnbottom watching her from the other side of the room, a smug smile on her pouty lips.

The duchess approached her. "I do hope you're enjoying yourself, my dear."

The woman's courtesy immediately put Aveline

on guard. "Of course I am, Your Grace. It was most generous of you to host this evening for us."

"Indeed. May I have a word with you?" One haughty look sent the ladies gathered around them scurrying to other parts of the room.

"Of course you may." Aveline focused on her manners and not on the anxiety that knotted in her stomach.

The duchess led her to a secluded corner of the room. The other ladies stayed beyond earshot out of deference to their hostess. The power the duchess wielded over others astonished Aveline, but at the same time, she admired it. The Duchess of Huntley was quite a formidable woman.

But so was Aveline DuFeron, country mouse or not.

"My dear child, I couldn't help but notice your distress at dinner." Clarissa patted her hand in a gesture no doubt intended to be maternal. "I understand your mother died several years ago."

"Yes." She fought the urge to yank her hand away from Clarissa's cold touch.

"Then you must allow me to guide you in this matter." She lowered her voice conspiratorially. "Men are such beastly creatures sometimes."

Aveline stiffened. "I beg your pardon?"

"I couldn't help but notice your husband's flirtation with Lady Turnbottom. Of course she is a dear friend of the family, but she is also a young, beautiful widow. Such women are often irresistible to men."

"I'm certain Lucien was just being kind." The good Lord would certainly strike her dead for such a lie, but she would shave her head bald before she would admit to this woman how Lucien's behavior had hurt her.

The duchess gave her another patronizing pat on the hand. "Now, dear, men will be men. And your husband, if I may be so bold, is well-known for his affection for the fairer sex. All a gently bred wife can do in a situation like this is to look the other way." She gave a sad sigh. "Of course, he might have waited until you were wed more than a fortnight before seeking other companionship. But such is the way of a rake, I'm afraid."

"I thank you for the advice," Aveline said stiffly. "If you will excuse me, Your Grace, I would like to refresh myself."

The duchess nodded. "Of course, dear. Just ask the maid to show you the way."

"Thank you." She hurried from the room, well aware of Clarissa's satisfied smirk behind her.

The maid showed her to a guest room where she could take care of her personal needs, then left again when Aveline assured her she could find her way back. As soon as the servant had departed, Aveline sank down on the chair before the vanity and stared at her pale face in the mirror.

She had known this might happen, had even expected it. Lucien was a man of strong appetites and would not go for long without a woman in his bed. But still, she had hoped that he cared more for their marriage than he did for physical satisfaction. She had hoped he might want to work out their differences, if only for Chloe's sake.

Tears stung her eyes. Damn him. She had hoped that he might care for her even a little, that he might want to have a real marriage and a real family. Yes, she was the one holding them apart. But if he would only relent on this obsession with revenge, if he would only meet her halfway, then perhaps they might yet have a chance.

But not if he went sniffing after every attractive woman who came into sight.

She shoved away from the vanity and paced the room, emotions churning until she felt she might explode. It was bad enough he was flirting with that widow, but to do so in front of his smug and superior family . . . to give them the opportunity to laugh at her . . . it was outside of enough.

She and Lucien would have words this night. *If* he came home with her, that is.

The window stood open, and a soothing breeze drifted into the room. Drawn by the scents of the night, Aveline pushed aside the drapes and looked down on the garden below. The Duke of Huntley was wealthy enough to own his own house in London, a mansion as grand as any to be found in Mayfair. The house included some lovely gardens, and the fragrance of roses drifted up to her, combining with the less appealing scents of the city. Still, the night air soothed her jangled nerves. The moon hung full in the sky like a Roman coin, allowing her to see down into the garden. Stone benches and statues glowed white in the darkness, surrounded by the dark shadows of the rosebushes.

Suddenly there was movement below her, and

two men appeared along one of the paths. They stopped near an arbor for what appeared to be a fierce, whispered conversation. Aveline ducked back behind the draperies so she wouldn't be seen, but continued to watch the scene below.

After a few moments one of the men turned away, and the moonlight lit his face so that she could clearly make out the features of the Duke of Huntley as he strolled back into the house. She'd never seen that cold, hard expression on his face before. It almost seemed as if he had two personalities, the boyish duke and another, darker side. Did he show a false face to the world, while behind the youthful lack of confidence lurked a more calculating individual? Why would he do such a thing?

The second man followed more slowly, and as he, too, passed through the shaft of moonlight, Aveline recognized Dante.

She stepped back from the window, brow furrowed in thought. Why were the two of them lurking in the garden together? She'd noticed that they never spoke, other than the required polite greetings, and she'd assumed that the duke's sense of his own consequence had been offended by the presence of the illegitimate gamester in his home. Still, Dante was Lucien's friend and was apparently championed by the Earl of Adminton, a friend of the duchess, which was why he'd been invited tonight. There was always the possibility that Dante had made some jesting remark that offended Robert, but she rather thought Dante smarter than that. As much as she mistrusted Lucien's best friend, she had to admit that such a man would not get very far in polite society unless he was very intelligent. And a smart man would not offend a duke in his own home.

Grateful that the puzzle took her mind off her marital confusion, Aveline turned ideas over in her mind as she went back to the drawing room.

The gentlemen had joined the ladies by the time she got back, and as soon as she set foot in the room Lucien came immediately to her side. His presence brought back all the disturbing emotions she had been trying to control, and she dared not look at him. The creature's perfume clung to him, and she knew if she opened her mouth, she would start ranting like a fishwife.

She took his arm out of necessity—merely resting the tips of her fingers on his sleeve—and remained by his side to exchange pleasantries with the guests who came forward to offer their congratulations. At the same time, she observed the others in the room.

Lady Turnbottom watched Lucien like a starving woman at a banquet. The duchess looked amused, malice glittering in her ice-blue eyes. Robert appeared unconcerned, but she caught the occasional look he sent in Dante's direction. Dante chatted comfortably with the Earl of Adminton, apparently oblivious to the emotional undercurrents surrounding him.

And Lucien never spoke to Dante at all.

Her head spinning, Aveline counted the minutes until they could depart.

* * *

Something was bothering Aveline.

As the door shut behind his valet, Lucien cast a glance in the direction of Aveline's room. She'd barely said a word to him all evening, and when they'd come home, she had merely wished him a polite good night and vanished into her bedchamber.

He hated it when she was polite. Aveline ranted at him, she lectured him, she flirted with him. She was *never* anything so mundane as polite unless she was vexed with him. Something was definitely wrong.

Still in his shirtsleeves and evening trousers, he waited until he heard her maid leave. Then he went to open the connecting door.

Locked.

He stared at the door latch, fury rising in him like a fire to dry tinder. How dared she lock the door against him! Hadn't he respected her wishes? Hadn't he acted the gentleman and not taken what by law belonged to him? Hadn't he tried to seduce her gently rather than insist on his rights as her husband? And in return she *locked him out*?

First Dante's betrayal, and now this. How much could a sane man take in one day?

For one crazed instant he fought the urge to simply kick down the door. If Aveline thought she could lock him away from her, she could think again! But then the noise would bring the servants running, and no doubt violence would simply push Aveline farther away from him.

She'd probably also locked the hallway door behind the maid. But there was another way.

Opening his window, he climbed out onto the narrow ledge. A mere two feet from where he stood, the curtains from Aveline's room fluttered in the breeze from the open casement. He nimbly leaped from his window ledge to hers. Then he swung inside.

As his feet hit the floor of her room, Aveline whirled away from the vanity mirror with a gasp. The stark surprise on her face made him grin even as her luscious curves encased in a clinging silk nightdress roused his body to instant alertness. "Good evening, my dear."

"What are you doing here?" She glanced around, grabbed a wrapper and shoved her arms into it. "Get out, Lucien."

"Now, now, is that any way to talk to your devoted husband?"

"Devoted?" she sneered.

"You seem put out with me, dearest." He strolled over to a chair and took a seat, stretching his long legs out in front of him, a congenial smile on his lips. "How did I offend?"

She looked like she wanted to rail at him, but for some reason she didn't, only made a low sound of impatience. "I'm tired, Lucien. I want to go to bed."

"Climb between the covers if you like," he said with a nod at the bed. "But know I'm not leaving until you tell me what's bothering you. *And why you locked that door*."

His last words came out as a near shout, and she blinked innocently. "Did I? I don't recall."

So, she wanted to play with him, did she? He rose from his seat, noting with satisfaction her nervous swallow before she fixed a look of polite inquiry on her pretty face. Didn't she realize he was a master at this sort of game?

"You tread on dangerous ground, my sweet. Haven't I been a good husband, despite your refusal to share my bed? Haven't I fed and sheltered you, provided you and our daughter with fine clothing?"

"You have."

"Then I am at a loss as to why you are angry with me."

"I'm not angry. Just tired. Please leave, Lucien, that I might go to bed."

"So stubborn." He approached her slowly, amused at the way she backed away from him. "There's nowhere to go, dear wife. You yourself locked the doors." He chuckled at her stricken look.

She stopped her retreat and stood firm even when he came to stand over her, abandoning her pretense of innocence. "Locks don't seem to stop you."

"There is nothing on this earth that will keep me from you, sweet Aveline." He stroked a finger down the center of her chest. "Except whatever you hide in that stubborn heart of yours."

She pushed his hand away. "We've discussed this, Lucien."

"Not enough apparently." He leaned closer, inhaled the scent of her hair. "Tell me what I've done to offend you, my love."

"Your *love*?" She shoved him in the chest with both hands. He actually fell back a step from the surprise of it. "How dare you call me that after you allowed that . . . that tart to hang all over you tonight?"

"What the devil . . . are you talking about Leticia?"

"Yes, I'm talking about *Leticia*," she mimicked. "I sat there all night watching the two of you. It was disgusting. If you must carry on with that sort of woman, kindly do so out of my sight!"

"You can't possibly think I was encouraging her?"

"Everyone thought it," she said tightly. "Even Her Grace the duchess remarked on it."

"I apologize if I have subjected you to any humiliation," he said, sincerely stunned. "I never encouraged Leticia."

"You never *dis*couraged her either."

"Perhaps not. But I am a man, Aveline, a man with a beautiful wife I cannot touch. You can't expect me to be blind and deaf to the interest of other women simply because you won't have me."

"I don't expect any such thing," she said, her tone icy. "I simply ask that you do not conduct your flirtations in my presence. I demand that much respect as your wife."

"So I may conduct my flirtations—my affairs even—*outside* of your presence?"

She gave a jerky nod. "Exactly."

"I see." She could have thrust a hot iron through his chest, and it would have hurt less. He thought they had been making progress. He'd been so certain she wanted him, scars not withstanding.

Rocked by her rejection, still torn by Dante's betrayal, he did the only thing he could to assuage his damaged sense of manhood. He took her into his arms and kissed her.

She struggled. He ignored the guilt tapping on his shoulder, the mewling protests coming from her throat, and tightened his embrace. She was his wife, by God, and he would not be sent from her chamber like a disobedient pup.

The scent of lavender made him dizzy with wanting her. He crushed her curves against his starved body, pressing her hips to his with a hand spread across her curvy bottom. After a moment her struggles died. Her arms came up around his neck. Her mouth opened beneath his, and she kissed him back.

His brain shut down as passion flared higher. He swept his hands along her back, cupping and stroking her soft flesh through her flimsy wrapper and night-dress. The thin silk took on the warmth of her body, and it was like having nothing at all between them.

He pulled his mouth from hers for an instant, gasping for breath, but then she grabbed his head in her two hands and brought him back for another hot, desperate kiss.

Now she made noises in her throat, whimpers of need, of a craving that he echoed with his own passionate sounds. She rubbed her body against him, tangled her fingers in his hair, edged her thigh between his to rest intimately against his rock-hard erection.

He nuzzled her neck, kissed her shoulder, buried his face between her breasts.

"Dear God, yes," she whispered. "Touch me, Lucien."

Her name on his lips snapped any restraint he may have had left. Her aroused nipples nearly poked through the silk, and he took one in his mouth right through the gown, clasping her other breast in his palm. She let her head fall back on a low, greedy moan, her hands holding his head in place, silently encouraging him.

He nibbled and suckled through the silk, dampening it until it was nearly transparent. But even that eventually proved too much of a barrier between him and her skin. His hands shook with near-crippling desire as he shoved the wrapper down her arms and off, then turned his attention to the nightdress.

Aveline eagerly reached for his shirt, pulling it out of the waistband of his trousers.

His scars. Curse it, but he didn't want her to be disgusted again. He finished removing her nightdress, letting it fall in a pool around her feet and leaving her naked before him. Then he caught her small hands in his just as they ventured beneath his shirt seeking the flesh of his chest.

She looked up at him, a question in her eyes, but he didn't want to answer. All he wanted was her. To know once and for all that the magic between them still existed. That there was some hope for this travesty of a marriage.

He lifted her into his arms and brought her to the bed. He saw the alarm flicker across her features and bent to kiss her before she could remember her principles. Before she could remember that she had sworn not to lie with him.

She gradually relaxed back against the pillows as

he kissed her with all the skill he possessed, stroking his hands over her soft, fragrant skin. Her body had matured with the birth of their child, grown more womanly, rounder in the hips and breast. Silvery lines trailed along her belly, reminders that she had borne a child. His child. How he wished he could have watched her body change, watched her grow ripe and beautiful in her confinement.

He bent and brushed his lips along those barely visible lines, making her gasp. She lifted her hips in silent invitation. But he trailed his mouth upward instead, settling once more at her breasts.

Her nipples pouted for his attention, and he applied it lavishly, teasing the sensitive nubs with teeth and tongue. She moaned his name, arched her back, cursed him even, especially when he insisted on taking his time worshiping her breasts. Finally, when she had taken to nearly tearing the hair from his head, did he shift to her mouth.

Lazily he kissed her, in no particular hurry even though his body throbbed with the frustration of abstinence. He deepened the kiss by degrees, playing with her, touching his tongue to hers, then retreating. Nipping her lower lip. Cupping her head in his hands and holding her still so he could plunder her mouth as he willed.

Sweat dampened her skin. More than once she tugged at his shirt, as if desperate to tear the thing from his body. Each time he distracted her—blowing on kiss-dampened nipples, nipping a sensitive part of her neck. Each time her hands fell away from their task as pleasure widened her eyes.

He slipped a hand between her thighs. She was warm and wet—just waiting for him. She gave a soft cry as he touched her sensitive folds, her legs falling open to give him better access. He stroked her with skilled fingers, pressing kisses to her belly or her fingers or her breasts or her mouth. Wherever he fancied.

Finally, he shifted and gave her the kiss they both craved.

She cried out at the first touch of his mouth, her hands seeking and finding his head between her thighs as he pleasured her intimately. Her fingers curled into his hair as if she needed to hang on to something. Anything.

He cupped her bottom in his hands and lifted her so he could better reach his target. With each stroke of his tongue she quivered, making soft, incomprehensible sounds of wanting. So aroused was she that it didn't take long for the climax to rip through her. She nearly screamed with it, clenching her fingers in his hair and her thighs around his head. Then she went limp.

He sat back on his knees. He could have her now, and she wouldn't deny him. Her sweet, feminine flesh beckoned, and his body answered, his cock twitching at the mere thought of sliding into that warm, welcoming sheath. She wouldn't say no tonight. But what would she say tomorrow?

Nothing was settled. He knew that. But at least he had learned that she did still want him. That the passion was still there, if they could ever resolve their differences.

He rose to his feet with a wince. Lust raged through his veins and tensed his every muscle to near pain. But he would not have her accuse him of forcing her. It was the hardest thing he had ever done, but he turned his back on all that succulent, aroused female flesh.

She leaned up on her elbows as he unlocked the door between their rooms, the click amazingly loud in the silence of the room. "Lucien? Where are you going?"

"To bed." He dared not even glance at her lest he lose his resolve. "Good night."

He stepped through the door and locked it behind him, resigned to a night of taunting dreams and self-satisfaction.

Chapter 17

She didn't know how she could face Lucien.

Aveline slowly approached the breakfast room, hoping that perhaps her husband had already eaten and left to conduct his business for the day. She didn't know how she could calmly regard him across the breakfast table after the events of the previous night.

A blush heated her face at the memory. After all her talk of principles, after her shrewish accusations regarding Lady Turnbottom, all Lucien had to do was touch her, and she fell panting into his arms like the veriest wanton.

Would he laugh at her this morning? Or would he smile smugly and say nothing? He'd pleasured her well, and both of them knew it. She wondered why he hadn't finished what he'd started, though she was grateful for it. If he'd completely made love to her, there was no way she would be able to continue to resist him.

Luck was not with her. When she peered into the breakfast room, her husband sat at the table with a plateful of eggs and sausage in front of him, reading the morning paper. She watched as he reached out to lift his coffee cup to his lips, his eyes never leaving the page.

Perhaps she should just have a tray sent to her room. But no, such an action would be cowardice, and Lucien would know she was nervous about facing him. Taking a deep breath, she stepped into the room. "Good morning, Lucien."

"Good morning," he replied, never looking away from his paper.

She waited to see if he would say anything else, but when he continued to read as if she didn't exist, she went over to the sideboard and helped herself to some breakfast. "Is there anything of interest in the news today?"

"Lady Fripley has snagged the Earl of Walton for her daughter Amelia," he said without so much as glancing at her. "The wedding is to be at the end of the Season."

"How nice." She sat down at the table, at a loss. She knew how to deal with Lucien when he raged. She knew how to deal with his sarcasm, with his seduction. She didn't know how to handle this man who barely acknowledged her. "Are you angry with me, Lucien?"

He looked at her then. "Should I be?"

Heat surged into her cheeks. "I thought you might be vexed about my behavior last night. I don't know what came over me. I can only apologize."

He folded the paper and laid it on the table beside his cup. "I assume you refer to your remarks about Lady Turnbottom."

"Yes."

"Then you did not mean to imply that you were jealous?"

"Of course I—what do you mean, *jealous*? I simply asked you for the basic respect due to me as your wife."

He held up a hand. "Calm yourself, Aveline. I'm only trying to clarify what it is you are sorry *about*."

"Locking the door for one thing."

"Ah." He gave her an intense look that belied his calm manner. "I admit that provoked my temper. But it wasn't entirely your fault. I had . . . other things on my mind."

"I see." Her heart sank. No doubt he'd been thinking about the beautiful, accommodating Leticia. She scooped a forkful of eggs into her mouth, tasting nothing.

"It's not what you think." He tapped his fingers on the table, his expression pensive. "I'd learned something distressing earlier in the day, and I'm afraid you were the one to take the brunt of my temper. Forgive me."

"I think you made up for any bad behavior," she whispered, then cleared her throat as his gaze warmed with shared memory. "I assume this distressing news has to do with Dante?"

He blinked in surprise, passion fading. "How did you know?"

"You barely spoke to him at the dinner party. You told me you'd had a disagreement."

"And so we did." He gave a weary sigh. "I discovered that Dante was the one who wrote that note to you."

"What?" Shocked, she dropped her fork, which clanked indelicately against her plate. "Why?"

He hesitated, watching her with dark, unreadable eyes. "From what I comprehend, he was worried about his livelihood after I came back from Cornwall."

"After you and I . . ."

"Yes." His intimate smile washed over her like a caress. "After our three nights together."

"Why was he worried?" Her voice sounded strange. Breathy. Flirtatious even.

He flashed her a wry look. "Apparently I became something of a hermit. Dante depended on me to gain entrée to the best social events so that he could game with the highborn. It's how he makes his living."

"I'm well aware of that. If you recall, he won a substantial sum from my father."

"Indeed." For once the mention of her father did not bring that brooding expression to his face. "At any rate, he found the note you had written to me before I ever opened it. Apparently he feared that once I knew you were with child, I would dash off to Cornwall to offer for you, which did not serve his plans at all."

"And would you have?"

"Of course." He raised his brows as if the answer should have been obvious. "I was abducted that night, but I did wed you as soon as I was able."

"I hardly think it was as simple as that." She turned her mind to the puzzle of Dante Wexford. "Lucien, do you suppose Dante had anything to do with your abduction?"

He narrowed his eyes. "I doubt it. We were together that night. He was assaulted as well, but he managed to escape."

"Or was allowed to."

"That doesn't mean he helped someone try to do away with me." He leaned forward. "I was Dante's entrée into Society, remember? I was his key to surviving."

"He seems to have done quite well these past five years without you."

"Dante and I have been in each other's pockets for years. He acted out of desperation for his own livelihood by writing that letter to you, but I cannot believe he would actually try to kill me."

"You said yourself that whoever arranged this must have deep pockets. Well, last night I witnessed Dante and the duke meeting in the garden."

"Robert? Now you think Robert was involved?" He gave a harsh laugh. "You'll accuse anyone to make me relent about your father."

"We're not talking about my family, we're talking about yours. I'm telling you to consider Robert as a suspect. He has some sort of grudge against you, if I recall."

"A trifling incident that happened long ago."

"How long ago?"

"Almost six years—" He glowered at her. "No, you don't. You won't accuse my half brother of try- ing to kill me because of an insignificant quarrel!"

"The quarrel hardly seems insignificant to Robert, as he still brings it up years later," she pointed out. "Your brother is young, and he's enough like you that he might harbor the grudge."

"What do you mean, enough like me? Robert and I are as different as day and night."

"Untrue," she scoffed. "You both possess the same stubborn pride and quick temper."

"You're daft," he pronounced with a scowl.

"Lucien, you share the same father. Of course you will both have some of the same characteristics."

"If Robert is so like me, then he wouldn't betray his brother."

She sighed with exasperation. "It seems far more likely than my father arranging the deed all the way from Cornwall. Must you always be right, Lucien? Can you never expand your reasoning to include the opinions of others?"

"Your opinion is that your father is innocent."

"You have no proof of Papa's guilt, and you refuse to see what's beneath your nose." She ticked off on her fingers. "Dante wrote the note. Dante was with you when you were attacked, but he escaped. Con- trary to your belief that he needs you, Dante has been able to survive without you these past five years. And Dante clearly has some connection with your half brother, who has both a grudge against you that he still harbors *and* enough money to arrange the deed."

"Dante's more my brother than Robert ever was."

"How can you defend him?" she cried, rising. "You know for certain that he is responsible for the act that left Chloe illegitimate. Had he not intercepted my letter to you, had he not written that cruel reply, you would have come to Cornwall. You would never have gone out with Dante, and you would never have been abducted."

Lucien raised his tortured gaze to hers. "I'm well aware of what he's done. I hate what he's done, especially the part that involves Chloe. And I intend to make him pay for that. But we've shared so much. I can't believe he'd try to harm me."

She let out a slow sigh. "You keep accusing me of blind loyalty, Lucien. But you suffer the same affliction with less cause."

He shoved back his chair. "I've heard enough of this."

"Where are you going?" she asked as he stalked past her.

"Out." He sneered. "Don't wait for me tonight, wife." Then he stormed from the room, leaving her staring after him.

Lucien strode down the street, barely noticing how people scurried out of the path of his long-legged pace. He didn't care where he was going; he walked to work off the frustration of his argument with Aveline. His tangled emotions nearly choked him.

She was right. He didn't want to admit it, wanted to pretend everything was right with the world, but his logical mind would not let him deny the obvious for long. All the pieces fit.

Dante had intercepted the letter and assured that Lucien never found out about Chloe, leaving her to be born out of wedlock. For that alone, he should call Dante out. And Aveline was right when she pointed out that Dante had gotten along well enough these past few years while Lucien slaved in hell beneath Sledge's cruelty. How had he managed it? He'd said something about Adminton sponsoring him.

Adminton, who was a friend of the Huntleys. And Aveline had seen Robert and Dante arguing about something. Could their quarrel have been about him? Robert certainly had the blunt—and the motive—to do away with an unwanted sibling.

Lucien had never had anything against Robert; even as a child his half brother had seemed amiable enough, just poisoned by his mother's hatred for Lucien. Then had come that incident nearly six years ago when Robert had been nineteen. Had the young duke then developed such loathing for Lucien that he'd arranged for him to disappear?

He didn't want to consider the possibility, but he knew he had to.

Someone screamed. Jerked from his thoughts, Lucien glanced around the bustling street, searching for the source of the cry. A rumbling reached his ears. He looked behind him just in time to see a runaway hack bearing down upon him. No driver manned the reins, which flapped uselessly behind the wild-eyed horse's thundering hooves. People scattered out of the way, shrieking.

No time to think. He dived into a fruit vendor's stand just as the hack raced over the place where he'd been standing. The wheels hit the curb of the walkway, and the coach tipped over, slowing down the stampeding horse. Lucien picked himself up out of the collapsed fruit stand, swiping crushed fruit from his clothing as two drivers from other nearby hacks managed to get control of the escaped horse before anyone was hurt.

"'At were a close 'un, sure enough," the elderly fruit vendor said, shaking his head at the overturned hack. "Ye nearly ended up like them apples there."

"Indeed." Lucien spared a glance for the smashed apples and tossed some coins to the old man, who nimbly caught them out of the air. "This should compensate you for the damage to your place of business. My apologies for the mess."

The old man called out his thanks as Lucien walked away, still wiping fruit pulp from his Bond Street trousers.

Aveline descended the stairs, pulling on her gloves as she went. She'd assembled the completed embroidery projects, and she was eager to sell the pieces and send some money to Mrs. Baines for her father's care. Elton came to meet her as she reached the bottom step.

"I'm going for a walk, Elton."

"Very good, madam." Before she could walk

away he added, "There are two gentlemen here to see you, Mr. Curtis and Mr. Whigby. I've put them in the Blue Salon."

"Mr. Curtis and Mr. Whigby? I know no such gentlemen."

"Shall I escort them out then?"

"No," she said after a moment. "I'll see what they want."

"Very good, madam." He bowed and walked away.

As Aveline entered the Blue Salon, two gentlemen rose from their seats. One stood tall and thin, with closely cropped silver-black hair. The other man was shorter and more portly, and had hardly any hair at all. Both wore impeccably tailored suits of the latest fashion. "Gentlemen, I am Mrs. DuFeron. How may I help you?"

The two men bowed. "Forgive the intrusion on your honeymoon, Mrs. DuFeron," the balding man said. "I'm Marcus Whigby. This is Mr. Curtis. We've come to discuss a matter of business with you."

"With me?" Completely puzzled, she looked from one to the other. "I'm afraid I don't understand, gentlemen. Perhaps you mean to talk to my husband."

"No, madam. We want to speak with you," the taller man said in a surprisingly deep voice. "We're here to discuss some of your father's financial obligations."

Cold fear spread over her. "Has something happened to my father?"

"Not at all!" Plump Mr. Whigby smiled, but she noticed it never reached his eyes. "We're old friends of your father's. We called on him in Cornwall, but—well, I'm certain you comprehend the situation. Since the baron is incapacitated, we are approaching you in regard to this matter."

"Which matter specifically?" she whispered.

The two men glanced at each other, then Mr. Whigby said, "The matter of your father's debts."

"His debts." She sank into a nearby chair, and the two men followed suit. "What about them?"

"I'm certain you're aware that your father incurred quite a few debts at the card tables," Whigby said. "Some of them to Mr. Curtis and myself. The sum is well past due."

"And we've come to collect," Curtis added.

"I see." She swallowed hard past the lump in her throat. "How much is it?"

"A thousand pounds. That's with interest, of course." He held up several sheets of paper she recognized as gambling markers. Each bore her father's distinctive scrawl.

"Of course." Panic screamed through her mind, but she kept her expression calm. "You do realize I don't have such a sum here in the house."

"Of course not." Whigby smiled. "But as you've married a wealthy man—"

"Indeed." She forced herself to smile back. "Will you leave your direction, Mr. Whigby, that I may send you the funds?"

Whigby and Curtis exchanged a quick glance. "It's better if I come back. Let's say three days from now. Is that agreeable?"

"It will have to be, won't it?" The stiff smile still on

her face, she rose, forcing both men to come to their feet as well. "Now if you'll excuse me, gentlemen, I have an appointment."

Both men bowed and headed toward the door, Aveline behind them. Just before stepping out of the salon, Mr. Whigby glanced back at Aveline. "You have a daughter, don't you, Mrs. DuFeron?"

She stopped dead in her tracks, alarmed by something in his tone. "I do."

"Children are so precious. It's such a tragedy when something happens to them." Whigby held her gaze for a long moment. "Three days, Mrs. DuFeron." Then he followed Mr. Curtis out.

Fear rooted her to the spot. They'd just threatened Chloe. Despite their polite manners and well-tailored suits, Mr. Whigby and Mr. Curtis were clearly members of the criminal element. She knew without a doubt that they would harm Chloe if she didn't produce a thousand pounds in three days. But where would she get such a large sum?

She remembered the pieces of embroidery she'd been about to sell. She would have to make more. A lot more. Both for Papa's care and for his debts.

Frantic, she hurried upstairs and into her sewing room. She would have to start right away to complete all the projects necessary. She took out her hoop, selected a piece of fabric. Yes, lovely. Now for thread. Where was the dratted thread?

She found it and sat down in her chair, picking up her needle. She tried to thread the needle, but her gloves made it awkward. Impatiently, she stripped them off and tossed them aside, then attempted to aim the thread once more through the eye of the needle. But her fingers shook too much.

She had to get control of her emotions. Lowering her hands, she closed her eyes and took deep breaths. But all she could see was Mr. Whigby's face as he subtly threatened Chloe. A thousand pounds. Dear Lord, how could she possibly accumulate such a sum in three days?

She still needed to send money to Mrs. Baines, but now she must first accommodate these criminals to whom her father owed money. And what if there were more? She gave a hoarse gasp as the possibility dawned. There could quite conceivably be more men out there holding her father's vowels. She could not possibly sew quickly enough to satisfy all of them.

"Papa, how could you?" she whispered, tears stinging her eyes. She loved her father dearly, but for the first time she faced the fact that he had not been as good a parent as he could have been. His incessant gaming was almost an illness; he'd been unable to stop. He'd constantly played the tables, even when they barely had enough to eat. He hadn't taken into account the effect his unchecked gambling would have on his family.

How many times had she been forced to find funds to support the household? Ever since her mother had died when she was fifteen, she had been cleaning up her father's financial messes. And never once had he shown regret. Never once had he recognized how cleverly his daughter was keeping the family afloat despite his damaging losses at the tables. Even when he'd found out that she'd gone to Lucien's bed to save him, he hadn't appreciated her sacrifice. Instead, he'd gone off to challenge Lucien to a duel and risk his life all over again.

Thank God Lucien had had the honor not to accept her father's challenge. She would ever be grateful that he had taken the letter of their bargain to heart. Their time together had brought her Chloe.

She dropped the needle and lowered her face into her hands. She couldn't let anything happen to Chloe. This problem was bigger than she could handle with mere embroidery. What was to stop others from following in Whigby's footsteps?

She would have to tell Lucien.

She didn't relish the thought, especially after their argument that morning. She knew he thought her father guilty of more than uncontrolled gaming. But she had no choice. Chloe's well-being was at stake.

She could count on Lucien to protect their daughter.

As the fear swelled up like an ocean wave, Aveline gave in to her despair and sobbed.

When Lucien arrived back at the house, Elton met him at the door. Being among the very best of London butlers, Elton didn't betray any surprise at his master's bedraggled appearance, merely held the door open, and asked, "Shall I send for Stokes, sir?"

"Absolutely. I only hope he doesn't ring a peal over my head at the state of my clothing."

"Indeed, sir." Elton closed the door. "Mrs. DuFeron had callers today."

Lucien stopped on his way to the staircase. The way the butler said the word "callers" gave it quite the sinister meaning. "What sort of callers, Elton?"

"Two gentlemen, sir. A Mr. Whigby and a Mr. Curtis."

"Whigby? What did that old reprobate want with my wife?"

"I'm certain I don't know, sir." Elton's face remained impassive. "However, Mrs. DuFeron seemed most distraught after their visit."

"She did?" What the devil did a moneylender like Whigby want with Aveline? The man patronized the worst gaming hells in London, lending money to poor sods who were too foolish to walk away from the tables when their luck changed. To pigeons too senseless to realize they were completely done up . . .

Of course. The baron.

"Elton, where's my wife now?"

"She's retired to her room, sir."

"Good. Let her calm her nerves while I take care of this. Send a footman to Mr. Whigby's rooms. My secretary will have the address. Tell him to present himself here within the hour. And make sure he understands this is not a request."

"Very good, sir." The barest trace of a smile flashed across Elton's lips, then vanished as if it had never been. He turned to summon a footman.

Lucien took the stairs at a run, fury burning through him. That bloody gullgroper Whigby had come to his home and harassed his wife for money owed by her father. He had no doubt of it. Apparently Whigby had a death wish.

He entered his room, shouting for Stokes as he shed his fruit-stained coat. When the valet appeared, Lucien waved aside the man's dismay at the state of his clothing. "Quickly, Stokes. I'm expecting a guest within the hour."

The valet leaped into action, laying out a new suit of clothes for his master.

Lucien jerked at his neckcloth and unbuttoned his vest, rage in every motion. Any respectable banker would have approached a lady's husband for funds owed, not terrorized a woman in her own drawing room. But Whigby was far from respectable.

And he would learn the hard way never to bother Lucien DuFeron's wife again.

Chapter 18

Lucien was waiting when Marcus Whigby arrived. Having changed into an elegantly tailored black coat and trousers accented with a bottle green waistcoat and white cravat, he sat behind his desk reading correspondence regarding his newest investments. He barely looked up when Whigby was announced.

"Sit down, Whigby. I'll be with you in a moment."

Out of the corner of his eye, he savored Whigby's wary expression. The moneylender had obviously not expected to hear from Lucien so soon—if at all. Lucien continued to read through his papers for another five minutes or so, then abruptly set them down and gave his guest the bare-toothed smile that had made pirates tremble. "Appreciate you coming, Whigby. I understand you paid a call on my wife today."

"Ah . . . yes, I did. Business matter."

"Really?" Lucien steepled his fingers. "Is it not the normal way of things to discuss matters of business with a lady's husband?"

The portly man squirmed. "I'd been given to understand that you'd not be interested in this particular matter."

"How curious. I'm interested in everything that has to do with my wife, Whigby. *Everything*."

"So I begin to comprehend." Whigby gave a weak smile. "I apologize, DuFeron, if I've offended you."

"Oh, you have offended me, Whigby. Greatly. I'm thinking of calling you out."

The man paled. "Now, DuFeron, no need for that—"

"Unless," Lucien continued in the same silky tone, "you tell me why you dared come here to harass my wife, and why you thought I would not be interested in the matter."

Whigby pulled out a handkerchief and dabbed at his perspiring brow. "The gossips say that you've quarreled with your father-in-law, and since it's his debt I've come to collect—"

"Ah, my father-in-law. You thought that because I've quarreled with Baron Chestwick that it would make more sense to confront my wife about the matter."

"Yes, exactly."

"You thought wrong." Lucien no longer attempted to hide his ire. "You, Whigby, came into my home and bothered my wife for a matter that can be handled more expediently through the two of us.

There is no excuse you can possibly give to absolve yourself."

Whigby twisted the handkerchief between his fingers. "I just had a word with the lady. Just explained that her father owed me a debt. I didn't hurt her."

"You upset her, Whigby, and I will not tolerate anyone upsetting my wife. How much does Chestwick owe you?"

"A . . . a thousand pounds."

Lucien opened his desk drawer and withdrew the bank draft he'd tucked in there. With a few quick scrawls, he allocated a thousand pounds to Marcus Whigby. Then he shoved the paper across the desk. "Here's your money, Whigby. I'd better never catch you anywhere near my family again."

Whigby snatched up the paper, scanned it quickly, then tucked it away in his coat pocket. "Thank you, DuFeron. Consider this paid in full."

"I'll have your signature on it." Lucien pushed another paper toward the moneylender. Whigby squinted at it. "It's an agreement that says I have paid you for Chestwick's debt and that you have no further claims on the baron. Sign it."

"O-of course." Whigby signed the paper and handed it back to Lucien, who tucked it into his desk drawer. Then he locked it. "It's been a pleasure doing business with you, DuFeron," Whigby said, backing away. "Give my regards to your wife."

Lucien came out from behind the desk so quickly that the moneylender fell back a step in surprise. Then he spun and raced for the door. Lucien followed at a more leisurely pace.

"Listen to me, Whigby," Lucien said in a low, menacing tone as the other man fumbled for the door latch. "If I ever hear of you anywhere near my wife, your days will come to an abrupt and painful end. Do you understand me?"

"Y-yes." Whigby finally got the door open.

Lucien followed the man out of his study. "And tell your associates that anyone who harasses my wife or any member of my household will be taking his life in his hands."

Whigby didn't answer, merely collected his hat from the waiting Elton and escaped the house with all possible speed. Amused, Lucien turned back to his study, but a movement on the stairs caught his attention. Aveline stood there, mouth agape.

He smiled. "Good afternoon, my dear. Were you looking for me?"

Good afternoon? That's all he had to say?

Aveline stared at her husband, hardly able to believe what she had just witnessed. She had been coming to tell him about Marcus Whigby's visit that afternoon—dreading telling him about it, in fact—but apparently he had already taken care of the matter!

Lucien came to the bottom of the stairs, his expression softening. "It's all right, Aveline," he said gently. "Everything's taken care of."

"You paid him?"

He began to ascend the stairs. "Yes, I did. You don't have to worry about him anymore."

"But what about Chloe?" Despite her resolve, her

voice climbed with panic. "Dear Lord, Lucien, he threatened to hurt Chloe."

"Did he?" A dangerous light came into his eyes. "No one's going to hurt Chloe. I'll see to that."

"But there may be more of them." She took hold of his arm as he reached her on the stairs. "Lucien, there's no telling how many men my father owes. He was mad for gaming."

"And if there are more, I will pay the debts." Gently, he swept a thumb along her cheek. "You've been crying."

"I was so frightened . . ."

A reassuring smile curved his lips. "I have plenty of money, Aveline, and paying your father's gaming debts is a small enough price for your peace of mind. I don't want you to worry about it anymore."

"I cannot fathom it. You hate my father."

"But I don't hate you. And I don't hate Chloe."

She closed her eyes as terror drained out of her and left her trembling. "Dear God, Lucien, when he said that about Chloe, I didn't know what to do. Then I realized I had to tell you." He folded her into his arms, and she clung to him gratefully, pressing her face into his coat. "I was coming to tell you, but you'd already taken care of the matter."

"How expedient of me." He tilted her face up to his. "Listen well, Aveline. No one will ever hurt you or Chloe. Not as long as I'm breathing."

She stared up at his resolute expression, his earnest dark eyes. "I believe you."

"Good." He gently turned her around, slipped his

arm around her waist, and guided her up the stairs. "I will assign a man to guard Chloe and her governess at all times if it sets your mind at ease, but I don't think we will have further difficulties. All these men really want is the money owed them. Once they're paid, they don't come back."

They reached the landing, and she had recovered her composure enough to give him a shaky smile. "You seem quite familiar with such underhanded doings."

"The results of my misspent youth. I've had unfortunate dealings with the dark elements of London before." He chuckled. "On the other hand, they've also had dealings with me and will not be quick to raise my ire."

"I don't doubt it."

He lifted her hand to his lips. "Go to your room and rest a while, my sweet. Your nerves are overset."

She let out a long sigh, but left her hand in his. "I must admit they are."

"What's this? Aveline DuFeron admitting weakness?" He widened his eyes in an exaggerated expression of astonishment.

She gave him a weak smile. "Today's events would have overset even your nerves, husband."

"Too true." He squeezed her hand. "I admit to a bad moment when Elton informed me Whigby had been here. But it's all taken care of now. Go rest, and I'll see you at dinner."

"Actually, I believe I'll have a tray in my room." She raised a hand to his cheek in a lingering caress.

"Thank you, Lucien." Then she turned and walked away, leaving him standing on the landing.

Aveline woke suddenly. For an instant dread took her by the throat, but then she remembered. Chloe was safe. Lucien had taken care of the threat.

She'd taken Lucien's advice and retired to her room, then called for her dinner to be brought on a tray. After she'd barely nibbled at Cook's tasty roast pheasant and done no justice at all to the delicious-looking pudding that accompanied it, she'd settled down for a nap. Now a glance at the window proved that she had slept longer than expected, for she could see the stars twinkling in the night sky beyond the curtains.

She rose from the bed and moved to the window, staring out at the peaceful night, such a contrast to her own jumbled emotions. She had only ever wanted to do the right thing, but now she wasn't so certain what that was.

She'd tried to be loyal to her father, but recent events had made her realize that Papa had never been the ideal parent she had always wanted him to be. He had been a greatly flawed parent in fact, not taking responsibility for his actions, always allowing Aveline to fix the financial tangles he created. After her mother's death, instead of putting the welfare of his child first, he had flung himself headlong into gaming to forget his grief. Instead of comforting Aveline, she'd had to comfort him. And no matter how many times she set his blunders to rights, he never learned his lesson and continued to make the same mistakes all over again.

She loved her father, but his weaknesses had changed the very course of her life. And she realized now that her loyalty had never been to the man Papa was, but to the man she thought he should be.

And what of Lucien? Here was a man who had never known love—not from his parents, not from his brother. He'd lived most of his adult life as a libertine and a gamester, yet always managed to remain responsible with his finances. He'd spent years in hell because someone wanted him gone from London. And yet after all that, he'd acted with honor.

Yes, five years ago he'd scandalously suggested she share his bed to save her father's life. And yes, he had kept the word of the bargain they'd made between them and cast her off at the end of their time together. But was it right to hold that against him? She'd seen it as abandonment. He'd seen it as an act of honor.

Then there was the fact that as soon as he'd discovered their child's existence, he'd immediately proposed marriage. He'd housed them and clothed them and provided a fine life for her and Chloe, even though it meant she had to turn her back on her father forever. At the time she had thought him the worst sort of blackguard.

But now she understood that Lucien thought himself justified in his action. He truly believed her father guilty of doing him a terrible wrong, and while any man in England would condone a punishment of death, he had chosen to let Papa live. She doubted that would have been the case had the accused been anyone but his potential father-in-law.

She still thought he was wrong about Papa. More and more, she believed that Dante and the duke were behind the plot to get rid of Lucien. But the point was, *Lucien* believed her father guilty.

Despite his beliefs, he had paid Papa's gambling debt. He said he would continue to pay them if only to provide her with some measure of relief. That was the first sign she'd seen that he cared more for her, for their marriage, than he did for his revenge. It gave her hope for the future.

For despite his unhappy childhood, despite his rakish past, despite the five years he'd spent being tortured so cruelly, he'd still stepped forward when it counted. He'd managed to do the right thing and protect her and Chloe in a way Aveline's father never had.

In that moment, she realized she had to let go of her blind allegiance to Papa. She would always love him. She would always defend his good name. But she could no longer punish Lucien for her father's failings.

Lucien was her husband. She loved him. She'd always loved him—had never stopped loving him even when she thought herself abandoned by him. And today he had shown her without a doubt that she had been doing him a disservice. He was more than worthy of her wifely devotion, and it was time she gave him his proper due.

Lucien sat before the fire in his study, watching the reflection from the flames flicker over the gleaming chess pieces set out on the board. He picked up the white queen, stared at it a moment, then closed his fingers around it and sat back in his chair.

How many times had this very act soothed him while he lay shivering on the cold floor of Sledge's brig?

When he'd been taken, he'd still had the chess piece he'd so foolishly slipped into his pocket. He'd known the brigands would no doubt steal his fine clothing, and as soon as they left him alone, he'd slipped the white queen into a knothole in his tiny cell. There she'd remained for most of his sentence aboard the *Sea Dragon*, a cold comfort in the times when his throat had been swollen with thirst and his back burned from the bite of Sledge's lash. He used to pull the piece from its hiding place and caress the smooth contours and remember the feel of Aveline's skin.

Then one night Denton, Sledge's first mate, had found him with it. He'd laughed and tossed the piece overboard into the churning sea. That easily, his last hope for sanity had vanished.

If the pirates hadn't shown up mere days later, he knew he would have gone completely mad in that tiny, dark cell.

Yet he'd escaped. He'd escaped and won back his fortune as a pirate aboard the *Revenge*, making his way back triumphantly to England to make Chestwick pay for what he'd done. And he'd accomplished that goal.

Never had he thought to see the day that he would willingly pay his enemy's gambling debts.

But never would he have imagined that he'd be married to Aveline, or father to a child, or considering the possibility that Chestwick might be innocent after all.

Dante's betrayal had stunned him. And Robert's possible involvement . . . Good God, had the incident with the Torrington chit all those years ago really turned his half brother against him? He had more evidence pointing to those two as the guilty parties than he did to Aveline's father. In fact, he wouldn't put it past Dante to deliberately mislead him into thinking it was Chestwick by having Sledge's men refer to an imaginary baron as their employer. After all, Dante had known that Aveline was expecting his child. He had known all about the bargain.

He let out a long breath and closed his eyes. He'd clung to the belief that the baron was guilty for so long that it felt strange to consider otherwise. But even if he were the one who'd arranged it all, what harm could the man do now? He couldn't move, couldn't speak. He'd destroyed himself far better than Lucien could have ever done.

He opened his eyes and looked down at the white queen in his palm. Chestwick be damned; Lucien had clearly walked away with all the winnings this time.

A soft knock at the door broke his train of thought. He glanced at the clock: nearly half past one in the morning. He'd thought the servants all abed. Had hoped they were. The knock came again. "Come in," he said, not disguising his annoyance at being disturbed.

The door creaked open. "Lucien?"

At the sound of his wife's voice, his entire body jerked to alertness. "Aveline? I thought you were sleeping."

"I was." She slipped into the room, a starving man's lusty fantasy with her honey-colored curls tumbling down her shoulders, her lush, siren's body clad in one of the tantalizing silk-and-lace creations she favored. "I hope I'm not disturbing you."

She certainly was, but not in the way she thought.

"Of course not." He gave her an appreciative smile. "A man would have to be a fool to turn away a beautiful woman who comes seeking him in the middle of the night."

Her lips curved as she leaned back against the door and shut it with a soft click. "And you're no fool."

"Sometimes I am," he replied, dazzled by the receptive light in her eyes. "Especially when you look so incredibly lovely."

She blushed and glanced away, a pleased smile still tugging at her lips, and it was all he could do not to leap from the chair and ravish her where she stood. The silk caressed her form like a second skin, the lace teasing him with glimpses of the treasures it covered. He wanted to unwrap her like a gift, slowly and one layer at a time.

"Is everything all right?" he asked, when she remained near the door. "Do you have need of me?"

"Oh, yes." She turned those luminous eyes back toward him, and his loins stiffened in immediate, hard-as-a-bone readiness at the warm invitation there. "Yes, Lucien, I definitely need you."

She reached behind her and turned the key in the lock, never looking away. The tiny click echoed with the force of a gunshot, and excitement roared through him.

She approached him slowly, her body swaying in a seductive female undulation that called to him, the silk nightdress making a soft swish in the near-silent room. Her hair glittered in the light from the fire, and her skin glowed gold. When she finally reached his chair and put her hand on his shoulder, he nearly embarrassed himself then and there.

He closed his eyes, let out a harsh breath. Aside from a few tavern doxies during his time with the pirates, he'd not made proper love to a woman since he'd been abducted. His scars had gotten enough comments from even the whores that he'd not been inclined to take a proper mistress. And when he'd returned to England, he'd had revenge on his mind, not sex.

But he had sex on his mind now.

"I want to tell you something," she said, stroking a hand through his hair.

He leaned into her touch, soothed and aroused at the same time. "You can tell me anything."

That mysterious smile touched her lips again. "I know."

Unable to resist, he reached out and stroked a hand down her silk-clad hip, the material warm from her flesh. "Tell me while my brain is still working."

She gave a delighted laugh that sent a shaft of pure lust straight through him. Not that he wasn't hard as granite already. "I want you to know something." She knelt in front of his chair, resting her hands on his thighs and looking up into his face. He swallowed a groan. Damn the woman. Didn't she know what images that position brought to mind?

"What?" he croaked.

"I want you to know that I think you an admirable man. What you did today showed a great deal of honor."

Admirable? Honor? Try lustful. Lascivious even. Starving for you, sweet wife, he thought.

"Paying my father's debts was the act of a true gentleman," she continued. "I know how you feel about him, and yet you still took care of it and protected Chloe and me."

"The matter wasn't as insurmountable as you thought it was," he said, wondering if it was a good time to ask her to move her hand up his thigh just a little . . .

"Perhaps not to you, a man with unlimited funds at his disposal," she replied, still wearing that earnest expression. "But to a woman with no funds to speak of, such debts are the stuff of nightmares. Especially when dealing with the criminal element such as Mr. Whigby."

"You're my wife, Aveline, and I have more money than I know how to spend. Paying your father's debts is simply part of my duty as your husband."

"Oh, no," she disagreed. "It's much more." She ran a fingernail down his thigh, her eyes luminous.

"When the situation is one like ours, it's nothing short of commendable."

"Commendable." He gritted his teeth at the trail of fire left by her teasing nail, amazed the buttons of his trousers hadn't already popped off.

"Commendable." She leaned forward, folding her arms on his thighs and resting her plump breasts against his knees. "Have I ever told you," she breathed, "how attractive I find a commendable man?"

He reached out, stroked a hand over her hair. "Have I ever told you how much I want to be inside you?"

Her soft gasp echoed the light of desire in her eyes. "I want that, too."

He gave her a wicked smile, for the first time feeling a bit like his old self. "Then what are we waiting for?"

"I don't know." She slanted him a glance from beneath her lashes. "I thought you were supposed to be a rake."

"I was, once."

"Not anymore?"

"Not for a long time. I've changed, Aveline. In ways you may not like."

"You've also changed in ways I like very much." She sat back on her heels, her flirtatious attitude taking on a more serious mien. "The man I met five years ago was selfish. Jaded. He would have shot my father with no compunction, not shown mercy enough to leave him alive as you have done."

"I admit I was a bastard, and not just in the literal

sense." He reached out a hand to her, and she took it, twined her fingers with his. "Dammit, Aveline, I was the worst kind of cad to make you trade your innocence for your father's life, for the stupid gaming debts. I was no better than Whigby."

"That was definitely not the act of a gentleman," she agreed. "But we were both different people then. And don't forget that those three nights we spent together gave us Chloe. For that alone, I can never regret it."

"You forgive too easily," he whispered.

"The past has brought us here. Let us not look back." She shifted with a soft swish of silk. "Shall we continue to discuss the subject," she asked, sliding a hand over the bulge in his trousers, "or are there more pressing matters in need of attention?"

"Definitely more pressing matters." He stood, tugging her to her feet with him. Tossing aside the chess piece he still held, he turned his full attention to the white queen in his arms. Cupping her face in his hands, he kissed her.

She melted against him, her mouth opening for him as she wrapped her arms around his neck with a little sound of pleasure. He demanded, and she gave. He wrapped his arms around her, her plump breasts crushed against his chest and her soft belly pressed against his erection. She wiggled even closer, as if trying to climb into his skin.

"I want you, Lucien," she whispered between kisses. "I want you inside me."

With a soft growl of need, he crushed his mouth to hers and gave over to his reckless need for her.

Desire made her knees weak and her hands shake.

He kissed her like he was starving, bunching the silk of her nightdress with desperate hands. She tugged at his coat, managed to get it open and shove it partway down his arms. He let go of her long enough to strip it off, then took her hands and placed them at the buttons of his waistcoat. "Unbutton it."

The wild look in his dark eyes reminded her of the Lucien of long ago. Accomplished seducer, masterful lover. Her fingers shook, but she managed to get the buttons of his waistcoat undone. He shrugged out of it, his heavily lidded gaze making silent promises that set fire to any of her remaining inhibitions. She tugged at his neckcloth and tossed it aside, unbuttoned his collar. Eagerly, she yanked his shirt out of his trousers.

"Aveline." Suddenly serious, he placed his hands over hers before she could jerk the shirt over his head. "I can leave it on if you like."

She frowned. "I don't understand."

"The shirt." Color crept into his face, but he held her gaze. "I can leave it on if it makes you more comfortable."

"Why would it make me more comfortable? Wouldn't you be more comfortable with it off?"

"Or we could go upstairs. Extinguish the candles . . ."

"Lucien, what is going on here?"

He closed his eyes on a sigh, then opened them again. "My scars, Aveline. If you can't bear to look at them, I can either keep my shirt on, or we can go upstairs where it's dark."

"Oh, Lucien." She caressed his cheek. "Your scars don't bother me. They never have."

His eyes widened. "But . . . you never said any-thing when you saw them the first time. I thought you repulsed."

"No. Not repulsed." Her voice broke with tender-ness for this strong, vulnerable man. "Saddened. Shocked, perhaps. Completely devastated by what must have happened to you. For the first time I un-derstood why you hated my father so, and I couldn't blame you for it."

He closed his eyes on a sigh of relief that visibly eased the tension of his body. "That morning when we almost made love in the breakfast room, it was only when you touched my scars that you pulled away." He opened his eyes, his every emotion laid bare for her to see, and the depth of his feelings rocked her. "I thought for certain that you were dis-gusted by them. That you wouldn't want me for a lover." He gave a self-mocking laugh. "That was a blow to the mighty Lucifer. I knew then I would never be the man I once was."

"I much prefer the man you are now." She leaned up and kissed him, but softly, to comfort, not to arouse. "I do want you for my lover, husband. I want you very much."

Chapter 19

⟨⟨⟨◦◦◦⟩⟩⟩

She reached for the hem of his shirt, but he beat her to it. Yanking the garment over his head, he hesitated only a second before casting the shirt aside. His muscular torso gleamed in the soft firelight, and Aveline couldn't suppress a purr of appreciation as she ran a hand through the crisp black hair sprinkled across his chest. She traced one of the shiny puckered scars that crisscrossed his body.

"How could you ever think this makes you less desirable?" she whispered. "In my eyes, it makes you so much more a man for having survived such cruelty."

"I . . ." His voice broke, and he glanced away, but not before she caught a hint of moisture in his eyes. "Before I came back—some women are not so receptive."

She felt a pang at the mention of other women, but then she reminded herself that he hadn't been her husband then. He'd had the right to bed anyone he pleased.

But now he was all hers.

"They were foolish to pass up the delights of your bed for something so trivial." He made a choking noise, something between a laugh and a sob. Pride kept his face turned away. Teasingly, she trailed a finger from the base of his throat down his chest, following the dark hair as it arrowed down, down, down to where skin gave way to fabric. There she lingered, tracing the rippling muscles of his abdomen and flicking her thumb playfully over the buttons of his trousers. "Make love to me, husband, before I go mad from wanting you."

He looked at her then, his face taut with emotion, and hooked a hand behind her head to pull her into his hot, needy kiss. She curled into his embrace, wrapping her arms around his warm, muscular torso. The crinkly hair on his chest pricked her skin right through the flimsy silk of her nightgown, and she rubbed against him, loving the stimulating friction.

He growled deep in his throat and shoved one flimsy sleeve down her arm, baring part of her shoulder. He dipped his head and kissed her there, then sank his teeth gently into the fleshy part near her neck. Her body roared to life. His greedy hands swept over her, one hand between her shoulder blades, locking her into his embrace, the other caressing the sensitive flesh of her bottom.

Lucien's unchained passion released any inhibitions she still possessed. She nipped at his throat, raked her fingers through his chest hair, teased his flat male nipples with her thumbs until he groaned. She pressed her open mouth to his chest while he tangled his fingers in her long hair and hoarsely whispered her name. Slowly she slid down his body in a soft hiss of silk, her mouth blazing a trail down his chest, pausing to press a kiss on each raised scar. She reached his waist, and his fingers tightened in her hair as she traced a teasing path along his waistband with her tongue. Flashing him a wicked smile, she continued downward to nuzzle her face against the front of his trousers.

With a rough sound of need, he tumbled them both to the floor, his heavy body coming down on top of hers. He stretched her arms above her head, holding her immobile while he took her mouth in a deep, carnal kiss that made her head spin.

His heart pounded against hers, his flesh hot even through the silk of her nightgown. She arched her hips against him, straining to feel more of his hard erection pressing against her thighs. He muttered something, then switched both her trapped wrists to one hand while the other swept down her body to cup her breast.

She whispered his name, closed her eyes as sensations roared through her body like a thunderstorm. He shoved his hand inside her gown, tearing the lace as he closed over her bare breast, working the nipple with his thumb. He feasted on her mouth, nipping her lips, tangling his tongue with hers.

She gave a cry of surprise when he took both

hands and tore open the bodice of her nightgown, but that cry turned to a moan as he immediately took one tight nipple in his warm mouth and sucked strongly. No gentleness here, but she didn't want gentleness. She wanted Lucien, in all his raw, unfettered passion.

She stroked her hands over his back, clasping his firm muscles with feminine appreciation. Then he took one nipple between his teeth and tugged, and her world spun out of control. She dug her nails into his back and arched into his mouth.

With a low groan, he shoved her nightdress up to her waist, his hand slipping between her thighs to discover the damp heat awaiting him. Willingly she let her knees fall open to give him access, trembling as he stroked her with exactly the right touch. The ache between her legs became an inferno.

He slipped a finger into her damp sheath, and she almost climaxed right there and then. But he retreated just in time, then came back, slower now, just grazing the part of her that craved his caress. She made a wild sound in the back of her throat and shifted her hips, chasing the heady pleasure just beyond her reach.

He laved her breasts with his tongue, worked his magic between her thighs. So many times he brought her almost to the brink, then stopped and waited for her quivering body to calm. Then he sent her up again.

Every inch of her burned for him, her skin rippling with reaction to the touch of a master. He knew just where and how to caress her, knew just when she was about to reach the pinnacle and when to pull back. Her breathing came in pants, her hair a tangle around them. Sweat misted his flesh and soaked the lock of hair falling over his forehead.

"Please, Lucien," she whispered in a near sob, locking her gaze with his. "Please—"

He swallowed the word with a kiss, reaching down to unbutton his trousers. She helped him shove his garments down until they got caught on his boots. But it was enough. His erection stood proud and hard in the firelight, a sheen of moisture at the tip. She reached out a hand and traced his hardness. He gave a shudder, then removed her hand and pressed her back against the carpet. She went willingly, spreading her thighs as he moved between them.

"Aveline," he murmured, stroking her hair out of her face. The way he said it made the simple word so much more than her name. Then he slowly slid inside her.

After the fierce passion that had driven them, she'd expected a frenzied coupling. But instead he moved slowly, pressing deep, then languidly withdrawing. She clung to his shoulders, wrapping her legs around him as he controlled the excruciatingly slow pace, his jaw clenched with restraint.

He cupped her bottom in his hands and thrust deeper, sending a flare of heat through her loins. Almost, almost—He withdrew at a snail's pace that left them both shaking, then entered her again with the same slowness. This time he remained buried inside her and began to rock, igniting a delicious friction in her loins that built and built until suddenly she was *there*. Pleasure ripped through her, tearing a hoarse scream from her throat.

Lucien was right behind her, throwing back his head as he thrust hard once, twice. His face twisted in concentration, a bead of sweat rolling down his temple, before he gave a shout of release, his body shuddering as he emptied himself inside her.

He collapsed on top of her in an exhausted heap, and Aveline smiled wearily, wrapping her arms around him.

Aveline's gasps for breath and her hands pushing against his chest woke him from his languor. With a muttered apology he rolled off her to lie supine on the rug. He heard her inhale deeply, then her fingers twined with his on the carpet between them. He turned his head to look at her, smiling a bit smugly at her disheveled appearance.

"You're looking untidy, wife."

"I've been ravished." She said it with a satisfied little smirk that made him want to ravish her all over again. She rolled on her side to face him, the remnants of her nightdress falling away from her lithe body. "It seems to me, Mr. DuFeron, that you remember quite a few of Lucifer's old tricks."

"And it seems to me, Mrs. DuFeron, that you are a woman of great passion and boldness."

She blushed prettily. "Blame yourself, sir, for you taught me."

"Then I commend myself on my teaching skills."

This time she laughed. "Truth be told, I was quite nervous. I've never seduced a man before."

"I'm honored to have been the first."

"As if anyone could hold a candle to the great Lucifer," she teased. "You quite ruined me."

At once his mood sobered. "I know I did. And for that I do apologize. I should have shown compassion that night, not used you for my selfish ends."

"We've agreed to forget the past." Her fingers tightened around his. "But if you'd like to prove your sincerity . . ."

He pulled her on top of him. "I do."

She leaned up on her elbows and grinned down at him. "You could take off your boots."

He joined in her laughter, then kissed her as her hair fell like a curtain of gold around them. And he showed her he was sincere indeed.

It was late morning by the time Aveline awoke in Lucien's bed.

Sometime before dawn they had crept up the stairs, giggling like children as they tried not to wake the servants. Since her nightdress had been completely destroyed, Aveline had wrapped herself in Lucien's coat as the two of them sneaked up to his bedchamber. That coat had been quickly tossed aside in the face of Lucien's passion, and she awoke now with a smile on her face and pleasant aches throughout her body.

Her smile faded as she noticed that she was alone

in the room. Obviously her husband had risen early and gone about his business.

She sat up in the bed, pushing her hair out of her face. She'd thought they'd shared something last night. That they'd forged a bond. But perhaps for Lucien it had been no more than a casual encounter.

Despair squeezed her heart as she recalled the night's events. There'd been no words of love spoken, no vows of undying devotion. Had she misjudged the situation? Perhaps nothing about their marriage had changed except that they now shared a bed. After all, she couldn't expect Lucien to share her feelings.

She let out a deep, shuddering sigh. Perhaps he didn't know how to love—and with his family, who could blame him? Someone close to him had betrayed him and sent him away to die aboard that ship. Only Lucien's strength of will had allowed him to survive. She didn't doubt that her husband's love might be hard to attain. If he was capable of loving at all.

Passion burned hot in the beginning, but it eventually faded. Without love to fuel it, passion turned to boredom and eventually to resentment. Was she doomed to an empty marriage in the years to come?

She gathered the sheets around her and stood, preparing to return to her own room. As she stepped away from the bed, something fell to the floor.

A white rose, barely open.

Slowly she bent and picked it up, lifting the flower to her nose to inhale the sweet fragrance. It must have been on the bed beside her, and she hadn't seen it.

She sniffed the flower again and was reminded of that lovely evening in the garden when she and her husband had seemed in perfect accord. Had he thought of that when he'd chosen this rose? Perhaps there was hope for their marriage after all.

Humming, she turned toward her own bedroom.

Lucien knocked on the door of Huntley House, half-expecting to be dismissed like the time he'd first come back to London. Instead the butler called him by name and opened the door wide.

"Is the duke in?" Lucien asked, taking off his hat and gloves.

"I shall inquire, Mr. DuFeron." The butler disappeared and reappeared in a matter of minutes. "His Grace has asked me to show you to his study."

Lucien passed his hat and gloves to a footman's waiting hands. "Thank you, Stinson."

"This way, sir."

Lucien followed the servant to Robert's study. How odd it felt to be back at Huntley House. He'd spent a good deal of his life in the elaborate town house, but he knew he wasn't imagining the museumlike coldness of the place. It was beautifully decorated and held a fortune's worth of antiques and artwork, but he much preferred the smaller home where he lived with Aveline and Chloe. Family, he realized, made all the difference.

Stinson took one step through the door of the duke's study. "Mr. DuFeron," he announced, then fell back to allow Lucien to enter.

"Thank you, Stinson." Robert stood in front of his desk, garbed in a fine blue coat and buff-colored trousers that could have been Lucien's own. Noticing the similarity in their clothing, the duke raised one blond brow. "Well," was all he said.

"Apparently we patronize the same tailor," Lucien drawled. "That can't be good for your reputation. Perhaps you should replace your entire wardrobe immediately."

"I rather like the fact you appear to have some sort of good taste," Robert replied. "It must run in the family."

"Are you admitting that we're related?"

"I never denied it." Robert folded his arms across his chest. "What brings you to call so early, Lucien? As I recall, you're a creature of the night. Have you even been to bed yet?"

Lucien couldn't stop the satisfied smile that spread across his face. "I have."

Robert held up a hand. "I don't care to hear the details."

"I have no intention of sharing them."

Robert exhaled with impatience. "Since I know nothing short of a dire emergency would entice you to come here voluntarily, please enlighten me as to the reason for your visit."

"Can you blame me?" Lucien glanced around the study, which hadn't changed much since his childhood. "This house holds little in the way of good memories for me. Speaking of which, where is your mother this morning?"

"She's gone shopping."

"Good. I wanted to talk to you alone."

"How extraordinary." Robert moved behind his desk and seated himself in the chair there. "Sit down, Lucien. I must admit you have me curious."

Lucien chose a chair near the desk and sat.

"What is it you'd like to talk about?" Robert asked.

"Victoria Torrington."

The duke shot to his feet. "Get out."

Lucien rose, too, more slowly. "I'm not leaving."

"Then I'll have you thrown out."

"Do it," Lucien taunted as his brother made for the door. "Then the *ton* can gossip about how the Duke of Huntley had his own brother ejected from the family home."

Halfway across the room, Robert spun back. "Half brother."

Lucien shrugged. "Whatever you like. I've already returned from the dead and married the mother of my illegitimate child. Isn't that enough talk for the family to withstand right now?"

"Unfortunately, you're right."

"We need to discuss Victoria, Robert," he said quietly. "We can't go on this way forever."

Robert gave him a look that said they certainly could, but he made his way back to the desk. Seating himself, he braced his hands on the arms of the chair. "If you're planning to apologize, it's a little late for that."

"I want to explain what happened. And then I'll apologize."

Robert leaned his head back, closing his eyes halfway in a practiced expression of ennui. "If you must," he sighed.

"Don't you want to know the truth?" Lucien asked. "Or do you prefer your own version of the facts?"

Robert opened his eyes and shot him a hostile look. "I know what happened. You tried to seduce the woman I was going to marry."

"I wasn't the first."

"How can you say that?" Robert leaped from the chair, slapping both hands on the desk as he leaned forward. "Victoria was the daughter of an earl. From the moment of her birth, our parents planned our betrothal. Victoria grew up knowing she would one day be my wife."

"And that made her careless. She thought she could dally where she wanted because her future was secure." Lucien gave a snort of derision. "The girl was a tart, and she would have made you a laughingstock. But I knew you'd never believe me unless I proved it to you. Damn it, Robert, think! Have you ever known me to tamper with innocents?"

Robert lifted a mocking brow. "What about your wife?"

"That was a different matter altogether. The circumstances . . . well, she was unique. And I made it right in the end."

Robert chuckled. "Dear me, how the mighty have fallen. It seems to me, Lucien, that your wife has you completely beguiled."

Lucien clenched his jaw, knowing Robert's remark was all too close to the truth. "We're not talking about Aveline. We're talking about Victoria. And she was no innocent."

"Not after you finished with her, certainly." Disgust heavy in his voice, Robert straightened and began to pointedly rearrange the papers on his desk.

"I never touched her, Robert."

"What's this? Changing the story now?"

"Lord Hardyston was her lover, not I." Lucien took hold of Robert's arm, forcing his brother to cease his paper shuffling and look at him. "I just arranged for you to see us together so you'd know her true nature."

"I knew her true nature. She was a beautiful lady with a sweet temperament who was supposed to have been my duchess."

"No, Robert. She was a beautiful whore who would have spent her life making you miserable with her many affairs."

"Get out!" Robert shook off Lucien's hold. "Get out of my house, you blackguard! You ruined the woman I loved!"

"I know you loved her," Lucien said quietly. "Which is why I had to save you from her. I'm sorry I had to hurt you."

"I should have called you out," Robert snapped. "But I had no desire to die at nineteen years of age."

"I wouldn't have killed you," Lucien said. "I would have refused the challenge."

"Coward!"

"You're my brother. That means something to me, even if it is an embarrassment to you." Lucien gave a brief bow. "Good day, Your Grace."

"Half brother," Robert muttered, as Lucien quit the room. But for some reason the comment didn't carry the sting it should have.

As the door of Huntley House closed behind him, Lucien was glad he'd chosen to walk the short distance to his brother's house rather than ride. He'd anticipated that his discussion with Robert would leave him frustrated, and he'd been right. With a last dark glance at the duke's residence, he set out for his own.

He'd known six years earlier that his demonstration of Victoria Torrington's true nature would wound his brother's pride and perhaps even sadden him for a short time, but he'd never imagined the boy's heart was that deeply engaged. And Robert *had* been a boy—barely nineteen—when Clarissa had encouraged him to become better acquainted with Victoria, the second daughter of the Earl of Plimington.

Their father had gone along with the match because the Plimington name and fortune went back almost as far as the Huntleys', but it had been Clarissa who engineered the actual betrothal. Lucien had always suspected that Clarissa insisted on arranging Robert's marriage so early because she wanted the future duchess to be a malleable girl whom she would be able to control. No one could have known that Victoria would turn out to be such a lightskirt, taking as her lover the married Lord Hardyston.

When Lucien found out about their affair, he'd realized that a woman like Victoria would make Robert miserable should the marriage come to pass. Already, the very proper Robert loved her and thought her the gentlest and most well bred of ladies. He'd gone out of his way not to offend his fiancée's delicate sensibilities. In the meantime, eighteen-year-old Victoria had managed several passionate assignations with Lord Hardyston—not her first lover by half, if Lucien's informants were correct.

He couldn't let his brother marry a woman who would not only submit him to ridicule as a cuckold but also humiliate the Huntley name. His opportunity to do something about it had come when, like everyone else in London, the chit had discovered the dissension between Lucien and the proper members of his family. *She'd* approached *him*, finding it amusing to try and seduce her betrothed's half brother.

But the little vixen had taken on more than she could handle by offering herself to Lucifer. Lucien had let her get him alone at the house party where the two families were to formalize the engagement. Claiming her fiancé bored her, she'd just thrown her arms around him and begged him to take her when Robert had walked in with both his parents and hers behind him.

The result had been pandemonium. Victoria had immediately acted the frightened virgin, but both families had heard her remarks to Lucien. Robert had instantly blamed his fiancée's change in behavior on Lucien, claiming he'd obviously set out to seduce her. Trying to salvage the betrothal, Lord

Plimington had gone along with Robert, shouting to the skies that his daughter had been ruined by a notorious rake. Clarissa, glaring daggers at Lucien, had been in favor of immediate marriage between Robert and Victoria, but the duke would not hear of it. Instead, he'd offered Lucien as an alternative to Robert, since it was he who had compromised Victoria.

The earl rejected the offer completely, indicating that he'd never allow his daughter to wed a bastard, even a duke's bastard. Thoroughly offended, the duke called off the engagement then and there. Lord Plimington's family had departed in high dudgeon mere hours thereafter.

Robert had taken the incident hard, and he and Lucien rarely exchanged a civil word after that. Lucien had repaired to Thornsgate to avoid the troublesome gossip, and three months later, he'd met Aveline.

Two months after that, he'd been imprisoned aboard Sledge's ship.

Could Robert have been so upset over losing Victoria that he'd arranged for the disposal of his troublesome half brother?

The idea disturbed him. He'd hoped time would calm Robert's ire, but apparently his brother had a long memory. More and more it was looking to Lucien as if people close to *him* had engineered his abduction and not Aveline's father. No longer could he in good conscience punish the baron. The man could harm no one in his current state, and the condition he'd set not allowing Aveline or Chloe to see their relative suddenly seemed to be hurting them more than it hurt the baron.

He would lift the restriction. There seemed no purpose for it now.

Heart lightened by the thought of Aveline's reaction to the news, he didn't see the footpad until the brigand was almost upon him.

He dodged to avoid the thief's outstretched arm, where the filthy fellow had poised to yank him down the alley, but another ruffian came at him from behind, shoving him off the main street and into the shadows.

Lucien cursed his poor timing as he spun to face the thieves. Because of the early hour, few people walked the streets. No one had seen the brigands shove Lucien down the alley—which was no doubt what they'd counted on.

"I've a small purse with me," he said, bracing for a fight. "You're welcome to it if you'll be on your way."

"Scared, are ye?" one said, waving a knife. "Ye should be."

"We'll have yer gold and yer fancy boots, too," the other chimed in, pointing a pistol at Lucien's chest. "Cause ye won't be needin' 'em anymore."

"And why is that?"

The one with the knife smiled, showing gaps where his teeth had been. "Cause ye'll be dead."

The thief with the knife, though smaller, looked to be the one to watch, he thought, shifting his weight in case they rushed him. The bigger one with the pistol looked less intelligent. "I don't die easily."

"We were warned about ye," the bigger one said.

"Indeed? By whom?"

"Shut yer hole," the smaller man hissed. "This is supposed to look like a normal fleecin'."

Lucien's blood ran cold at the words. "You've been sent to kill me?"

"Now ye've done it," the bigger man said.

"Someone doesn't like ye, milord," the smaller one sneered.

Someone doesn't like you at all, laddie. He could still hear Sledge's voice the night of his abduction.

Not again.

"I'm not a lord," he said to the smaller man. "And I have no intention of dying today."

"Ye'll be nothin' but fish bait soon enough," the larger one jeered.

"We shall see."

"Get 'im!" the younger one cried, lunging with the knife.

Lucien moved. His time with the pirates of the *Revenge* served him well as he dodged the swipe of the knife and tripped the smaller brigand. The little man went tumbling, the knife skidding out of his hand. The bigger one cried out and fired the pistol. Lucien dived to the ground. The pistol ball flew overhead and lodged in the wall behind him.

The smaller man reached for the knife, but Lucien got there first, grabbing the knife and stabbing the man in the back of the hand. The footpad gave a screech of pain and cradled his injured hand.

The bigger fellow fumbled with the pistol, trying to reload it. Lucien got to his feet, knife still clutched in his fingers, and charged him. They fell to the ground, Lucien's arms locked around the ruffian's large middle. The pistol flew out of the thief's hand, and as they hit the ground, the impact jarred the knife from Lucien's fingers.

Unarmed, the two men rolled on the ground, switching to fists. Lucien took a hard left to the jaw and retaliated with a punishing right to the face. He and the big brigand seemed evenly matched in a fist-fight, exchanging blow for blow.

Not again, he kept thinking. *Never again.*

A flash of light out of the corner of his eye warned him. He rolled aside just as the smaller thief brought the knife down. Instead of embedding itself in his back as its wielder no doubt intended, the blade plunged into the chest of the big brigand.

"Jack!" the smaller one cried. He fell to his knees beside his fallen comrade.

While he was distracted, Lucien tackled him, flattening him on his back and shoving an arm against his windpipe. The man's eyes bulged, and he clawed at Lucien's arm.

"Who hired you?" he demanded. "Who sent you to kill me?"

The thief gasped for breath. "I . . . don't . . . know."

"You lie." Lucien leaned harder on his arm. "Try again."

"Hired . . . at . . . the docks." The thug's face reddened as his breathing grew shallower. "Some . . . baron."

"The baron, was it? What did he look like?"

"Never . . . saw him."

Lucien relaxed his arm a bit. "Then who delivered the message?"

The thief took a deep breath, his eyes watery. "A bloke I know. Said some gent wanted to do another gent, no questions asked. I took the job. Never saw this baron fella."

"How do you get paid then?"

" 'E's to leave my money at the Rose 'n' Hound after the job is done."

"Well, you won't be collecting it." Lucien rose to his feet, jerking the little man with him. "If I were you, I'd rethink my profession."

Chapter 20

After handing his would-be assassin over to the local constable, Lucien had gone to seek out Dante.

He hadn't believed the brigand's story about the baron. Aveline's father was in no condition to arrange an attempt on Lucien's life, but obviously news of his condition had not yet reached everyone in London. This time, his enemy had made a grievous mistake.

Aveline had been right; Baron Chestwick had never arranged his abduction. Though Lucien had already decided to let go of his desire for revenge against the baron, he now owed Aveline an apology. She had remained loyal to her father even in the face of her husband's condemnation.

It had been *his* friends—*his* family—who had ru-ined his life. His own best friend had written the letter that had resulted in his child's illegitimacy, and it looked as if his half brother the duke wanted him dead. Vengeance stirred to life once more as he walked up the steps to Dante's living quarters.

But Dante's rooms were empty, and no one had seen him for the last couple of days at his usual haunts. That disturbed Lucien, for Dante only went to ground when he had something to hide. Had he simply been scared off by Lucien's earlier visit about the letter? Or had he participated in hiring the thieves and fled once he'd realized they'd failed in their mission?

It was with a heavy heart that Lucien arrived home near dinnertime.

As he stepped through the door, Elton dropped his impassive butler's guise when he saw Lucien's bloody coat and torn trousers. "Sir! What happened?"

"An encounter with footpads, Elton. Have no fear; I'm quite all right. Do ring for Stokes before my wife sees—"

"Lucien!" From the staircase, Aveline stared at him in shock, one hand creeping to her throat. "Good heavens, what happened to you?"

"Just a scuffle with a pickpocket. Nothing to worry about."

"Nothing to worry about!" She grasped the skirts of her pale pink dinner dress and hurried down the stairs. "You're filthy! And is that *blood*?"

"It's not mine." Glancing around at the listening servants, he took her arm and led her to the nearby drawing room. "I will tell you what happened," he murmured, "but only in private."

"Fine." She waited until he closed the door behind them. Then she leaped forward, running her hands down his arms and across his chest. "Where are you hurt?"

"I'm not hurt." He took her wandering hands in his. "I was attacked by two footpads as I left Huntley House. I killed one, and the other confessed they had been sent to kill me."

"What!" Her face paled. "Lucien, we must contact Bow Street at once."

"Listen to what I have to say first." He sighed and leaned forward to rest his forehead against hers. "I believe Robert may be behind these attempts on my life," he said, "and I think Dante is involved, too."

"Attempts? There's been more than one?"

"Yesterday I almost got run over by a runaway hack. I think you were right. I think Dante and Robert worked together five years ago to arrange my abduction."

"Oh, Lucien." She wrapped her arms around his neck and hugged him tight. "I'm so sorry."

Her compassion unmanned him. A great wave of relief and misery swept him at the same time, and he clung to her, burying his face in her hair. He'd been betrayed by the very people who were supposed to care for him. But he still had Aveline.

He would always have Aveline.

"I looked for Dante," he murmured, his voice muffled by her hair. "He wasn't in his rooms. No one's seen him."

"What about your brother?"

Lucien gave another sigh and stepped back from the embrace. "I will deal with him, but it is much more complicated because of his status."

"Of course. He's a duke, and you're—"

"—his bastard brother. No amount of money in the world can compete with the Huntley title." He gave a harsh laugh. "Robert even bought Thornsgate, did I tell you that? After I was declared dead, he purchased the house but never lived there. I loved that house."

"I know you did." She smoothed his hair. "But we'll find another house. One that can be a home for the three of us."

"Yes, we will." He turned away, walked to the other side of the room. "There's something else, Aveline. Something I must say to you."

"What?" She folded her hands at her waist, watching him calmly, as nothing he said would bother her.

His Aveline. Always accepting him as he was, always there to argue with him or reason with him. Beautiful, stubborn, brave, and intelligent. Bit by bit, she'd brought Lucifer home from hell and made him human again.

Damn, but he loved her.

He loved her. The truth of his own feelings overwhelmed him, and he stared blindly up at the watercolor landscape hanging over the mantel. If he looked at her, he was afraid he'd say the words. And he wasn't ready.

He cleared his throat. "You were right about your father. I'd already decided to forget about revenge, but today's incident proves his innocence beyond a doubt."

"How is that?"

Controlled now, Lucien faced her again. "The thief claimed to be sent by the baron. And we both know your father is in no condition to arrange anything of the sort."

"Ah." Her eyes sparkled. "It seems the real culprit made a serious mistake."

"Quite." He grew serious once more. "I'm sorry I didn't listen to you. I thought you blind where your father is concerned."

"I was." She met his gaze squarely. "I love my father, Lucien, but he was a slave to his weaknesses, and it ruined our lives. Your actions of late have proven you to be quite the opposite."

"Because of me you ended up alone and with child."

"But you saw your mistake and tried to correct it. My father never saw his mistakes." Her lips curved in a smile of fond exasperation. "For Papa, the answer was always in the next turn of the card or throw of the dice."

"He was a poor father, but not a bad man."

"No," she agreed. "He's not a bad man. But he stumbled and fell in the face of his difficulties, whereas yours have made you stronger."

"I sent for him, you know." He shifted uncomfortably as her face lit with pleasure. "I sent a coach for him this morning before I left to speak with Robert. I'd already decided, you see, that revenge was not worth the sacrifice."

"What sacrifice?"

"You."

"Oh, Lucien." She flew into his arms and hugged him. "Chloe will be so excited when I tell her. She's been asking for him."

And how hard had it been, he wondered, for Aveline to deflect the little girl's requests to see her grandfather?

"Perhaps there is a doctor here in London who can help your father." Gently he moved her back to arm's length. "In the meantime, have a care for your dress. I'm filthy."

"Dresses can be replaced." She cupped his cheek and kissed his lips. "Thank you, Lucien," she whispered, her eyes aglow with happiness.

His heart swelled in his chest. Uncomfortable, he waggled his eyebrows in a playful leer. "You can demonstrate your gratitude later tonight." He glanced down at his ruined trousers. "I suppose I'd better change for dinner. You do realize Stokes is going to die of apoplexy when he sees the condition of my clothing."

"You will survive his wrath." Her lighthearted expression faded. "Lucien, I'm afraid for you. What if they try again to kill you?"

"My darling wife." He came to her and with a wicked smile, lifted her hand to his lips. "Haven't I already proven that I am notoriously hard to kill?"

"It only takes one time." She closed her fingers over his. "Be careful, Lucien. I lost you once. I do not think I could stand to do so again."

He turned his hand over to twine his fingers with

hers. "I have no intention of ever leaving you, madam. I'm afraid you're saddled with me."

Her lips curved in a soft smile. "Good."

That night he came to her as soon as her maid had left the room. She'd hoped he would come, and when the connecting door clicked open, she nearly dropped the brush she held in her eagerness.

"Now isn't this a lovely sight." In his shirtsleeves with his cravat dangling untied around his neck, he leaned in the doorway and folded his arms. He crossed one stockinged foot over the other, and appreciation warmed his gaze as it swept over her. "I believe you're more beautiful now than the day I first saw you."

"And you haven't changed." Amused, she met his gaze in the mirror and once more resumed brushing out her hair. "You're still a rogue."

"Only with you, madam. Only with you." He straightened and approached her. "May I assist you?"

"If you wish." She surrendered the brush to him, then closed her eyes in pleasure as he began to stroke it through her hair.

"I've always loved your hair," he said quietly. "It looks like spun gold when it's loose about your shoulders like this. I'd like to wrap myself up in it."

"You're welcome to do so."

He chuckled. "Ah, temptress. I do believe I've taught you too well, wife."

"Is it so unnatural for a woman to enjoy the sensual arts when her husband is such a master at them?" She opened her eyes, met his gaze in the mirror again. "I believe in honesty between us, Lucien. There has been too much deception not of our making that has come between us."

"True enough." He pulled the brush slowly through her hair, and she let her head fall back as a purr of pleasure escaped her throat. "There is nothing wrong with a woman who enjoys her husband's attentions," he added.

"If it is wrong, I hope never to be right."

"I will teach you to be wicked," he whispered, sweeping her hair away from her ear with the brush. "But only with me."

"I want no one else." She smiled. "I never have."

He exhaled with a hiss. "You make it hard to control myself."

"I didn't say you had to."

He laughed. "I want to make love to my wife in a leisurely manner, not jump upon her like a boar in rut."

"At least you're not a boring boar."

He groaned. "That was pitiful."

She gave a low, husky laugh, reveling in her power as a woman. "I thought it rather clever."

"Do you want to trade quips, Aveline?" He swept her hair over one shoulder and trailed the brush along the bared skin of the other, the soft bristles making her flesh ripple with arousal. "I had something else in mind."

"You don't find my conversation interesting?"

He leaned down to place his mouth near her ear. "I find everything about you *fascinating*."

A quiver ran through her. There was no one else like him, no one who made her feel so beautiful in such a basic, feminine way. She had the feeling she could be the most physically ugly woman in the world, yet he would still make her feel as if she were the only woman who could ever satisfy him.

And she'd almost lost him today.

She turned her head to look at him, to stare into his eyes—into his soul—as she said the words she could no longer hide. "I love you, Lucien."

He inhaled sharply, then he closed his eyes.

"I wasn't going to tell you," she continued. Her heart beat like a rabbit's; she couldn't read his expression. "But when you came home today, and I realized you could have been killed . . . I just wanted you to know." She cupped his cheek with one hand. "I love you, Lucien. I loved you five years ago, and I will love you years from now."

"How could you love me after what I did?" He opened his eyes, fierce emotion glowing in the dark depths. "I took your innocence for your father's sins. You must have been terrified, but you followed through on the bargain."

"How could I not love you? You live your life with passion and bend it to your will." While he hadn't returned her declaration, he hadn't rejected her either. Thrilled, she spoke from the heart. "You've survived incredible torment and rebuilt from nothing. You taught me to do the same."

"I don't deserve you," he muttered roughly, pulling her off the chair and into his embrace.

"But you have me."

"Thank God for it." He lifted her into his arms, surprising a squeal of laughter from her, and stepped through the connecting doorway.

"Where are you taking me?"

"To my bed." He laid her on the mattress, satisfaction etched upon his face as he looked down at her. "I like the sight of you here."

She stretched lazily, knowing how the silk of her nightdress would follow the movement. "I like being here."

"Siren." He swept his knuckles along her cheek. "Are you trying to tempt me?"

"Not at all." She leaned up on her elbows, lips curving smugly as his gaze dropped to her hardened nipples poking against the silk. "I *am* tempting you."

"Indeed you are." He bent and kissed her, going willingly as she wrapped her arms around him and pulled him onto the bed with her.

Their loving seemed more like a symphony than a fire, with gentle caresses and sweet murmurings and sweet gasps of pleasure. Eager hands pushed aside clothing. Mouths kissed and caressed and whispered words of praise. Higher and higher their pleasure built, always close but not quite to the pinnacle. Finally, he poised himself at the entry to her body, teasing her with the hard heat of him. He took her face in his hands and kissed her softly, staring deeply into her eyes. "I love you," he murmured, then joined their bodies.

She climaxed immediately, overcome by a rush of passion and emotion. She clung to him, tears streaming from her eyes, as he whispered the words again and again with the rhythm of his thrusts until he, too, threw his head back and shouted his pleasure.

Then they settled into each other's arms and slept.

Lady Tripton's ball should have proven the most enjoyable event Aveline had attended that Season. After all, her husband had confessed his love for her, and the Duchess of Huntley was not in attendance to freeze her from across the room with her cold stare. But as happy as she was that her marriage had now evolved into something approaching a normal relationship, she was also terrified—terrified that it would all be taken away with one assassin's bullet.

How could Lucien calmly talk business with the gentlemen in attendance when he knew someone was trying to kill him? And that the most likely suspect was his best friend, Dante? Yet that was exactly what he was doing. When she'd tried to stay with him, clinging to his arm while on the lookout for enemies behind every potted palm, he'd gently asked her to take herself off to enjoy the delights of the ball. Apparently some of his business associates had difficulty discussing important matters in the presence of a female.

And what could she do but comply?

Reluctantly Aveline left him to it, taking a seat at the edge of the dance floor with the dowagers. She tried to keep Lucien in her line of sight, but it was difficult with the crush of people crammed into Lady Tripton's ballroom. She had visions of one of his enemies lurking in the crowd, ready to stick a knife through his ribs.

They'd only just found each other again. She had no intention of losing him.

The Duke of Huntley appeared out of nowhere, bowing and holding out his hand. "Would you take a turn around the ballroom with me, Mrs. DuFeron?"

The matrons ceased their gossiping, waiting with unconcealed curiosity for her reply. Aveline hesitated. Robert was also on the list of suspects behind Lucien's attacks, which made her wary, but then she realized that if she went with him, at least he'd not be able to enact any plots to kill Lucien while in her company. Perhaps she could even earn a confession from him. "Of course, Your Grace."

Placing her hand on his outstretched arm, she allowed him to lead her in a turn around the ballroom.

"I have not seen your mother this evening," Aveline remarked after a few moments of awkward silence.

"She left this afternoon for Havenmeade, my country estate. Our French chef left our employ rather abruptly."

"I'm sorry to hear that."

"Mother acts as my hostess until I wed." Robert flashed her a meaningful glance. "In fact, I was betrothed once, to a lady handpicked by my parents when I was a babe."

"Your Grace," she said, slowing her steps, "is there something you want to say to me?"

He looked nonplussed for a moment, as if she'd stumbled on a secret. Then he sighed and gave a short nod. "Come, allow me to fetch you a glass of punch."

"Punch is unnecessary. Perhaps we could find a quiet corner instead so you might tell me what you want."

"You're a very practical woman, madam." Robert led her along the edge of the dance floor to a more sparsely populated area of the ballroom. Few ladies lingered there as the smell of smoke drifted unpleasantly from the nearby gentlemen's card room.

Robert stopped, and a haughty look cleared the area of the two young bucks who had paused to debate the merits of their favorite hunting steeds.

"You do that very well," Aveline said, watching the gangly gentlemen scurry away.

"Thank you. One of the benefits of being a duke."

She nearly smiled at his youthful arrogance. It was hard to comprehend that she and the young duke were the same age. "I assume you sought me out for a reason, Your Grace."

He raised one blond eyebrow. "Perhaps I just wanted the company of a beautiful woman."

"You're very charming, but do not expect me to fall for such flummery. You are not the sort of man to confess his family secrets in the middle of a crowded ballroom."

"True enough. But I wanted to get your attention."

"You could have paid a call."

He gave a bitter laugh. "I didn't know if you would receive me."

Her heart leaped into her throat. Did he know of their suspicions? "Whatever gave you that idea,

Your Grace?" she asked as casually as she could manage.

"Lucien came to see me today. We . . . discussed an incident from the past. I thought he might forbid you to see me if I should call."

"Discussed?"

He gave her a long-suffering look. "Very well. We quarreled."

Distrustful of him, she glanced back over the crowd, looking for Lucien. "Brothers always quarrel."

"Half brother."

She sighed with exasperation. "What did you want to tell me?"

"I wanted to talk to you about Lucien."

"Botheration. What now?"

He looked taken aback at her tone. "I would think a wife would be eager to know her husband's past."

"I know all about my husband's past, Your Grace. And it does not cast you in a flattering light."

Anger kindled in his eyes. "Indeed? Perhaps you don't really know what sort of man you married."

She narrowed her eyes as anger swept through her. Did he think to blacken Lucien's name to her? They'd been through enough, by God. Why could no one leave them in peace? "I know *exactly* what kind of man I married."

"Are you certain? He ruined my fiancée."

"I doubt that."

"It's the truth."

"Your truth. I'm sure there's more to the story. Good evening, Your Grace."

He took her arm when she would have turned

away. "Wait. I want to tell you what happened."

"For heaven's sake!" She gave him a look of profound annoyance. "All right, I will listen, but do not think to turn me against my husband."

His features tightened in frustration, but he nodded. "Very well. I was betrothed to Victoria since the day of her birth. She was always meant to be my duchess, but on the night we were to announce our wedding date, Lucien attempted to seduce her."

"Oh, please. Why would he do such a thing?"

"Because he's always been jealous of the fact that I am the true-born heir." He looked down his nose as if the answer should be obvious.

"Where did you get such nonsense?" she scoffed.

"I've always known."

"Did he say such a thing?" she demanded. "Or was this an assumption you made on your own?"

"I—"

"My husband is a man of honor," she interrupted fiercely. "And if he did this thing, he must have had a reason."

Robert's expression grew mulish. "The man's a rakehell. That was all the reason he needed."

"Not," she hissed, "anymore. Now he's my husband."

"Until his eye wanders."

She pressed her lips together in annoyance. "Is this the history between you? This woman?"

"It is."

She shook her head in pity. "It's been almost six years, Robert. He's a different man now."

"You're besotted with him," Robert sneered. "Look at you, more blindly loyal than my best hunting dog."

She lifted her chin proudly. "I've been told that before."

"What will you do when he breaks your heart?" Robert shot back. "He's a rake. We both know that. I was trying to open your eyes to the truth."

"Let's do talk about the truth," she shot back. "Perhaps you might tell me what you know about the attempts on Lucien's life."

"What the devil are you talking about?" He paled when she just stared at him. "Someone has tried to kill Lucien?"

"Someone tried to kill him five years ago, but he survived." She snatched her hand from his arm. "And someone tried again twice more since he came back to London. I don't suppose you'd know anything about that, *Your Grace*?"

"Are you accusing *me*?" Fury and astonishment warred on his face. "Are you mad?"

"You make no secret of your anger over what happened with your betrothal. So yes, perhaps I *am* accusing you. Because someone hates Lucien enough to try to kill him, and right now you have the most reason."

"I wanted . . . Good God, this conversation is not what I intended."

"I'm sure it's not."

"Don't take that tone with me," he snarled. "Who are you to be flinging about unfounded accusations?"

"I'm Lucien's wife." She pointed a finger at him. "And if anyone thinks to separate us, he'd best think again."

He grabbed her wrist, leaning closer in a posture of intimidation "Are you threatening me, madam? I warn you, I'm no longer a boy. Not so easily made a fool of any longer."

"And who is making a fool of you?" Lucien appeared out of nowhere, frowning as he noticed Robert's grip on Aveline's wrist. "Kindly release my wife."

Robert let go, and Aveline darted to Lucien's side, comforted by the hand he placed at the small of her back. "We were talking about the past," Robert said, once more the genial, urbane duke.

"The past is over and gone. Better to think of the present." Lucien smiled down at her. "And presently, the orchestra is about to play a waltz. Would you care to dance, wife?"

"I would."

Lucien nodded once at his half brother. "If you'll excuse us, Your Grace."

"Of course." Robert waved a dismissal, but he gave Aveline a last, meaningful look as Lucien turned her away.

"What was that about?" Lucien asked, leading her back to the dance floor.

"I'm not certain." She gave him a worried look. "Be careful of him, Lucien. He's a very angry young man."

"I know." Taking his wife's hand, he swept them into the waltz. "He blames me for losing his fiancée."

"He says you ruined her."

"She was a tart," he said bluntly. "I just showed him her true colors before he married her."

"He thinks you're jealous of him."

"Hardly." His lips curved in a wicked grin. "What use have I for a title when I already have everything I want?"

"Everything?" She slanted him a glance from beneath her lashes, then slowly licked her lips.

He sucked in a breath. "Perhaps not everything," he murmured, drawing her a bit closer.

"We will have to correct that this evening."

"We certainly shall."

As she danced with her husband, Aveline noticed the duke leaving the ball. His departure alleviated some of the tension that had possessed her all evening. She relaxed in Lucien's arms, allowing him to draw her into a world of tantalizing flirtation as he skillfully whirled her around the room. The dance became a seduction, made all the more exciting because they already knew what pleasures awaited them in the bedchamber.

"There's something scandalous about being in your arms in front of all of Society," she murmured, as the music ended.

"You must save every waltz for me."

"Done." Her lips curved. "It would not do to have you call someone out over a mere dance."

He raised her hand to his lips. "My only dawn appointment is with you, my love."

She sent him a playful look. "Bring your pistol."

Chapter 21

A pounding on the door woke them just after dawn the next morning.

"Who the devil could that be?" Lucien muttered.

Aveline snuggled closer to her husband, burying her face in his chest. "Tell them to go away."

He stroked a hand down her back as the pounding continued. "Must be urgent if they're trying to knock the door down." He pressed a kiss beneath her ear. "I'll be right back."

She made a sleepy protest as he slipped out of bed, reaching out to lay her hand on the sheet where the warmth from his body lingered. Opening her eyes, she watched with appreciation as he padded naked to the wardrobe and removed his dressing gown.

The banging on the door came again. "Sir!" someone cried. "Are you awake, sir?"

"Yes, blast you! One moment." The knocking stopped, and Lucien cast his wife a lazy smile as he slipped into the garment and fastened it. "I'll be right back."

Her lips curved in response to the gleam in his eyes. "I'll be right here."

Chuckling, he went to fling open the door. "What?" he roared.

From the bed, Aveline could see Elton, dressed to perfection despite the early hour. There was someone with him, but she couldn't see who it was past Lucien's broad shoulders. She closed her eyes, smiling as she pondered how long it would take Lucien to get rid of the servants so they might return to more important matters.

"Sir! Miss Chloe is gone!"

"Gone? What do you mean, gone?"

Terror struck at the words. Bolting upright in bed, Aveline struggled to wrap the sheets around her naked body as Lucien barked questions at the servants. Stumbling to her feet with the bedding wrapped around her, she could see that Chloe's governess was standing beside Elton.

"She's not in her bed, sir." Miss Edgerton's voice quavered with distress. "I woke to get a drink of water, and when I looked in on her, she was not in her bed!"

"Have you searched the house?"

"No, sir." Elton held out a piece of paper. "We found this on her pillow."

Aveline hurried to Lucien's side, uncaring of her state of dishabille. "What does it say?"

Lucien's expression darkened. "It says if I want to see our daughter again, I must bring twenty thousand pounds to a location stated here at noon today."

"Twenty thousand pounds!" Her head spun. "Do you have such a sum?"

"The money is not a problem." He crumpled the letter in his fist. "But someone is going to rue the day they touched my daughter."

"How could this happen?" She trembled from head to toe and laid her hand on Lucien's arm for support. "How could someone snatch her from her bed? From inside this house?"

"That, my dear wife, is what we will find out."

"Shall I summon Bow Street, sir?" Elton asked.

"Yes. And Fenworthy. I shall be down directly."

"Very good, sir."

"Miss Edgerton," Lucien said in a gentler tone, "please get dressed and meet us downstairs in the parlor. I'm certain the runner will have questions about Chloe's daily routine that you can answer."

"Yes, sir." Eyes reddened with tears, the governess sniffled and turned away.

Lucien closed the door as the servants departed and leaned back against it. He met Aveline's gaze, his eyes dark with torment. She stepped into his embrace just as he reached for her. His arms tightened around her, and when he buried his face in her neck, she realized he was trembling, too.

"What are we going to do?" she asked, stroking his hair with her free hand.

"Pay the ransom and get her back."

"Do you suppose this has anything to do with the attempts on your life recently?"

"I'd thought of that." He raised his head and looked at her, a ruthless light entering his eyes. "And if it does, someone will pay dearly."

"Do you think it was Robert? He left the ball early last night."

"I will definitely find out about my dear brother's activities last night."

"What about Dante?" she asked softly.

His jaw clenched. "I'll be looking for him, as well."

"I'm frightened, Lucien." She clenched her fingers more tightly in the sheet wrapped around her body. "What if these are the same people who tried to kill you? Chloe's just a little girl."

He smoothed his hands soothingly down her back. "They have no quarrel with the child; it's me they want. She's just bait."

"What about the money?"

"My man of business will assemble the funds for me."

"So quickly?"

His mouth quirked in a semblance of a smile. "Fenworthy thinks me a god. He will do it."

She reluctantly stepped out of his arms. "I suppose I'd best get dressed. Everyone will be here soon."

"Yes." He caressed her cheek. "I swear to you, I will get her back."

She took his hand and squeezed it reassuringly. "I know you will. I trust you, Lucien."

* * *

Fenworthy arrived just after the runner from Bow Street had come and gone. Aveline came into Lucien's study just as Fenworthy was taking his leave. The short, bespectacled man gave her a polite good morning, then hurried off, a satchel full of papers authorizing the liquidation of several of Lucien's assets clutched in his arms.

Lucien sat back in his chair, staring at his desk as if he'd never seen it before.

"It never amazes me that you can summon a fortune with nothing more than your signature," she said, crossing the room to him.

He glanced up and gave her a rueful smile, but weariness and worry haunted his eyes. "I wish every problem could be handled so simply."

"You regard money a simple matter?" She stopped beside him and leaned her hip against the edge of the desk.

"It's always been that way for me. I have a talent for turning straw into gold." He took her hand and just held it, as if he needed the connection. "Had this been a plain case of abduction for ransom, I would have paid ten times as much to get our daughter back."

"But it's not. It's much more complicated."

"Much," he agreed. He lifted her hand to his cheek and closed his eyes. "I'm terrified," he confessed. "This enemy of mine, whoever he is, has set out to ruin my life. And by stealing our daughter, he may well have succeeded."

"You'll find her." She summoned a weak smile

and twined her fingers with his. "You're a man of influence and wealth. You have all the tools at your disposal to bring Chloe home."

He gave a humorless laugh. "Fine lot of good it's doing me."

"Mr. Harris from Bow Street seemed confident. When does he return?"

"Half past ten."

"Where are you supposed to bring the money?"

"A place in Kent, about an hour's ride from London. Appears to be a hunting box of some sort. Fenworthy says he'll have the money in an hour, then the runner and I will go meet these vermin."

She tightened her fingers in his. "I'm coming with you."

"The hell you are."

She met his glare with one of her own. "I'll stay out of the way, but I have to be there. I can take care of Chloe while you deal with her abductor."

"I don't want you in danger." He lifted their entwined hands and pressed a lingering kiss to the back of her hand. "I can't lose you, too. Not again."

"I'll stay in the coach. But I can't sit idly by and wait for you to bring our daughter home. The worry would kill me." She saw another protest forming. "Damn you, Lucien! We're in this together."

A genuine chuckle escaped his lips. "Do my ears deceive me, or did a foul curse just escape my lady wife's lips?"

"I'm the daughter of a gamester, husband, and I have plenty more words where that came from if you think to leave me behind."

"Very well." He grew serious. "But you must stay in the coach as you promised. I'll brook no disobedience in this matter."

"I will."

Elton came to the door. "Pardon me, sir, but the Duke of Huntley has just arrived."

"What the devil—?" Lucien glanced at Aveline.

"What's he doing here?" she whispered.

"Come to gloat, no doubt. Show him in," Lucien said to the butler.

Aveline moved to stand beside Lucien's chair, slipping her hand from his and laying it instead on his shoulder in a sign of solidarity. He reached up to briefly caress her fingers and then dropped his hand as the duke appeared in the doorway.

"Lucien, I just heard from the servants that your daughter has been abducted." Robert strode into the room, the picture of concern. "Is there anything I can do? Do you need money?"

"I have funds enough for the ransom, Robert." Lucien rose, never taking his eyes from his half brother. "But you can certainly tell me what you know of this villainy."

"What *I* know?" Robert glanced from one to the other, alarm dawning in his eyes. "Good God, you don't think *I* had anything to do with this?"

"You tell me," Lucien replied softly.

"Are you mad?" Robert's gaze flicked to Aveline. "Has your wife been telling you of her wild accusations?"

"My wife and I are partners, Robert, and we tell each other everything."

"Does that mean you believe . . ." He shook his head as if to clear it. "Lucien, I cannot fathom this."

"Where were you last night, Robert?" Lucien sat on the edge of the desk, and while his voice sounded mild, his expression was anything but.

"At the Tripton ball, the same as you." He sent a glare at Aveline. "You both saw me there."

"But you left," Aveline pointed out. "Where did you go after that?"

Robert's face reddened. "How dare you question my whereabouts. Remember who I am!"

"I know exactly who you are," Lucien growled. "You're a wet-behind-the-ears boy who plays at being a man because he has a title."

"I am the Duke of Huntley!"

"You're my little brother," Lucien corrected. And when Robert opened his mouth to retort, he added derisively, "Half brother."

"I don't have to stand for this." Hands fisted at his sides, Robert glared at both of them. "I came to see if I could help, and instead you insult me!"

"You're not leaving." Lucien came around the desk to loom menacingly over the younger man. "Not until I have some answers."

Robert didn't back down. "I can't tell you what I don't know."

"Who arranged to have me abducted?" he demanded. "Who's been trying to kill me? *Who stole my daughter?*"

Robert flinched at Lucien's roar. "It wasn't me. Dammit, Lucien." He shoved at his brother's chest, his face twisting with emotion. "I've been trying to find a way to get *closer* to you, not rid myself of you!"

"Liar."

"I am *not* lying." Robert lifted his chin and surprised all of them by scowling right back at Lucien. "I treated you horribly when we were children."

"I know what you did. I was there."

"I'm not proud of it." Robert glanced from Aveline back to Lucien, a plea in his eyes. "It was my mother's influence. She always told me I was better because I would be the duke someday. And you were just a bastard."

"You're not endearing yourself to me, Robert."

"Will you just listen to me for once? I'm not good with words." The duke paced away from Lucien, then turned back to face him. "I've been trying to make my peace with you, but I keep blundering it."

"You've a fine way of making peace."

"Lucien," Aveline said, "let's hear what he has to say."

Her husband cast her an irritated look. "Aveline, this young pup has demonstrated his hatred of me for years. I'll not fall for his Banbury tales at this late date."

"I don't hate you. I never did." Robert glanced from one to the other. "I know you don't believe me."

"You're right," Lucien snarled.

"The truth is, I've always looked up to you, Lucien." He gave a self-mocking laugh. "I had the title, but you had the admiration of Society, earned on your own merits. Even our father commented on it."

"How touching."

"You were successful in everything that you did, from business to women," he went on, sending an apologetic look to Aveline. "You were a crack shot and always talked about in the most deferential of ways. I wanted to be more like you. But I was to be the duke."

"And I could never be the duke."

"You would have made a far better duke than I," Robert whispered.

"What has that to do with now?" Lucien pulled out his pocketwatch. "In an hour, I am supposed to take the ransom to get my daughter back. Unless you care to tell me where she is . . . ?"

"Why don't you listen to me? I didn't take your daughter. She's my niece, man! How could I harm her?"

"The same way you could try and kill your own brother."

"I didn't try to kill you. I *mourned* you, Lucien. I grieved when I thought you'd died." His voice broke, and he sank down into a chair.

"I think—"

"Lucien." Aveline came around and laid a hand on his arm, stopping whatever blistering comment he'd been about to utter. "I think he's telling the truth."

"Of course, I'm telling the truth!" Frustration etched Robert's young face. "I hated you over the incident with Victoria. And I hated you even more when I realized that I was *glad* you had ruined my engagement. I was too young to wed."

"You seemed hell-bent on it." Soothed by Aveline's hand stroking his arm, Lucien leaned back against the desk.

"My mother had spent years telling me how Victoria was to be my duchess. I got used to the idea, but when the time came to formally announce our wedding date, I realized I didn't want to get married yet. I was only nineteen. But Mother insisted."

"Yet you acted the outraged bridegroom."

"I couldn't show how I really felt. My mother would have been furious."

"You're a man now, Robert. Stop letting her control your life."

"My mother can be a formidable woman," Robert said with a sigh. "But while I couldn't let her see my grief when we thought you'd died, I did buy Thornsgate to hold in memory of you. I haven't changed anything about that house. It's exactly the way you left it five years ago."

Lucien stiffened. "You bought my house as a remembrance?"

"Yes." Robert patted his pockets. "In fact . . . ah, here it is." He pulled a piece of paper from his coat pocket. "I'm deeding it back to you as a wedding gift. I just haven't had the chance to present it to you."

"You were too busy arguing," Aveline said wryly.

Lucien slowly took the paper Robert held out to him. "You didn't arrange for my disappearance?"

"Good God, no. I admired you." Robert shrugged as they both cast him disbelieving looks. "I did. I just couldn't show it. It wouldn't have been quite the thing to admit how much I cared for my illegitimate brother, especially in my mother's hearing."

"You're the duke now, Robert. Perhaps you should consider banishing your mother to the dower house."

Robert winced. "That wouldn't be easy."

"Try." Lucien stared down at the deed as if someone had just handed him the sun. "I don't know what to think of all this. I thought you had paid to have me killed."

"I didn't." Robert stood. "I know I haven't been the best of brothers, but I want to forget the history between us and go forward as true brothers should." He rose and held out a hand.

Lucien stared at that hand for so long that Aveline feared he wouldn't take it. But, finally, he clasped Robert's hand, mutely accepting the offer of peace.

"So you were serious when you told me you wanted to mend things with your brother," Aveline said.

"I was." Robert gave her a crooked smile. "Unfortunately, words don't come easily to me. Many times I let my temper guide me from my course."

"A characteristic that seems to run in your family," Aveline said, with a meaningful glance at Lucien.

"This leaves us with something of a quandary, however." Lucien placed the deed to Thornsgate on his desk. "If you're not the villain of the piece, then who is?"

"If only you could find Dante," Aveline said with a sigh.

"Wexford? What does he have to do with this?" the duke demanded.

Lucien glanced at Aveline, who nodded. "Just before I disappeared, Dante intercepted Aveline's correspondence telling me she was with child. Unknown to me, he also responded by sending a letter to cast her off."

"The blackguard!" Robert exclaimed. "I don't know how you remained friends with a rapscallion like that, Lucien."

"Unfortunately, I only found out about his perfidy a few days ago. I confronted Dante, and now he's disappeared."

"Probably left the country," Robert said.

"Perhaps. But the timing of the letter coincides with the timing of my abduction."

"We believe Dante may have had something to do with Lucien's disappearance," Aveline said. "The night of the dinner party you held in our honor, I saw you and Dante arguing out in the garden."

"So you assumed that meant that I was involved with his schemes?"

"Well, given your attitude toward my husband, and the fact that it costs a great deal of money to arrange the abduction of a man with Lucien's social prominence, it wasn't such a ridiculous notion."

"I must agree with you there," Robert said. "But my argument with Wexford had nothing to do with Lucien. The rogue was sniffing around my mother again. I'd warned him to stay away from her."

Lucien stiffened. "Your mother?"

"Yes, disgusting, isn't it?" Robert made a face. "Young fellow like that from his social class thinking to have a flirtation with a woman of my mother's age and station."

Lucien and Aveline glanced at each other. "This has happened before?" Lucien asked.

Robert nodded. "A few years ago, Wexford suddenly started calling daily, taking carriage rides with Mother, murmuring in her ear at social events. It was horribly embarrassing. Adminton is a much more sensible companion for her."

"Perhaps their association was not what you think," Lucien said. "What if they weren't having an affair?"

"What other explanation . . . You don't think—"

"There is no one who hates me more than the Duchess of Huntley," Lucien said grimly.

"Impossible." Robert shook his head. "I know she's never liked you, Lucien, but I find it hard to believe she would go to such lengths to be rid of you."

"I don't find it hard to believe at all. She has the money to do the deed, and how strange is it that as soon as I disappeared, her friend Adminton took it into his head to sponsor Dante in Society?"

"Perhaps it wasn't Mother at all. Perhaps it was Adminton."

"I'm sorry, Robert, but Adminton has nothing against me," Lucien said. "In fact, we were even business partners in a very lucrative investment some years ago. He would be the last person to try and be rid of me. It *must* be Clarissa."

"Dear God," the duke whispered, shock evident on his face.

"Didn't you say your mother was not in Town?" Aveline asked.

"She left yesterday morning for Havenmeade."

Aveline met Lucien's gaze. "Convenient, don't you think?"

"Agreed." Lucien grabbed the ransom note from the desk. "This meeting place is a hunting box in Kent."

"One of my mother's family estates is in Kent. It was part of her dowry when she married my father."

"Do you recognize this place?" Lucien shoved the note into Robert's hand.

The younger man paled. "Yes. It's part of Mother's estate."

"That's it, then." Lucien strode to the door and shouted for Elton.

"What are you going to do?" Aveline asked.

"I'm riding out to this place, and I'm going to find our daughter."

"Not without me, you're not."

He paused a beat, then nodded. "Remember our agreement."

"I'll just fetch my cloak." She started for the door.

"I'm coming, too." Robert tossed the note on the desk and matched Lucien stare for stare. "I might be able to help. I can talk to Mother, whereas she won't listen to you."

"True enough." Lucien took Aveline's hand as she reached him and squeezed it. "Promise me you'll not do anything foolish."

"As long as you make the same promise."

Before he could reply, Elton appeared at the door. "Yes, sir?"

"Summon Mr. Harris from Bow Street immediately and send a note to Mr. Fenworthy telling him to disregard his instructions from this morning."

"Yes, sir." The butler vanished to carry out his orders.

Lucien turned away from the door and went to the desk to unlock a drawer. He pulled out a handsome mahogany case. "Before we go, we'd best take these." He flipped open the lid to reveal two pistols resting on red velvet.

Robert came to his side and stared grimly at the weapons. "Do you think this is necessary?"

"Yes." Lucien glanced at Aveline, who still hovered near the door. "I'm taking no chances with the lives of my family."

Robert reached out to stay Lucien's hand when he would have taken a pistol from the case. "And I'll take no chances with mine. Promise me you will not harm my mother."

The two men locked gazes for a long moment. "I don't know if I can do that."

Robert clenched his jaw in determination. "I swear to you I will deal with her appropriately. All I am asking is that you not hurt her."

Lucien shook off Robert's hand and lifted the pistol from its resting place. "As long as she does no harm, I will keep that promise. But if I have to choose between your mother and my wife or child, you know what my choice will be."

Robert nodded slowly and took the other pistol from the box. "Then at least don't shoot to kill. You're a marksman, Lucien. You can wound without killing."

"I'll do my best." He laid a hand on Robert's shoulder.

Touched by this first evidence of brotherly affection, Aveline opened the door. "I'll get my cloak," she said, and slipped from the room.

Chapter 22

⌒◦◦⌒

They reached the hunting box with a quarter hour to spare.

From the coach, Lucien looked out at the innocent-looking hunting lodge. His daughter was in there, probably terrified. His fingers tightened around the handles of the empty satchel he carried.

"Mr. DuFeron, you approach the house," Harris from Bow Street said, drawing an imaginary map with his finger on the seat. "I'll circle around this side, and, Your Grace, if you'll go around the other way . . . ?"

Robert nodded grimly, his hand firm on the pistol in his pocket.

"And Mrs. DuFeron will stay in the coach," Lucien said, sending his wife a warning look.

"Yes, husband," she replied with a sweet smile.

"Your Grace, let's take our positions. Mr. DuFeron, as soon as we're set, you come out."

"Agreed."

Harris and Robert slipped out of the coach. The sun gleamed off his brother's hair like a newly minted coin. Or like a bright and shining target, Lucien thought.

"Robert!" he hissed. When his brother halted, Lucien tossed him his own hat. "Watch yourself."

Robert caught the hat and placed it on his head, then gave Lucien a wave of reassurance before he slipped into the brush.

"Some duke," he muttered. "In his rush to save the day, he forgot his blasted hat."

"This is as difficult for him as it is for you," Aveline said. "His mother is the villain behind all our miseries. How do you think that makes him feel?"

"I know, I know." Lucien swept a hand over his face. "I just wish this were over. I wish Chloe was back with us and we were home having a tea party in the nursery."

She gave him a tender smile that eased some of the ache around his heart. "I'll tell Chloe that it is your turn to pour."

"Do that." He glanced outside the coach. "Looks like they're in position." Scooping her close with a hand behind her neck, he kissed her, trying to infuse all the love he felt for her in that one caress. When their lips parted, he rested his forehead against hers. "Stay in the coach."

"Don't get killed."

"Promise me."

"*You* promise *me*." That stubborn gleam lit her green eyes.

"How about we promise each other."

Her lips curved. "Done."

He stroked her cheek. "I love you." Then he stepped out of the coach and focused on what he had to do.

Aveline watched Lucien walking toward the house, his blue coat making him an easy target amongst the greenery. She glanced at the darkened windows of the house, but saw no threat. Saw no one at all, in fact.

Suddenly, the door on the other side of the coach opened. Aveline gave a cry of alarm as Dante stuck his head inside.

"Call him back!" Dante whispered. "It's a trap!"

"Where's my daughter?" she demanded.

"Right here." He moved to the side.

"Hello, Mama." Sucking on a piece of peppermint, Chloe held Dante's hand and smiled as if nothing were wrong.

"Come here, poppet." Aveline held out her arms, and Dante helped the child scramble into the coach and into her mother's embrace.

"Now call him back," he hissed. "She's going to kill him!"

She stuck her head out the window. "Lucien, come back! I've got Chloe!"

Nearly at the door, Lucien spun to face her. At the same time the front window of the house shattered, and a pistol appeared. He dodged to avoid the threat, and a shot rang out, hitting the satchel he carried. He dived into the bushes.

"Lucien!" she screamed. Chloe whimpered, and Aveline absently comforted her, her eyes darting back and forth in search of her husband.

"Damn it all," Dante muttered. He pulled a pistol out of his coat pocket. "Move to the other seat," he demanded. "Hurry!"

She didn't want to move, didn't want to give him a clear shot at Lucien. How did she know this wasn't part of the trap? But she couldn't endanger Chloe.

"I'm trying to *help* him, blast it! Now *move!*" He gave her a shove, and she scooted across to the other seat so he could sit near the window.

"If you hurt him," she said in a low voice, "you won't leave this coach alive."

He cast her a startled look, which swiftly changed into one of admiration. With a cocky grin, he leaned out the window, sighting down the barrel of the pistol. "Come out," he murmured to himself. "Show yourself, you Frenchie coward."

Long moments of silence ticked by, broken only by Chloe's tuneless humming as she sucked on her candy.

"Come on out," Dante muttered. "That's it."

Aveline shifted back to the other seat so she could see past Dante's shoulder. The door to the house was slowly creeping open. Dante aimed the pistol at the door, his finger hovering on the trigger.

A screech rang out, and a bird suddenly launched itself from the bushes where Lucien had disappeared, followed by a very human curse. A large man with a black mustache and a pistol jumped into the doorway and fired at the bush. Someone cried out.

Dear God, no. Aveline crushed Chloe to her, tears all but choking her.

"Bastard!" Dante spat, and fired.

A red stain appeared on the large man's chest. With a startled expression that was almost comical, he crumpled to the ground.

Dante kicked open the door to the coach and set off at a run for the bush from which the cry had come. Aveline followed on his heels, carrying Chloe. Mr. Harris appeared out of the woods and sped in the same direction.

And then Lucien rose up out of the brush at the side of the path and hurried over to the same spot.

"Lucien!" Aveline cried.

Lucien spun to face her, then his expression darkened as he saw Dante. He pulled out his pistol. Dante skidded to a halt, dropping his empty pistol to the ground and slowly raising his hands.

"Lucien, no!" Aveline rushed to stand in front of Dante. "He brought Chloe back. He tried to save you. Don't do it."

Lucien's eyes narrowed, but his aim never wavered. "Move out of the way, Aveline."

"No."

He spared her a glance. "He shot my brother."

"He didn't." She started walking toward him, keeping herself between them. "I was watching, Lucien. That man there"—she indicated the fallen man in the doorway—"*he* shot your brother. Dante shot *him*."

Chloe raised her head. "Don't shoot Mr. Wexford, Papa," she said. "He gave me sweets." She indicated her peppermint stick.

Lucien swallowed hard. "Did he indeed?"

Chloe nodded vigorously, her dark curls bouncing.

Lucien lowered the pistol to his side, but sent Dante a dark look. "You and I will settle our differences at a later date."

Dante gave a stiff nod. "Name your seconds at your convenience."

"Lucien—"

Her husband held up a hand to silence her. "This is not your affair, Aveline." He turned to where Harris had eased Robert into a sitting position. Blood oozed from a nasty wound in his shoulder. "How's my brother?"

"Hard to tell," Harris said, examining the wound. "He's lost a lot of blood. Best get him to a doctor."

Robert looked up at Lucien, pain twisting his features. "Shot by my own chef," he said. "How extraordinary."

"Is the man hurt?" Chloe asked.

"That's your uncle Robert," Aveline said. "And yes, he's hurt."

"He needs candy," Chloe pronounced. Even Robert chuckled, though the movement caused him pain.

"Let's get him to the carriage," Lucien said.

"I'll help." Dante stepped forward.

A shriek rang out from the house.

"*Robert!*" The Duchess of Huntley rushed through the doorway. Gone was the coolly elegant social hostess. Her blue eyes burned with mad fury as she stepped right over the body of the dead French chef and hurried to her son's side, dropping to her knees beside him. "What happened? Why are you here? You weren't supposed to be here!"

Despite his evident pain, Robert managed a steely look. "My brother was in peril, Mother. What else would you have me do?"

"Your brother!" she spat. "How can you call him that? You're better than he is."

"No," Robert whispered, pain glazing his eyes. "I'm not."

"Don't die! Robert, don't die!" Her son's eyes drifted shut, and his head fell back. The duchess threw back her head and screamed.

Aveline winced at the piercing wail and tried to cover Chloe's ears.

"He's not dead, Clarissa." Lucien stepped forward. "He's just unconscious from the blood loss."

"You killed my son!" The duchess leaped to her feet and threw herself at him, grabbing the pistol from his relaxed grip. She gave him a shove that unbalanced him, sending him crashing to the ground. Then she spun and sighted down the barrel at Aveline and Chloe. "You killed my child," she hissed. "So I'll kill yours."

"No!" Lucien shouted, pushing himself to his feet. He leaped at the duchess. The pistol fired as he tackled her, and someone cried out. He untangled himself from the fallen woman and turned, certain he would see his family lying in a bloody heap.

But Aveline stood untouched, hugging a crying Chloe. Dante lay sprawled on the ground at her feet.

As Harris took custody of the hysterical duchess, Lucien stumbled to where his friend lay bleeding on the ground. A red stain spread across the center of his pink satin waistcoat.

"Gut shot," Dante whispered, then coughed. "Ruined my waistcoat."

"That's what you get for selecting pink." Lucien tore open the garment to see the injury. Blood seeped steadily from the undeniably mortal wound.

"He threw himself in front of us," Aveline said softly.

"Trying to be the hero again?" Lucien asked, but his own voice broke.

"Have to impress the ladies."

"You did that," Aveline said. "For what it's worth, I forgive you. Thank you for my daughter's life."

She gave Lucien a look of profound sorrow, then carried Chloe away from the bloodshed.

"She wanted to kill you," Dante whispered.

"Don't try to talk." Lucien stripped off his coat and bunched it up, then gently slipped it beneath Dante's head.

"Not much time." Dante reached out and grasped Lucien's hand. "Five years ago . . . she said to kill you."

"Dante, you don't have to—"

"*Yes, I do.*" He swallowed hard. "I couldn't do it. Faked your death. Sent you away." He attempted a smile. "My best friend."

"She got Adminton to sponsor you in Society, didn't she?"

"Yes." He coughed, and blood trickled from his mouth. "I was . . . in dire straits. Lenders were going to kill me."

"So you did the duchess's dirty work, but instead of killing me, you sentenced me to hell on board the *Sea Dragon*."

Dante gave a little smile. "Knew you'd survive." His eyes slid closed.

"Dante!" Lucien shook him, and his friend's eyes flickered open again.

"Sorry about . . . the letter."

"Never mind the dratted letter!"

"Took care of Chloe for you." Dante gasped for breath. "The bitch never saw her. Told me to take her, but—" He was seized by a fit of coughing, blood bubbling at his lips.

"Dammit, Dante!"

Dante gave him the gentlest of smiles. "You win the game, Luce. Better this way. At least you . . . won't . . . have to kill me . . . at dawn . . ."

His words drifted away, his eyes staring up at the sky as the breath slowly whooshed out of his lungs.

Then, silence.

Grief rose up, stinging his eyes with unmanly tears. He reached out with a shaking hand and gently closed Dante's lifeless eyes.

Hell's Brethren existed no more.

"Mr. DuFeron," Harris said quietly, "we must get the duke to a doctor."

"Of course." Clearing his throat and blinking away the moisture in his eyes, Lucien stood and turned to his injured half brother. Robert had regained consciousness and watched him somberly.

"I'm sorry, Lucien," he said with genuine sympathy.

"Me too." Lucien pulled Robert's uninjured arm around his shoulders and assisted him to his feet. Harris escorted the duchess, who stared straight ahead as if in a trance. Harris had bound her hands behind her back.

"I'll take this one in the duke's carriage, if that's all right with His Grace," Harris said.

Robert nodded.

"And if we could move the ... your friend ... into the house, I'll send a man back for him and the Frenchman."

"I'll send my coachman to assist you." Lucien cast a glance at Dante's motionless body. "I'll handle the funeral arrangements for Mr. Wexford."

"Very good, Mr. DuFeron." Harris led the duchess away to the back of the house, where her conveyance awaited.

"My mother is not well," Robert murmured, as they picked their way slowly down the path toward Lucien's coach.

"Hatred eats away at some people over the years."

"That's generous of you, considering she tried to kill you more than once." Robert gave a hiss of pain as he stepped on a rock and jarred his injured shoulder. "I'll handle my mother. I've an estate in Scotland where I can lock her away. She won't hurt anyone ever again."

"I'm sorry it turned out like this."

"I am, too." Robert stopped walking, forcing Lucien to halt with him. "Lucien, I know I have no right to ask this of you after what my mother did, but as the head of the family I must think of the Huntley name. I'll speak to Harris about what happened to-day, but will you keep silent as well, for the sake of our family's reputation?"

"Our family?"

"Yes, our family." Robert smiled. "I can't think of anyone I'd rather have for a brother."

"Don't you mean half brother?"

"No." Robert squeezed the shoulder that sup-ported him. "I mean brother."

"Of course I'll keep silent." He started walking again, compelling Robert to come with him. "I'm done scandalizing the family, in case you didn't notice."

"How dull."

Lucien laughed. "If there's anything my marriage is not, it's dull."

"I envy you your wife." Robert gave a weak laugh. "She's an amazing woman."

"I consider myself lucky to have her."

"You seem to have better taste in brides than I do. Now if you'd like to share some of your secrets re-garding the fairer sex with your dear brother . . ."

Lucien chuckled. "Perhaps when you grow up, Your Grace."

They were almost to the coach when Aveline threw open the door, her face creased with concern for Robert. Her worry visibly eased when she no-ticed the young duke walking on his own feet. But then she turned her gaze to her husband. In one shared moment of silent communication, she under-stood what had happened, what he was feeling.

She came to assist him with Robert, tucking her

arm around his brother's waist on the opposite side. Over Robert's bent head she sent him a look of deep compassion, then gave a swift squeeze to his arm before turning her complete attention to his brother.

Lucien took a shaky breath and felt some of the grief fade. He was a lucky man, indeed.

Epilogue

Aveline found him in the study, staring into the fire as usual.

Dante's funeral had been earlier that day, and the only attendees had been Lucien, Robert, and herself. Lucien was taking Dante's death hard, though he'd fully intended to call the jackanapes out for the actions that had left Chloe illegitimate. But apparently killing a rival in a duel of honor was much different than having a friend sacrifice himself to save your wife and child.

She walked over to him and rested a hand on his shoulder. He looked up, taking a deep breath as he shook off his melancholy. "Is Chloe in bed?"

"Sound asleep." She slipped into his lap, linking her arms around his neck. "Now it's time to put you to bed."

"Indeed?" A wicked gleam sparked in his eye, warming her heart. As long as he never stopped looking at her like that, they'd be all right.

"Unless you'd like to cuddle by the fire." She squirmed in his lap, well aware of the affect her silk-clad body had on him.

He tugged playfully at the tie of her wrapper, peeling back the lacy garment to reveal the sleek silk nightdress beneath. "I like cuddling."

"So do I." She tucked her head into the hollow of his shoulder as he swept his hand down the curve of her hip. "My father is comfortably settled as well. Dr. Wells thinks he might be able to help him."

"Good news indeed." He trailed his hand upward to gently cup one breast.

A shaky sigh escaped her lips. "Have I thanked you," she asked breathlessly, "for bringing my father to London?"

"You know, I don't believe you have." He grinned, stroking his thumb over her nipple.

"What can I do . . ." She kissed his neck. ". . . to show . . ." She kissed his ear. ". . . my gratitude?" Her mouth met his in a kiss that sizzled down to her toes.

Their lips slowly parted, and Lucien stared down into her eyes, his own serious and intent. "Give me a son," he whispered. "Let me watch you through all the stages of your confinement. Let me witness what I missed with Chloe."

Her heart melted in her chest, and she cupped his face tenderly. "I would love to give you a son." Her lips curved. "But what if it's a daughter?"

He arched his brows with a rakish grin and stood,

lifting her into his arms. "Then we try again."

She laughed and clung to him, but as he shifted his grip, something dug into her thigh. "Ow. What's that you have in your hand?"

"Just an old game piece." He opened his fingers and dropped the white chess queen on the carpet. "I don't need it anymore."

"Did you win the game?" she asked flirtatiously as he carried her toward the door.

"You know, I believe I did." He swept her out of the study and toward the stairs. "And you're my prize."

Her delighted laughter echoed throughout the house as he carried her off to his bedchamber.

In the study, the white queen gleamed in the firelight, forgotten.